THEM DAMN EASTERNERS

"I done made up my mind 'bout this stupid hunt, Morgan." The gunhand grunted and took a sip of beer.

"Oh?"

"Yeah. I'm out of it. I'll stick around till the road is open, then I'm gone."

"What changed your mind?"

"A number of things. I've hired my gun out many times, for a lot of reasons. But never for nothin' like this here. It's stupid. And I just flat out don't like them damn Easterners."

Frank smiled. "Neither do I."

The gunslick laughed softly. "I reckon you don't." He looked down at his drink, then lifted his glass. "Luck to you, Frank."

"Thanks." Frank watched the man drain his glass and then walk away.

Through the front glass of the saloon, Frank watched lightning dart across the skies, listened as thunder rumbled, and then heard the rain increase in intensity.

"When the hell are we gonna get this show goin'?" a man yelled out. "I'm gettin' damn tired of waitin'."

"Patience, patience!" Horace Vanderhoot shouted from the doorway leading from the hotel to the saloon. "As soon as the rain ceases, the hunt will begin. Fifty thousand dollars will go to the man who kills the notorious murderer and gunfighter Frank Morgan. But if he's killed before I officially announce the start of the hunt, not one penny will go to that man. Here is something that might pique your interest: With the exception of Frank Morgan, the last man standing will be declared the winner of the hunt. At last count, there were almost sixty of you men in town. Only one will ride out fifty thousand dollars richer. Think about that and act accordingly. For now, I bid you all a very pleasant good night."

You bloodthirsty son of a bitch! Frank thought as he watched the foyer door close behind Vanderhoot. *You have just opened the gates of hell.*

THE LAST GUNFIGHTER:

SHOWDOWN

William W. Johnstone

PINNACLE BOOKS
Kensington Publishing Corp.

http://www.pinnaclebooks.com

PINNACLE BOOKS are published by

Kensington Publishing Corp.
850 Third Avenue
New York, NY 10022

All Kensington Titles, Imprints, and Distributed Lines are available at special quantity discounts for bulk purchases for sales promotions, premiums, fund-raising, and educational or institutional use. Special book excerpts or customized printings can also be created to fit specific needs. For details, write or phone the office of the Kensington special sales manager: Kensington Publishing Corp., 850 Third Avenue, New York, NY 10022, attn: Special Sales Department, Phone: 1-800-221-2647.

Pinnacle and the P logo Reg. U.S. Pat. & TM Off.

First Printing: March 2002
10 9 8 7 6 5 4 3 2 1

Printed in the United States of America

Nothing on earth consumes a man more quickly than the passion of resentment.

—Nietzsche

One

The town had grown quite a bit—it had been no more than a wide spot in the road the last time Frank Morgan had ridden through. About ten years back, he thought with a smile. He didn't remember the name of the town.

Still not much to it, Frank thought, looking down at the buildings from a hill. But maybe there's a barbershop with a bathhouse. Hard winter was fast approaching, and Frank was out of supplies and needed a bath, a rest, and a meal he didn't have to fix himself. He looked down at Dog, sitting a few yards away.

"And you need a good scrubbing too, Dog," he told the cur.

Dog wagged his tail without much enthusiasm at the mention of the word "scrubbing."

A few weeks had passed without incident since Frank left the valley of contention and the twin towns of Heaven and Hell. But peaceful times were coming to a close, and events were now in motion that would forever change the life of the gunfighter known as The Drifter.

They were events that Frank could not alter even had he known about them. Events that had taken place in a private men's club in New York City; a club to which only the very wealthy could belong.

Frank had intended to head southwest when he

left the valley, but instead he headed northwest. Why, he didn't know; he just did. He rode slowly toward the town, passing a weather-beaten sign that read: SOUTH RAVEN.

Frank shook his head at the name. "I wonder where North Raven is."

It took Frank about a minute to ride the entire length of the town, passing a general store, a saloon, a leather and gun shop, a barbershop/bath-house/undertaker's combination, a small cafe, a stage office/telegraph office, and several other stores, and finally reining up in front of the livery stable.

Frank swung wearily down from the saddle. An old man walked out of the shadows of the livery, sized up Frank for a few seconds, and said, "Howdy, boy. You look plumb tuckered out."

"I am," Frank replied.

"Come a ways, have you?"

"A good piece, for a fact. Did I miss the hotel coming in?"

The old man chuckled. "Ain't nary. But they's rooms for hire over the saloon."

"Where's North Raven?"

"You're funny, boy, you know that? There ain't no North Raven. Never has been. Town is named for the local doctor. He's from the South. That's how the town got its name."

"What part of the South?"

"Alabama. Raven was a doctor in the Confeder-ate Army. I think he was a colonel."

"There were a lot of them, for a fact."

"You was a Rebel?"

"I was."

"I was on the other side. That make a difference to you?"

"Not a bit. War's over."

"We'll get along then. I hate a sore loser. You want me to take care of your horse?"

"And my dog. I'll stable them and feed them."

"You don't think I can do that?"

"I don't want you kicked or bitten."

"I'll shore keep that in mind. Them animals got names?"

"Horse and Dog."

The liveryman smiled. "That ain't very original."

"It suits them."

"I reckon so. You look sort of familiar to me, boy. You been here 'fore?"

"Can't say I have. But I appreciate you calling me 'boy.' "

"I'm older than dirt, boy. Everybody's younger than me." He stared hard at Frank for a few seconds. "I've seen you 'fore. I know I have. It'll come to me."

"Let me know when it does. Is there anyone in town who does laundry?"

"The Widder Barlow. The barber'll get your stuff to her."

"All right. My gear will be safe here?"

"Shore will. I got a room with a lock on the door.

"The cafe serve good food?"

"Best in town," the liveryman said with a wide smile.

"It's the *only* cafe in town," Frank reminded him.

"That's why it's the best!"

Frank smiled and led Horse into the big barn, Dog following along. Dog would stay in the stall with Horse. Frank left his saddle in the storeroom and walked across the street to the barbershop. He arranged for the washerwoman to launder his trail-worn clothes, and then took a long soapy bath in a tub of hot water. He dressed in his last clean set of long-handle underwear and clean but slightly wrinkled jeans and shirt, and then got a shave and a haircut. He stepped out onto the boardwalk smelling and feeling a lot better, and walked over to the cafe for some lunch.

"Beef stew, hot bread, and apple pie," the waitress told him. "It's all we got, but it's good and there's plenty of it."

"Sounds good to me," Frank told her. "And keep my coffee cup filled, please."

Frank ate two full bowls of the very good stew and drank several cups of coffee before his hunger was appeased. He walked across the street and signed for a room, then went into the bar for another cup of coffee and to listen to the local gossip, if any. The patrons fell silent when he entered, everyone giving him the once-over. Frank ignored them, took a table in the rear of the room, and ordered a pot of coffee.

"I know who you are," a man said from across the room. Frank sipped his coffee and offered no reply to the statement.

"What are you talkin' about, Ned?" another patron asked.

"The gunfighter who just walked in," Ned said.

"What gunfighter?"

"Frank Morgan."

'Frank Morgan! Here in South Raven? You're crazy, Ned."

"That's him what just walked in, Mark," Ned stated. "Sittin' over yonder drinkin' coffee."

Frank took another sip of the strong coffee and remained silent.

"Is that true, mister?" Mark asked. "Are you Frank Morgan?"

"Yes," Frank said quietly.

"Oh, my God!" another patron blurted out as the front door opened, letting in a burst of cool air. "He's here to kill someone."

"I don't think so," the old liveryman said, stepping into the saloon. "Seems like a right nice feller to me." He walked to the bar and ordered a beer. "Your name come to me, Mr. Morgan. I knowed it would."

Frank lifted his coffee cup in acknowledgment.

"I seen Doc Raven right after you stored your stuff. Told him 'bout you. I reckon he'll be along any time now."

"Why are you here in our town, Frank Morgan?" another bar patron asked.

"To spend a couple of days resting my horse," Frank said. "To eat a meal I didn't cook and to get my clothes washed. Is that all right with you men?"

"Shore suits me," the liveryman said.

"You're not lookin' to kill no one?" Mark asked.

"No."

"By God, it is you," a man said, stepping into the saloon from a side door. "I thought Old Bob was seeing things."

"Told you it was him, Doc," the liveryman said. "Dr. Raven, Mr. Morgan."

Frank nodded at the man. "Do I know you?"

"No,"the doctor replied. "But I've seen your picture dozens of times and read a couple of books about you."

"Don't believe everything you read," Frank told him. "According to those books I've killed about a thousand white men, been wounded fifty times, been in gunfights all over the world, and been received in royal courts and knighted by kings and queens."

The doctor laughed. "And you're still a young man."

"I'm forty-five, Doc. And feel every year of it."

Dr. Raven walked over and sat down at the table with Frank. "Coffee," he called to the barkeep. He looked at Frank. "You're very relaxed, Mr. Morgan."

"The name is Frank, Doc. And why shouldn't I be relaxed?"

"You're not aware of what's been planned back East?"

"No. Something that concerns me?"

"I would certainly say so. It's been in the works for . . . I'd guess six months, at least. Probably longer than that. You're about to become the prey in what some are calling the ultimate hunt."

Frank's eyes narrowed for a few seconds; that was the only betrayal of his inner emotions. "You want to explain that? And also, how did you find out about it?"

"I have a doctor friend in New York City. We went to college together; graduated just in time to serve in opposing sides during the Northern Aggression Against the South. He wrote me months ago asking if I knew you. Of course, I told him I didn't. In his next letter, which was not long in coming, he told me about a group of wealthy sportsmen who had each put up thousands of dollars for this hunt. To be blunt, the money goes to the man who kills you."

"The authorities haven't stepped in to stop this . . . nonsense?"

"Obviously not. The so-called sportsmen are on their way west as we speak."

"The West is a big place, Doc. How do they propose to find me?"

"I understand the group has hired private detectives to do just that."

Frank hottened up his coffee and sugared it. "Doc, this is the damnest thing I ever heard of. Hell, it's *illegal.*"

"Of course, it is. But you're a known gunfighter. In the minds of many people, the world would be a better place without you in it."

Frank sighed heavily. "This is going to bring out every two-bit gunslinger west of the Mississippi."

"Well, we have a couple of gunfighters right here in this community. They'll be in town later on today, you can bet on that."

"You know that for sure?"

"It's Friday, Frank. And they always come in for drinks on Friday."

"Ranch hands?"

"They occasionally hire on to some ranch, when they're not stealing cattle or horses."

"I'm surprised anyone will hire them."

"Oh, they're careful not to steal from any of the ranchers in this area. But they've already heard about the other money being offered for your head."

"Sounds like everyone in the West has heard of that," Frank said sourly. Then he took a sip of coffee and smiled. "But no one's collected it yet."

"Obviously," Doc Raven replied. "But don't sell these two men short, Frank. I'm told they're fast, and good shots to boot."

"Young?"

"Mid-twenties."

"The worst age. They're full of piss and vinegar and think they're ten feet tall and bullet-proof."

"That's an interesting way of putting it, but accurate, I would say."

"Doc, if I could have one wish granted me by the Almighty, it would be that I could live out the rest of my years in peace and never have another gunfight. And that's the God's truth."

Doc Raven stared into Frank's pale eyes for a few seconds. He took in the dark brown hair, peppered with gray. The thick wrists and big hands. "I believe that, Frank. But it doesn't change anything."

"No, it doesn't. Doc, do you have a marshal here?"

Doc Raven smiled. "No. We had one, but he died several years ago. Not much goes on here, Frank. It's a very peaceful town."

"If you want it to remain peaceful, then I'd better move on, Doc."

"Nonsense. You're welcome to stay here for as long as you like."

"The mayor and town council might have something to say about that."

"I'm the mayor, Frank. And we don't have a town council."

"Interesting. How about a bank?"

"A small one, located in the stage office."

"Do you own it too?"

Raven laughed. "As a matter of fact I do. Would you like to open an account?"

"Not really. I have ample funds with me."

The doctor pushed back his chair and stood up. "Enjoy your stay in South Raven, Frank. I've got to see about a patient. We'll visit again soon."

"I'm sure."

The doctor walked out of the saloon and into the crisp fall air of Southern Idaho. Frank poured another cup of coffee and rolled a cigarette.

Old Bob, the liveryman, came over to Frank's table, a beer mug in his hand, and sat down. "The doc tell you about the Olsen boys?"

"The horse thieves?"

Bob laughed. "That's them. They're cousins, and worthless. But both of them pretty good with a pistol."

"Maybe I can avoid them."

"Doubtful, Mr. Morgan. Them two is lookin' for a reputation."

A man turned away from the front window of the saloon. "Here comes Brooks and Martin. They're reinin' up now. Oh, Lordy, the lead is goin' to fly for sure."

"The Olsen boys?" Frank asked.

"That's them," Bob said.

The front door open and two young men swaggered in, both of them wearing tied-down pistols.

Bob pushed his chair to one side, giving Frank a clear field of fire. Frank sipped his coffee and waited.

Two

Frank remained seated at the table as the front door was opened and two young men walked into the saloon, both of them all full of confidence and false toughness. Frank had seen their type many times before. Bullies, for the most part, and to Frank, very unimpressive. Frank could tell by the way they walked both were primed and cocked for trouble.

Brooks and Martin strolled over to the bar and ordered whiskey, then turned and gave the patrons a once-over. Both their gazes settled on Frank.

The old liveryman, Bob, moved further away from Frank's table.

"You somebody important?" Brooks called to Frank.

"Are you speaking to me?" Frank asked.

"Yeah. Who are you?"

"A man enjoying a pot of good coffee. Does that bother you? Not that it's any of your business," Frank added.

The pair of trouble-hunters both stiffened at that, Martin saying, "We might decide to make it our business."

"Why?" Frank asked.

"Huh?" Brooks blurted.

Frank smiled tightly, his eyes never leaving the pair. "I said, why?"

Brooks and Martin exchanged glances. " 'Cause we wants to know who you is, that's why!" Martin spoke.

"The name is Frank. And I assure you, any pleasure in this meeting is all yours. Now leave me alone." Frank had taken an immediate dislike to Brooks and Martin. Frank had never liked bullies, and that dislike had heightened over the years.

"You got a real smart-alecky mouth, you know that?" Brooks said.

"You have my totally insincere apologies."

The bartender smiled at that.

"I don't think I like you," Martin said.

"It's a free country," Frank replied. "Like or dislike whoever you choose. Now, if you have nothing else to contribute to this small exchange, shut up."

"Huh?" Brooks asked.

"I said shut up!"

"Who the hell do you think you is?" Martin shouted.

"A man who is rapidly losing patience with a couple of pushy loudmouths."

"You think you somebody special or somethin'?" Brooks yelled.

Frank smiled and said nothing.

"I'll tell you who he is," a saloon loafer said. "He's Frank Morgan."

Brooks and Martin stood silent for a few seconds as that statement sank in. Brooks was the first to speak. "You lie! That ain't Frank Morgan. Cain't be."

"Well, it damn shore is him," Bob said.

"Frank Morgan's an old man," Martin said. "That feller sittin' yonder ain't old enough to be him."

" 'Sides," Brooks added, "what would Frank Morgan be doin' in a dump like South Raven?"

"Resting and having a cup of coffee," Frank said.

"And minding my own business. Why don't you two shut the hell up, try minding your own business, and leave me alone?"

That shut the cousins up for a moment. They looked at one another. Martin opened and closed his mouth a couple of times, then said, "You cain't talk to me like that, mister, whoever you are. Why . . . I've called men out for less than that."

Not to be undone, Brooks said, "Yeah. Me too."

"Go away," Frank told the pair, a note of weariness in his voice. "I didn't come here looking for trouble."

"Well, now," Martin said. "That's some better. Now you're bein' smart, mister. Nobody with any sense wants to tangle with us."

"I'm sure," Frank replied. "Now go away."

"Maybe we don't want to go away," Brooks said. "Maybe we want to stay and have a drink."

"Then, damnit, drink!" Frank said, raising his voice. "But do it quietly."

"What if we want to talk?" Martin asked, a smirk on his face. "That allowed?"

Frank slowly pushed back his chair and stood up. He was growing very weary of the Olsen boys, and wanted nothing more than to get away from the pair before the situation deteriorated into gunplay.

Martin and Brooks tensed, their hands dropping close to the butts of their guns.

Frank kept his hand away from his .45. "I'll be leaving now."

"Maybe we want you to stay and talk to us," Brooks said. "I mean, you're such a famous person and all that."

"Yeah," Martin said. "It ain't often we get to talk with someone like you. Maybe you can show us how fast you are, Mr. Has-Been. How about it?"

"I really don't think you boys want me to do that," Frank said softly.

"Oh, but we do, Mr. Famous Gunfighter," Brooks said. "As a matter of fact, we insist on it."

The cousins began to giggle like a couple of schoolgirls.

Frank stepped away from the table, his hand dropping to the butt of his pistol. From long experience, he knew the situation was very close to a showdown. He didn't like it, didn't want it, but there it was.

"All right, boys," Frank said. "Here it is. I'm going to walk out that front door. You want to slap iron, do it. Do it right now, or shut your damned mouths."

Brooks and Martin suddenly found the situation had lost all humor. They were facing a man who had never been beaten in a hook-and-draw confrontation. The pair exchanged quick glances. "Easy now, Mr. Morgan," Martin said. "We was only funnin' with you."

Frank offered no reply as he began walking toward the front of the saloon.

"But we'll be around," Brooks said in an effort to save some face.

"So will I," Frank said. He opened the door, shoved open the batwings, and stepped out onto the boardwalk. The batwings clicked and clacked behind him.

"Good thing he left," Martin said. "I'd hate to have had to put lead in him."

"Yeah," Brooks said. "Him bein' kind of a legend and all that. You know he's slowed down to nothin' with age and all."

Liveryman Bob began laughing at that, and the other patrons quickly joined in. Both Brooks and Martin flushed with anger and frustration and turned away, facing the bar. "It ain't over," Martin whispered. "Not by a long shot."

"Damn shore ain't," Brooks said.

"You boys best settle down," Bob told them. "And enjoy life. 'Cause if you push Frank Morgan again, they'll be guns goin' off . . . with the lead flyin' in your direction."

"We ain't scared of that has-been!" Martin blurted out.

"Then you're a couple of damned young fools," Bob replied.

Outside, Frank paused for a moment on the boardwalk long enough to roll a smoke and light it. The chilly wind blew around him unnoticed while Frank was deep in thought. A group of Eastern businessmen were going to hire men, or had hired men, to hunt him for sport? Incredible.

Frank had heard of this happening just once before, but he never knew if it was fact or just some rumor. "I guess it's true," he muttered, and walked on. "What am I, some sort of beast of prey?"

Frank bought some food at the cafe for Dog, and went back to the livery and fed him, making sure he had plenty of water. Stepping outside the livery, he stood and watched as two men rode slowly into town and reined up in front of the saloon. They both stepped stiffly from the saddle and stood for a moment, looking around them. Frank did not recognize them, but he did know the type: gunhandlers. Both of them wore tied-down guns and they were acting wary, carefully looking over the area before moving away from their horses and stepping up onto the boardwalk.

Frank stayed in the shadows of the livery and watched the pair. They stepped onto the boardwalk and stood for a moment, visually checking all around them before disappearing from sight into the saloon.

"Well, I'm not going to stand out in the cold because two strangers rode into town," Frank muttered. He headed for the saloon, intending to go to his room and relax, perhaps read some from a book he'd picked up from a traveling peddler. Frank was not an educated man, in the sense of formal education, but he was well read and always had a couple of books in his saddlebags. He walked back to the saloon. He wanted to avoid trouble, but damned if he was going to sleep in the barn when a warm room was bought and paid for.

The liveryman stepped out just as Frank approached the side door. "Gunslicks in there, Mr. Morgan," Bob said, jerking his thumb toward the batwings.

"I saw them. You know them?"

"Never seen 'em 'fore. But I know what they are."

"They're trouble-hunters, for a fact. Did you hear a name?"

"No. They ain't said nothin' to nobody 'ceptin' the bartender. They ordered coffee and asked about someplace to eat."

"I imagine the Olsen boys will have something to say before long."

"You can bet your bankroll on that. Them boys got mouths that would put an alligator's snout to shame."

Frank smiled at that.

"You gonna ride out, Mr. Morgan?"

"No. I probably should, but I want to find out more about this so-called sporting game those idiots back East dreamed up."

"You think them two gunslicks that rode in is a part of it?"

"I don't know. But I'm going to find out."

"I got to see about my animals. Don't start no

shooting till I get back. It ain't often we get any excitement in this town. I don't wanna miss nothin'."

Frank laughed softly. "I'll do my best, Bob."

Frank stepped inside the saloon and paused for a moment, sizing things up. The Olsen cousins were sitting at a table across the room, the other patrons scattered around the big room. The two gun-handlers were at the bar, drinking coffee. All conversation ceased when Frank entered, all eyes turning to watch him.

Frank walked to the end of the bar closest to the door and ordered a beer. His eyes touched the two gunhands. "Howdy, boys," he greeted them.

Both men nodded their heads in greeting, one saying, "I thought the men in here were joking when they told us Frank Morgan was in town."

"In person," Frank replied. "You boys looking for me?"

"No," the second gun-handler said. "But they's about fifty people who are lookin' for you."

"So I heard. How close are they?"

"Hard to say. Damn detectives are all over the West, snoopin' and askin' questions, tryin' to pinpoint you."

His friend said, "Big money goes to the man who locates you, Morgan."

"You boys interested in that money?" Frank asked casually.

"We could use it, but it'd be tainted, far as I'm concerned. I've hired my gun for a lot of reasons, but"—he shook his head—"this here huntin' a man for sport is stupid. I ain't takin' no part in it."

"Nor me," his saddle partner said. "They's a little nothin' town 'bout fifty miles east of here that's fillin' up with bounty hunters. I 'spect they'll be in this area in a week."

"Was I you, Morgan," his partner said, "I'd head

west, for California maybe. Get the hell out of this
area. Your life ain't worth spit 'round here."

"I never was much for running," Frank said
softly, then took a sip of beer.

"Us neither. But man, they's a whole damn mob
after you."

"How much money on my head?" Frank asked.

"Thousands of dollars. I don't rightly know the
exact figure. We've heard everything from ten
thousand to fifty thousand dollars."

"And that'll draw the trash out of the garbage
pile," the other gunslick said. "Along with the ants
and the flies and the maggots."

Frank nodded his head in agreement. "You boys
want a drink? On me?"

"Appreciate it. Right after this coffee. It's a tad
chilly outside. We're warmin' our innards some."

"Give them what they want," Frank told the barkeep. "And put it on my tab."

"If I knew who was payin' the money for your
dead stinkin' butt and how to collect it," Brooks
Olsen said, "I'd brace you right now, Morgan."

"That's whiskey talkin', boy," the bartender
called. "Shut your mouth."

"Don't tell me what to do, Pops," Brooks said.
"And mind your own business."

"Suit yourself," the bartender said with a shrug.
"It's your funeral."

Frank leaned against the bar and sipped his beer
in silence.

"It's damn shore gonna be somebody's funeral,"
Martin said. "But it ain't gonna be ours."

The two gunslicks glanced at Frank and smiled
knowingly. Frank acknowledged the smile with an
arched eyebrow.

The door opened with a rush of cold wind and
Dr. Raven walked into the saloon and up to the
bar, taking a position beside Frank. "Getting colder

outside," the doctor said after telling the bartender to bring him a cup of coffee.

"How's your patient?" Frank asked.

"Complaining," the doctor said. "Which is a good sign." He glanced at the clock behind the bar. "Stage is due anytime now."

"Expecting somebody?"

"No. Just some newspapers from back East. This time tomorrow we'll only be a couple of months behind times."

"Late for a stage, isn't it?" Frank asked.

"It's a regular stop. They'll spend the night here. And the driver always has more news. The stage layover is always a big event."

"Daily stop?"

"Twice a week. Sometimes three times a week. Supply wagons roll in twice a month."

"You have a telegraph here, don't you?"

"When the wires are up. You want to send a message?"

"Nothing urgent. Just asking."

"Maybe he wants to call in some help," Brooks said. "Like maybe the Army."

Doc Raven turned to look at the young man. "You have a big mouth, Brooks. And big ears. Why don't you mind your own business?"

"Why don't you go to hell, Doc?" Brooks popped right back. He stood up, his right hand dropping to his side, close to the butt of his pistol.

"The doc ain't armed, Brooks," the bartender said. "And you know it."

"Morgan is," Brooks said.

Frank turned to face the young man. "Why are you pushing me, boy?"

"I ain't no boy, Morgan. And I'll tell you something else. I don't like you at all. What do you think about that?"

Frank smiled. "I think, boy, that I've had all your

damn mouth I intend to take. Now either drag iron or shut the hell up. It's your choice."

The saloon became as silent as the grave as the wall clock began chiming the hour.

Three

"Stage coming!" someone shouted from outside. "And it's full of passengers."

The tense moment was shattered when all the bar patrons began rushing toward the front door. One of the men bumped into Brooks Olsen. Brooks was wound up tight as a drumhead and lost his balance. He cursed and put out a hand to grab the edge of the table. His eyes were wide, suspecting that Frank would take that time to shoot him.

Frank leaned against the bar.

"They'll be another day, Morgan," Brooks said.

"Take your time, boy," Frank cautioned him. "You've got a long life ahead of you."

"Hell with you!"

"Whatever," Frank replied. He turned his back to the angry young man and signaled the barkeep to bring him a cup of coffee.

Brooks and Martin stomped out of the saloon.

"Stage arrival is a big event in this town," Frank said.

"You bet," the barkeep replied, pouring Frank a cup of coffee. "Although it usually don't amount to a hill of beans when it comes to people gettin' off. Newspapers is what the folks want. News is mighty scarce around here."

The front door opened and the liveryman, Bob,

yelled, "They's two stages this run, boys. Both of them full of folks. Git some rooms ready, Phil."

"Phil?" Frank asked.

"That's me," the barkeep said. "Help yourself to the coffee, boys. I got to get some rooms ready for the crowd."

"We'll look after the bar, Phil," Doc Raven assured him.

"Trusting person," Frank remarked.

"Small town, Frank. Full of good people."

"For a while, Doc. But they'll get tired of me pretty fast."

"Nonsense!"

"You'll see. I've been through it many times. If it's one thing I know, it's human nature."

"We'll see. Frank, where is your home?"

"The West, Doc. Wherever I choose to hang my hat."

"I hear you're a man of some means."

"I'm not going to miss any meals because of lack of funds."

Doc Raven laughed. "That's an interesting way of putting it."

"You hustling cash for your bank, Doc?" Frank asked with a smile.

"Hell, yes!" the doctor responded with a matching smile.

The conversation came to a close as the batwings squeaked and the front door opened, the entrance filling up with passengers from the two stages. Six men and four women trooped into the saloon. The passengers were all dressed to the nines: all but one of the men in suits and stiff collars, the women in fancy traveling dresses.

"Easterners," Frank said in a low voice. "Most of them."

"City folks for sure," Doc Raven agreed.

"I am exhausted," one of the fancy men exclaimed. "I insist upon a hot bath immediately. Where is the proprietor of this wretched hovel?"

"Bringin' in all your damn travelin' bags," Phil said, dumping a pile of luggage on the floor. "Sort it out, folks. I got to bring in all them trunks now."

"Well!" one of the women said in a huffy voice. "Hospitality is very thin here."

"What the hell is a wretched hovel?" Bob asked, walking up to the bar. "Is that somethin' good?"

"You there!" a passenger said, waggling a finger at Frank. "Get us something to drink and be quick about it."

"Go sit on a cactus," Frank told him.

"You obviously don't realize whom you are addressing," the man said.

"Nope. I sure don't. And furthermore, I don't care."

"What an impudent fellow," another passenger said.

Doc Raven smiled at the exchange. He turned to face the weary travelers. "I'm Dr. Raven," he announced. "Welcome to South Raven. But I must warn you, this is not New York City. There are no doormen or valets here."

"That much is quite obvious," one of the ladies said. "You're Dr. Raven and the town is South Raven. The . . . village is named after you?"

"Yes."

"How wonderful," another of the ladies said. "Perhaps you could tell us where we register for our rooms?"

"Through that door right over there," Doc Raven replied, pointing. "Just sign your names to the register and grab a key."

"And tote your own luggage," Frank added.

"You, sir," one of the men said, "are a most disagreeable fellow."

"There is a saying out here, folks," Frank replied. "You stomp your own snakes and saddle your own horses."

"How quaint," another of the men said. "I'm sure I will treasure that rather pithy remark forever."

Frank started to tell him where he could shove his reply, then decided against it. He turned his back to the Easterners and sipped his coffee.

"There are bathing facilities in the rooms?" one of the ladies inquired hopefully.

"No," Doc Raven told her. "Sorry. You can have a bath behind the barbershop. If you don't want to share the water, you'd better tell the barber now so he can get ready."

"Share the water?" a man said. "How primitive."

"Save some water for me," Frank said, hiding his smile. "I got to bathe my dog."

"Bathe your *dog?*" a woman almost shouted.

"He don't have many fleas," Frank replied, fighting back his laughter, his back to the travelers. "They'll be dead 'fore you strip off anyways."

"Civilization has not yet reached this outpost," a man said.

"Do you have savage red Indians here?" a woman questioned.

"Not many," Frank said. "But you don't have to worry about Injuns. Most of them don't like white women. Y'all smell funny to them."

"I beg your pardon!" the woman shouted, stamping her foot.

"I never seen so much crap in all my life," Phil said, carrying in a heavy trunk and dumping it on the floor. "It's gonna take me an hour to tote all this junk in. You men come on out here and give me a hand."

The one male passenger who was not dressed as fancy as the others had taken a seat at a table and had said nothing. But his eyes had never left Frank.

Frank had singled him out immediately. He was not wearing a pistol . . . that could be seen. Frank didn't know the man, but he knew the type. The two gunslicks that had been standing at the bar had taken their drinks and moved to another table.

Conversation waned as the men went outside to help with the luggage. The women waited impatiently.

The trunks began piling up in the front of the saloon as the men struggled them into the large drinking area.

"We can't get them through the door to the hotel lobby," one of the men complained. "This is the worst hostel I have ever experienced."

"With the rudest counter help," another man added.

"What counter help?" yet another traveler asked.

"Where's the newspapers and magazines?" someone shouted from the outside.

"I can't imagine these people actually read," one of the women said disdainfully. "It's so primitive here."

"Do you suppose we could have something to drink while we're waiting?" a woman inquired.

"Coffee or water?" Doc Raven asked.

"Coffee would be wonderful," the woman replied. "Two lumps and a splash."

"Two lumps and a splash of what?" one of the locals asked.

"Sugar and cream," Frank told him.

The woman looked at Frank, a strange glint in her eyes. "The man actually has some knowledge of genteel behavior, ladies. How curious."

"Quite, Margaret. You there!" she called to Frank.

Frank turned away from the bar. "What do you want, lady?"

"Don't speak to Mrs. Dunbar in that tone of voice," the man at the table warned Frank.

Frank ignored him and continued looking at Mrs. Dunbar.

"You seem to possess some level of education . . . rudimentary, I'm sure. What do you do for a living? Are you a cowboy?"

"No," Frank replied shortly, and turned back to his coffee. This entire gaggle of Easterners irritated him with their superior attitude.

"Well," Mrs. Dunbar pressed, "are you going to answer my question?"

"I'm independently wealthy," Frank said with a small smile. The truth was, he was extremely wealthy. He owned railroad stock, holdings in several producing gold mines, and many, many shares in other companies, thanks to his ex-wife, who, after her father had driven Frank away with false accusations, remarried into a very wealthy family. Before Vivian Browning was killed, she'd set Frank up for life . . . as well as a son who didn't have a whole lot of use for Frank.

"Yes," Mrs. Dunbar said haughtily, "you certainly look wealthy." Then she laughed very mockingly.

"Do you have a name?" Margaret asked.

"Frank."

"Frank . . . what?"

"Frank will do."

"You're not very friendly, Frank," Margaret said.

The man who had warned Frank about addressing Mrs. Dunbar abruptly stood up. "That's Frank Morgan!"

Frank stood quietly at the bar, but he had turned slightly, his right hand dropping to his side, not far from the butt of his .45 Peacemaker.

The men had just reentered the saloon, burdened with heavy trunks. They froze at the shouted announcement.

"Is that true?" Margaret asked in a soft voice. "Are you Frank Morgan?"

"Yes," Frank said.

"My God," Mrs. Dunbar whispered. "Hugh? There he is, in person."

"I see him, Colette," Hugh replied, carefully setting the trunk on the floor.

Frank cut his eyes to the man. Nothing extraordinary about him. Just another Easterner, all duded up.

"You want me to take him now, Mr. Knox?" the man who had first recognized Frank asked.

"No, Sonny," the Easterner said. "That would spoil the game for everyone."

Frank ignored Knox and cut his eyes to Sonny. "Just where are you figuring to take me, Sonny?"

"Anywhere and anytime I choose, Morgan."

"And how are you planning on doing that, Sonny? Fists or guns?" Frank moved his hand to the metal coffeepot Phil had placed on the bar. Frank had poured his own coffee, and guessed the pot was about half full.

"Sonny . . ." Knox said.

Sonny ignored the man. "I'll show you people that this so-called tough-as-nails gunfighter is nothing but a washed-up has-been."

Sonny took several steps toward Frank, and with one fluid movement, Frank closed his hand around the handle of the coffeepot, took one step, and smacked Sonny in the center of the forehead with the heavy pot. Hot coffee splattered as the pot impacted against Sonny's head with a dull clunking sound and Sonny stretched out on the floor, out cold.

Frank put the dented pot back on the bar. "Damn shame to waste good coffee like that," he said. "But coffee's easier to clean up than blood."

Four

A wicked cut of lightning flashed outside, followed by a tremendous clap of thunder. The thunder rattled the windows of the saloon.

"My word!" one of the Eastern men exclaimed.

"It's gonna rain like a bull pissin' on a flat rock," Bob said. He looked at the women. " 'Cuse my language, ladies. I forgot you was here."

"Clouds have been building all day," Frank said as Sonny groaned on the floor. "I suspect the storm is going to be a bad one."

"How do you know that?" a woman asked.

"Because it's building from the east. Anytime a storm blows in here from that direction, it's a bad one."

The stage driver walked in, carrying the last of the luggage. "Startin' to rain," he said. He glanced at the man on the barroom floor. "What happened to him?"

"He got tired and decided to take a nap," Bob told him.

"Well, somebody step over him and get me a drink," the driver said. "I got me a hunch we're all gonna get to know each other right well if this storm is as bad as it looks."

"What do you mean?" one of the traveling men asked.

"We're sometimes cut off here after a bad

storm," Doc Raven explained. "Sometimes for a couple of weeks. The passes are closed due to rock slides, and bridges wash out. While your rooms are being readied, why don't we introduce ourselves and have a drink? You people might be here for several days."

"There is a man lying unconscious and perhaps badly hurt on the floor!" a woman said, her voice filled with indignation. "And nothing is being done to help him."

"He's all right," Doc Raven said. "But he'll have a headache when he wakes up. What is your name, madam?"

"Nora Greene. That is my husband," she said, pointing, "Edmund."

Sonny groaned and put a hand to his head. He made no attempt to rise from the barroom floor.

"I'm John Garver," a man said. "My wife decided at the last minute not to accompany us on this Western adventure."

"The manhunt, you mean?" Raven asked.

"Well . . . yes."

"Are you one of the men who put up money to hunt me like some sort of rabid animal?" Frank asked.

"Ah . . . well . . . yes," John said.

"What kind of people are you?" Frank questioned. "I'm not a criminal. I'm not wanted by any court. What kind of mind considers a manhunt sport?"

Sonny groaned and managed to sit up on the floor. There was a trickle of blood and a swelling knot in the center of his forehead. His glazed eyes found Frank. "You bastard! I'll kill you," he mumbled.

"I doubt it," Frank replied. "Now just sit there and shut up." He looked at the group of men and women and pointed to Sonny. "Is this dude in your employ?"

"He is our bodyguard," Margaret said. "He is one of the finest bodyguards in all of New York City."

"Well, if your fine bodyguard isn't careful, he's going to be a dead bodyguard," Frank told her. "This isn't New York City, folks. Out here, the rules of conduct are somewhat different."

"I should have you arrested," a man blurted out. "I believe I shall summon a police officer right now."

"Yeah, you do that," the stage driver said, looking up from his mug of beer. "I think they's a deputy 'bout a hundred miles east of here. If the rain was to stop right now, and the telegraph wires ain't down, and the passes ain't closed by slides, or the bridges ain't washed out, I figure he'd get here in 'bout a week or so."

"That is incredible," the man responded.

"Welcome to Idaho Territory," Frank said.

Outside, lightning and thunder hissed and boomed and the rains came pouring down, hammering on the roof.

"Gonna be a bad one," Bob said. "Good thing the supply wagons just run. 'Cause we're damn sure gonna be cut off for a spell."

"This is dreadful," Nora said.

"Not as dreadful as it's going to be when some of your gunfighters catch up with me," Frank said, his voice hard.

"It's uncommonly warm," Doc Raven said to Frank the next morning. The men were having breakfast in the cafe. The heavy rains had not abated. "I've seen it like this a couple of times over the years. Both times during a heavy rain. The slides are going to be bad—bet on it."

The telegrapher walked in, waved at the waitress, and took a seat at the table with Frank and Doc Raven. "Wires just went down," he said. "That means the slides have started."

"We're cut off?" Frank asked.

"We sure are. Thirty miles to the east and thirty miles to the west. The last wire I received was informing me that about a dozen or so wagons were on the way from the east. No way of knowing whether they made it through Wildhorse Pass."

"Wildhorse Pass is where the slides start?" Frank asked.

"Not necessarily," Doc Raven replied. "But it's the worst place coming from the east. If they made it past that point, they'll probably be rolling in here late today or tomorrow."

"Supply wagons?" Frank asked.

"Maybe one or two of them," the telegrapher said. "The others are probably settlers. No way of knowin' till they roll in."

"I didn't stick to the roads," Frank said, "and followed old trails over the Divide. I don't know much about what lies west of here. How about that way?"

"The way west on the main road is worse," Doc Raven said. "If any travelers made it to the old trading post about twenty five miles west of here, they can get through to South Raven. If not, they're stuck."

"So there is a possibility this town is going to fill up with men looking to gun me down," Frank said softly.

"Could be," Doc Raven said. "Things might get real interesting about here."

"Interesting is not the word I would use, Doc."

"You best sharpen your tools, Doc," the telegrapher said with a smile. "Odds are good that you're gonna get real busy diggin' out lead."

"Not if I pull out right now," Frank said.

"Are you considering that?" Raven asked.

Frank shook his head. "Not really. It was just a thought."

"It would be a tough pull over the mountains in this weather," the telegrapher said. "And dangerous. No matter which direction you headed."

Frank smiled at that. "Any more dangerous than me staying here and possibly facing several dozen guns?"

"Good point," Raven said. "So what are you going to do?"

"I'm going to wait until the rains ease up, then pull out."

"It'll be several days at least, maybe even a week or more, after the rains stop before the road is cleared. Believe me, we've been through this before."

"I'm sure you have," Frank said. "Say, back about ten years ago, there was a little town north of here. Along the Payette. Is it still there?"

"The buildings are," Doc Raven replied. "The last of the people pulled out, oh, five years ago, I guess. Red Rock was the name of the place."

"Yeah, that's it. I stopped there for supplies. Gold-mining town, I recall."

"Gold-mining fiasco was what it was. There never was any gold there, except what was salted in a couple of caves by that thieving ne'er-do-well who bilked a lot of people out of their money."

"Whatever happened to him?"

"Some folks down in Utah hanged him a few years ago."

Frank smiled. "Don't tell me he tried to pull something over on the Mormons?"

"Yes. And he didn't make it. They were on to him like a weevil to flour. Strung him up."

"Probably deserved it."

"Ten times over," Doc Raven said.

A local stuck his head into the cafe. "Wagons and riders coming in from the east."

The three men stepped outside to the boardwalk to watch the arrival of the travelers.

"Those sure are some fancy wagons," the telegrapher remarked. "I never seen anything like them."

"Made to order," Frank said. "For the rich to travel in comfort and style."

"More Easterners," Doc Raven said. "You suppose those are more of the men who put up the money for the hunt, Frank?"

"Probably. And the outriders are hired bodyguards."

"You know any of them?"

Frank shook his head. "No."

"Tough-looking bunch."

"Wonder where they're gonna stay," the telegrapher declared. "There ain't no more rooms to be had at the saloon."

"Who cares?" Doc Raven replied.

Frank leaned against a support post and rolled a smoke as the fancy wagons rolled slowly past. The men on horseback all gave Frank hard looks. Frank returned the looks.

"They're sure giving you the once-over," Doc Raven said.

"They know who I am," Frank replied. "I suspect they've been thoroughly briefed. I imagine it won't be long before some of the good citizens of the town will approach me, or you, asking that I please leave town."

"There might be a few who will ask that," Doc

Raven replied softly. "But they will be in the minority."

"Wait until the streets get bloody," Frank said.

The telegrapher walked back to his small office as the wagons continued to roll slowly through the town.

"Maxwell Crawford!" a man shouted, walking out of the saloon/hotel and waving to a wagon.

The wagon lurched to a stop.

"Maxwell Industries," Doc Raven said. "I don't believe it."

"You know him?" Frank asked.

"We went to school together back East. Both of us sparked the same girl for a time. Wilma Lewis. I heard they got married right after the war."

"My, my. This might turn out to be quite a reunion for you."

"Maxwell was a pacifist, or so he claimed at the time. I heard he bought his way out of serving in the war."

"A lot of men did."

"More in the North than in the South," Raven challenged.

Frank did not reply. He was not interested in the politics of the War of the Northern Aggression. The war was over and the country had healed many of the open wounds that lingered after that violent upheaval.

"Bernard!" a man shouted, climbing out of the wagon. "I'm glad you made it. Where is Margaret?"

Maxwell Crawford stepped up onto the boardwalk and the two men shook hands. Their conversation did not carry across the street to Doc Raven and Frank.

Frank watched as a lone rider stepped his horse up the street. "Now, there is a man I do know."

"Where?"

"Riding into town. His name is Dolan. Damn! I

thought he was dead. Rumor has it that he was killed in a range war."

"Gunfighter?" Doc Raven asked.

"One of the best."

"Better than you?"

"I don't know. He's quick. I'll give him that."

Raven studied the man as he drew closer. "You two are about the same age, I'd guess."

"Just about."

Dolan reined up in front of the cafe and sat his saddle, staring at Frank for a moment before saying, "Morgan. It's been a few years."

"About ten years, Dolan. I heard you finally caught some lead and got planted."

"It was close, for sure. But I fooled the Reaper again."

"I'll leave you two to reminisce about old times," Doc Raven said. He walked away after a curt nod to Dolan.

"Friend of yours, Morgan?" Dolan asked.

"The town's doctor and namesake. Raven."

"Interesting name. Wonder if it's really his."

Frank shrugged. "It'll do. You know how it is out here, Dolan."

"For a fact, I do. I've plumb forgot the name my parents give me." He smiled. "Ah . . . you do know that we're cut off here, Morgan?"

"So I'm told. With a bunch of rich men from back East and their hoity-toity women."

"They all put up money for this hunt, Morgan, and yet here you are, standing around like nothing important is taking place."

"How much money is on my head, Dolan?"

"I ain't sure. Thousands of dollars, I'm told. The last man standin' after you hit the ground is the winner, so I'm told."

"So it's not just me that'll have to watch his back."

"What do you mean, Morgan?"

"You said it yourself, Dolan. 'The last man standing.' "

Dolan frowned. "Yeah. That do put a different light on things, don't it?"

"I would say so."

"I reckon I better start clearin' the herd some."

"Why don't you do that."

"I will, in due time, Morgan. You ain't plannin' on cuttin' out, are you?"

"I'm going to stick around. I wouldn't miss this show for the world."

"You're a strange man, Morgan. Mighty strange. See you."

Morgan nodded and watched as the man lifted the reins and rode away. Boot-steps sounded on the boardwalk to his left. A cold voice said, "Turn around and face me, Drifter. I got dollar signs in my eyes."

Five

Frank turned slowly. The man only a few steps away was a stranger, but he had the hard-bitten stamp of a hired gun on his face and in his eyes. "Has the hunt begun already?" Frank asked softly, his right hand near the butt of his Peacemaker.

"I ain't been told otherwise, so I reckon so."

"You got any kin?"

"Huh? What business is it of yourn whether I do or not?"

"Someone's going to have to be notified of your death, stranger."

"My death! What the hell are you talkin' 'bout?"

"You pull on me and you're a dead man," Frank said, his voice cold as the grave.

The stranger hesitated, then said, "You damn sure of yourself, ain't you, Drifter?"

"I sure am. Now turn around and walk away from me and live."

"Naw," the man said, shaking his head. "I done made my brags. So grab iron, Drifter."

"After you," Frank replied, meeting the man's eyes. "It's your show."

Across the street, the occupants of the newly arrived wagons had climbed down and were silent, watching the life-and-death standoff between the two men on the boardwalk.

"So that's Frank Morgan?" Maxwell Crawford asked his friend Bernard Harrison.

"That's him. A rather unimposing chap, isn't he?"

"Certainly seems that way from here. Who is that lout confronting him?"

"I have no idea."

"Hi-ho, chums," Horace Vanderhoot said, walking up, his wife, Nellie, with him.

"Horace!" Maxwell and Bernard both said at once.

"What a dismal little village," Nellie remarked, looking around her. "I am told there is no hotel."

"Only a few rooms above the saloon," Bernard said. "But I was just informed there is a boarding-house on a side street."

"We anticipated few accommodations," Aaron Steele said, walking up to the group, his wife, Ethel, by his side. "Which is why we endeavored to have our wagons equipped as lavishly as was humanly possible."

"Is there a place to bathe in this depressing mud hole?" Ethel inquired.

"A bathhouse behind the barbershop," Bernard told her. "It's primitive, but functional. You must bring your own soap, however."

"Are those two fellows going to shoot one another?" Aaron asked, staring at Frank and the challenger.

"I rather believe the moment has passed," Bernard said. "From here, it seems Frank Morgan is unwilling to draw his pistol."

"Well, poo!" Ethel said. "I wanted to see a Wild West shoot-out."

"Oh, you will, my dear," her husband assured her. "Before this is over, we'll see several, I'm sure."

Frank's challenger lost his grit. His shoulders sagged and he took several deep breaths. "All right,

Drifter," he said. "You win this round. But they's gonna be another day."

"There usually is," Frank said. "But like the Indians say: Any day is a good day to die."

The stranger turned and walked away. Frank stepped off the boardwalk and into the light drizzle that continued to fall. The sky had cleared a bit that morning; now clouds were once more rolling in and the drizzle would be only a precursor to more heavy rain.

Frank walked over to the growing crowd of Easterners and stopped in front of Maxwell Crawford. He stood for a moment, staring at the rich Yankee. "You one of the men who put up money to hunt me?"

"There are several rifles trained on you right now, Morgan," Maxwell said. "Accost me and you're dead in the street."

"Too damn yellow to do your own fighting, are you?"

"I'll have you know I'm quite a good boxer, Morgan. I daresay you're never fought with your fists, so if I were you, I'd not push too hard."

Frank stared at the man for a moment, then began laughing. The more he laughed, the madder Maxwell Crawford became.

"Here now, you dolt!" Maxwell demanded. "Stop that!"

Frank took off his hat and wiped his eyes with the back of his hand, his laughter gradually fading to a chuckle. "I needed that, Tough Man," Frank said. "Thanks for brightening my day."

"Needed that?" Maxwell almost shouted the words. "What do you mean by that, you . . . you . . . misbegotten cretin?"

"A good laugh, that's what I mean. Thanks for that."

"You were laughing at *me?"* Maxwell said, his face

deepening with a flush. "That 'Tough Man' remark was fraught with sarcasm. I demand an apology!"

Frank looked at the man, then quietly told him where he could stick his demand . . . sideways and with great force.

"Oh, my stars and garters!" Wilma said, putting a hand to her forehead. "How crude!"

Several locals who were standing on the boardwalk began laughing.

"Stop that!" Bernard shouted, whirling around. "Vulgarity is not in the least amusing."

"I should thrash you!" Maxwell shouted at Frank.

"In your dreams, Cream Puff," Frank told him.

"Cream Puff?" Maxwell yelled. "Cream Puff! That does it. Prepare to defend yourself, you ignorant oaf!"

"I'll be your second," Bernard offered.

"That's fair," Horace Vanderhoot said. "After all, they were fraternity brothers."

"Done," Maxwell declared. He stepped back and took off his coat, handing it to his wife, Wilma. "Hold this, dear. I shan't be long."

Frank stood a few feet in front of the rich industrialist, waiting for the man to make the first aggressive move.

"Do try not to roll about in the mud, dear," Wilma said. "It's dreadful out here."

Across the street, Doc Raven had reappeared, standing under a boardwalk awning, watching and listening to the crowd. "Maxwell," he muttered. "You're just as arrogant as you were in school. And now you're about to get your ass whipped." He looked long at Wilma. "Still a lovely woman," he muttered.

"Are you ready to take your thrashing, Morgan?" Maxwell bellowed as he did a couple of stretching exercises. He held his arms up, hands clenched into fists. His left arm was stretched out in front of him and his left fist held close to his chin.

"If you insist on this nonsense, come on," Frank told him.

Maxwell waggled his left fist under Frank's nose in the hopes of drawing a swing from Frank, thus enabling him to uncork a left.

Frank didn't take the bait. He stood with his fists half raised, a faint smile on his lips. Frank was the veteran of dozens of brawls—kick, bite, and gouge types—and he also knew a bit about the N art of boxing. Maxwell Crawford looked to be in good physical shape; probably worked out in some sort of gym. But he was about to tangle with a man who was strong as an ox and didn't have an ounce of back-up in him.

Maxwell tried a sharp quick right, and Frank moved his head ever so slightly and the right whistled by him.

Maxwell grunted and his eyes narrowed. He was beginning to realize that he was facing a man who knew something about boxing. Then he knew for a fact he was when Frank's gloved right fist suddenly smacked him in the mouth. Maxwell shook his head and backed up, spitting away blood from busted lips.

"Knock his block off, Maxwell!" one of his supporters yelled.

Maxwell did not reply. He did not take his eyes off Frank, knowing now that he was facing a man who could box and punch like a pile driver. Maxwell spat away more blood and tried a left. Frank blocked it easily.

More wagons had pulled in, stopping in the middle of the muddy and rutted street so their passengers could watch the fight. Another half-dozen or so wagons were just entering the town, followed by a dozen or so mounted men. The riders rode on around the wagons and reined up across the street and down a few stores from the fight.

Maxwell slipped a left through that jarred Frank. The man could punch, Frank would sure give him that. Maxwell's friends roared their approval at his scoring a wicked blow. But their roars of approval turned to sudden silence when Frank blasted Maxwell with a left and a right. The blows knocked Maxwell back several steps, and he lost his balance and sat down on the edge of the boardwalk, blood seeping from his nose.

Frank would have normally stepped in while his aggressor was addled and finished the fight. But this time he didn't. He simply took a couple of paces back and waited for the Easterner to regain his senses and stand up.

"I say," Bernard Harrison said. "The man does have some sporting blood in him. Quite fair of you, Gunfighter."

"Yes," Aaron Steele said. "Really white of you, old boy."

Frank cut his eyes at the men and said nothing. But he was thinking, What a pack of nincompoops.

"Time, time!" another man shouted from the crowd. "Time for a one-minute rest period."

"Good God!" Frank muttered.

"What the hell's all that about?" a local questioned.

"New rules," Bernard announced. "A rest period every few minutes."

"Well, ain't that just spiffy?" another local said. "Frank, why don't you just shoot the feller and be done with it?"

"Here now!" Aaron said. "There'll be none of that."

"Relax," Frank told him. "This is fists until someone pulls a gun."

Maxwell stood up and jabbed at the air a couple of times. "I'm ready. Round two coming up."

"Well, come on then," Frank said. "I got things to do."

"Are you in that big a hurry for a thrashing?" Maxwell asked.

"Maxwell," Frank said, "just get your fists up and fight, will you? And shut that damn big mouth."

"I'm really going to whip you proper for that uncalled-for remark."

"Bring your ass on, Rich Boy!"

Maxwell flushed and rushed in, ready to pummel Frank to the ground, and Frank promptly knocked him on his butt in the mud. Maxwell floundered around for half a minute, his lips bloody from the blow, before he slowly crawled to his feet. He stood for a moment in the cold drizzle, glaring at Frank, the mud dripping off him.

"What's the matter, Rich Boy? You ready to admit you're facing the better man and quit?"

"You insolent cretin!" Maxwell shouted. "How dare you speak to me in such a tone of voice?"

"Well, come on, then, Puke Face! Fight!"

"Puke Face?" Maxwell yelled.

"That's you, Maxie Baby."

"Damn you!" Maxwell shouted. He took a run at Frank and Frank sidestepped, stuck out a boot, and tripped the man. Maxwell went sprawling face-first into the mud. Frank stood and laughed at him.

Maxwell slowly got to his knees and tried to wipe the mud from his face. All he succeeded in doing was spreading it around. The man was covered with mud, from his shoes to his face, all mixed in with a bit of horse crap.

Someone in the crowd of locals began laughing, and soon it became infectious. Maxwell's anger grew the louder the crowd laughed.

"Damn you!" Maxwell shouted at Frank and the crowd of locals. "Stop laughing at me!"

The laughter grew louder.

"You ready to quit now?" Frank asked the Easterner.

"Hell, no!" Maxwell shouted.

"Well, come on then," Frank told him. "Let's get this over with."

Maxwell struggled to get to his feet. He almost made it before he lost his balance and fell face-first into the muddy street.

That set the crowd off again. Peals of laughter ripped the cool, drizzly air. Children had joined their parents along the boardwalk, and their pointing and giggling seemed to infuriate Maxwell.

"Brats!" he screamed at the kids. "Incorrigible ragamuffins!"

"Fall down again," one little girl called. "You're a funny man."

"Oh . . ." Maxwell flailed his arms as he got to his knees. He could not find the words to express his anger.

Frank walked out into the street just as Maxwell was getting to his feet. Maxwell took a wild swing at Frank and Frank sidestepped. Maxwell could not check his forward momentum. He again went face-first into the mud and horse crap of the street. The locals cheered and applauded and laughed.

"Hell, it's over," Frank said, and turned to walk away.

"You stop right where you are!" Maxwell shouted, after spitting out a mouthful of mud. "I will dictate the conclusion of this match."

"You've got to be joking," Frank said, pausing and turning around. "You can't even stand up."

Maxwell slowly and carefully rose to his feet and lifted his fists. "Now, fight, you oaf!" he shouted.

Frank sighed and walked out to face Maxwell.

He took one long look at the man and popped him on the jaw with a quick, hard right. Maxwell's eyes rolled back in his head and he stretched out in the mud and did not move.

"Now it's over," Frank said. He walked back to the boardwalk to the cheers and applause of the locals.

Six

Frank slopped across the muddy street, just making it to the other side and stepping up under the boardwalk as the skies opened up and torrents of rain came pouring down.

Maxwell's friends dragged him unceremoniously out of the street by the feet, and hoisted him up onto the boardwalk.

"Somebody get a pitcher of water," Bernard said, as Maxwell's wife, Wilma, hovered nearby, sobbing and moaning about her poor, poor poopsie.

"Poopsie?" a local questioned. "Did she say poopsie?"

"She did," another local said. "Poopsie. Ain't that pitiful?"

In his room, Frank poured water into the basin and washed up, then spread a paper sack he'd gotten from the lobby, took off his boots, and scraped the mud from them. "Well," he muttered, "at least I didn't have to shoot anyone."

But he had made a very bitter enemy. He realized that for a fact.

He pulled a rocking chair over to the window that looked out over the street, and checked the scene out. More gunslicks had ridden into town with the newly arrived wagons.

"I should slip out of here quietly and head into the timber and just vanish for a few months," Frank said while the rain drummed against the side of the building.

But he knew he wouldn't do that. He couldn't do that. It just wasn't in him to run away. Besides, he had his doubts the Easterners would give up; they'd just wait until he resurfaced, and the hunt would be on again.

And there was this too: He just couldn't believe in this day and time the authorities would allow something like this hunt to continue. The West was still wild, sure, but this hunt was ridiculous. It was savage. And illegal.

"I insist you march right up to that barbarian's room and demand that he vacate it immediately!" The woman's voice reached Frank from the small lobby.

A man said something that Frank couldn't catch.

"But he's a notorious murderer!" the woman persisted.

Again, the man's voice, probably the bartender/desk clerk, couldn't be heard.

"But we need that room for some of our friends!" the woman yelled.

This time, the man's voice could be heard. "Well, damnit, lady, you can't have it. It's signed and paid for."

Frank smiled at that.

"You are a very impolite man!" the woman yelled.

The conversation faded from earshot, and Frank once more turned his attention back to the rainy street. The wagons had been moved out to the end of the street, and the newly arrived gunfighters were nowhere in sight. Probably all downstairs in the saloon, Frank thought. He pulled on his boots and slung his gunbelt around him. He checked the loads in his Peacemaker and then, after a short pause, rummaged in his saddlebags and took out a short-barreled .45, loaded it up, and stuck it behind his belt, left side, butt forward. He slipped on his coat and exited the room, carefully locking the door behind him.

He went out to the street through the small hotel lobby, and walked over to the cafe to buy some food for Dog, then strolled down to Bob's livery. The stagecoaches were parked by the side of the building, the horses in the corral. Frank forked some hay for Horse, gave Dog his food, and filled up the water bucket. After he ate his fill, Dog went outside for a few minutes to do his business, then returned to the stall, circled his bed a half dozen times, and then curled up and went to sleep.

Frank stood in the huge open entrance to the livery for a few minutes, just out of the steady drizzle, looking up and down the street. Foot traffic was, at this time, very light.

"I can't hide all day," Frank muttered. "And I sure have no intention of running." He checked his watch, then snapped the lid closed. Far too early for a drink. "Think I'll have some coffee," he whispered. "And let the chips fall."

He walked to the boardwalk and stepped up, slowly making his way toward the saloon, under the protective cover of the awning.

Frank entered the saloon and as soon as he did, all conversation ceased and all eyes turned toward him. He walked over to the bar and took his place at the far end, his back protected.

"What'll it be, Frank?" Phil asked.

"Got some fresh-made coffee?"

"Just fixed a pot. I'll get you a cup." Phil leaned close and whispered, "Lonesome Howard is here."

Frank's eyes narrowed. "Where?"

"Sittin' in the shadows to your left, against the wall."

"I thought he retired about five years ago,"

Frank replied in a low voice. "And was ranching down in Arizona Territory."

"I guess the big money drawed him out. I'll get your coffee."

Frank took his coffee and walked across the large, crowded room to the table where Lonesome was sitting by himself, a bottle of whiskey and a Bible in front of him. Frank sat down and stared at the man for a few silent seconds.

"Frank." Lonesome broke the silence. "You're looking well."

"And you, Howard."

"Thank you. Time has treated me well, I must admit." He stared at Frank for a short time. "Why are you still here, Frank?"

"Running is something I don't do well."

"I understand."

"I thought you gave up gunslinging."

"The money is too good this time, Frank. I hope you realize this is nothing personal."

"I know. How much goes to the man who kills me?"

"Many thousands of dollars."

"And you think you can take me, Howard?"

Lonesome smiled and tapped the closed Bible. "There is a time to kill, Frank. Says so right here in the Good Book."

Frank returned the smile. "Don't tell me you think you're doing God's work?"

"I reckon perhaps I am. You've killed a lot of men in your time here on this earth."

"They were trying to kill me."

Lonesome shook his head. "Perhaps that was true in a few cases, but not always. You have a sickness, Frank. And the only way it can be cured is with a bullet."

"From your gun?"

"I hope so."

"You'll understand if I don't wish you luck." It was not a question, and was delivered with a flatness of tone that caused Lonesome to look up and meet Frank's eyes.

"I could take that as a threat, Frank."

"Take it any damn way you like. You even act as though you're goin' to pull on me and I'll kill you, Howard."

"I should kill you right here and now, Frank."

"Try it."

The man known throughout the West as Lonesome Howard stared hard at Frank for a few seconds. Then he relaxed and put both hands on the table. "Not yet, Frank. The hunt has not officially started."

"When does it start?"

Lonesome shrugged. "I really don't know. I believe an Easterner named Vanderhoot is the man who began all this."

"Did you say Vanderhoot?"

"Horace Vanderhoot. He's spent thousands of dollars on detectives searchin' for you."

"He's in town."

"Then I must look him up and introduce myself. Perhaps this small adventure can be ended quickly."

"And you'll be thousands of dollars richer."

"Yes. Of course."

"Or dead."

Lonesome smiled. "You can't take me, Frank. You're not that quick."

"We'll see, won't we?"

"I suppose we will. Have you made your peace with God, Frank?"

"I talk to the man occasionally."

"Do you want me to pray for you?"

Frank laughed softly and leaned back in his

chair. "Howard, you are a walking contradiction. Are you aware of that?"

"I don't think so," Lonesome said, an edge to his voice.

"Well, you are. Either that or you're crazy as a bessie bug. One or the other."

"You're callin' me insane?"

"If the boot fits . . . You know the rest."

Howard closed his Bible and put one hand on the Word of God. "I shall enjoy killing you, Frank. That is a sin, and I know it, but it's the truth. I must remember to pray for my own weaknesses."

"And a practicing hypocrite too."

"What?"

"That's you, Lonesome. You do know the meaning of the word, don't you?"

"You've very insulting, Frank. Of course I do. And I am most certainly not a hypocrite."

"Then you're a fool. Take your choice."

Lonesome pulled back his chair and stood up. He looked down at Frank. "Make your peace with God, Frank Morgan. Your time is near."

Frank softly and calmly told Lonesome Howard where he could shove his Bible, ending with, "I say that because it means nothing to you, Howard. It's just words on paper to you. Nothing more."

"You speak blasphemy, Frank."

"I speak the truth."

"The next time we meet, Frank, might be the moment you meet God."

"Or you meet the Devil."

Lonesome Howard blinked a couple of times, then turned and walked away.

Frank signaled for the barkeep to bring him more coffee. While waiting for the coffee to cool down some, he rolled a cigarette and studied the crowd of gun-handlers that lined the bar and filled the tables. A few of them glanced his way and nodded their head in greeting. Most just ignored him even though they knew him—some casually, others had known him for years.

"Reckon what they're waitin' for?" Old Bob asked, sitting down at the table with Frank. He jerked his thumb toward the gunslicks.

"The hunt is about to officially begin," Frank told him. "That's what Lonesome just told me."

"That was Lonesome Howard?"

"In person."

"I thought he was retired."

"He was, for a number of years. But the money for killing me pulled him back into the game."

Bob looked the crowd over. "Too many for one man, Frank. There must be thirty-five or forty gunmen in here."

"With more coming in."

"Some of them yahoos look older than me."

"I think some of them are. That grizzled old hombre standing at the very end of the bar, at the curve, is called Rogers. He's in his late sixties, at least. He was a well-known highwayman in California before the War Between the States. And that's been over for many years."

"Who is the dude with the pearl-handled guns? The one standin' in the center of the bar."

"His name is Olmstead. Made his reputation down in Oklahoma Territory. No-man's-land. He's a back-shooter."

"You go to hell!" a man standing at the bar shouted.

"I'll take you with me," a man standing next to him yelled.

The two men stepped away from the bar to face each other, their hands hovering over their gun butts.

"Get ready to hit the floor," Frank whispered.

"I been ready," Bob told him.

"You been makin' your brags behind my back, Les," one said. "I'm damn tired of it. Now fill your hand or shut the hell up."

Both men grabbed for their guns. Les was quicker. He fired once, the bullet striking his challenger in the center of the chest. The mortally wounded man fell back against the bar and clung there for a few seconds, then slumped to the dirty barroom floor. He died without uttering another word.

"I warned him about that damn mouth of his'n," the other man said. "I told him I'd shut it permanent someday, and by God I done it."

"One less for you to have to deal with," Bob said softly.

Frank nodded his head in agreement and sipped his cooling coffee. He set the cup down on the table and said, "I'm hoping a lot of that will go on before the actual hunt begins."

"It would shore cut the odds down some, for a fact."

The body of the dead man was dragged out of the saloon and the barkeep tossed some sawdust on the blood spots on the floor.

The gunslingers resumed their drinking, talking, and playing cards.

The Easterners had not made an appearance since retiring to their rooms and wagons. Bob finished his drink and left, saying he had to get back to his livery.

Frank sat alone at the table, drinking coffee and smoking, his eyes constantly moving, studying the crowd in the packed saloon.

The rain continued to come down from the dark, sullen skies. Not a hard downpour, but a quiet steady drizzle.

The Olsen cousins, Brooks and Martin, entered the saloon and found a place at the crowded bar.

They had cleaned up, including changing their clothing. Both of them were dressed in black suits, with black shirts, open at the collar, and both were wearing two guns, tied down. Frank sensed they both were primed and cocked, hunting trouble.

Damn good place to find it, Frank mused.

Brooks bumped into the man standing next to him—accidentally or deliberately, Frank couldn't tell—causing the man to spill some of his drink.

"Watch what the hell you're doin', boy!" the man snarled at Brooks.

"Don't call me boy, Skunk Breath!" Brooks popped right back.

"Skunk Breath?" the gunslinger yelled, turning to fully face the younger man. "Why, you damn mouthy little punk!"

Brooks stepped away a couple of steps, brushing back his coat. "What'd you call me, Skunk Breath?"

"I called you a mouthy punk!" the gunfighter said. "Are you hard of hearin' or just plain stupid?"

"I'll kill you for that!" Brooks said, his face flushing and his eyes narrowing down. His hands were poised just above the butts of his guns.

"You damn shore got it to do, boy," the older man said.

Brooks backed up, putting a few more feet between them. The crowd at the bar stepped away, out of the line of fire.

Frank watched the building confrontation without moving or changing expression. He was sure Brooks had intentionally provoked this moment. He did not know the older gun-handler, had never seen him before.

"Drag iron," Brooks told the man.

"After you, boy. I ain't never pulled on no damn punk kid and I shore don't intend to start now."

"You got a big fat mouth, mister," Brooks said.

"Fill your hand, kid," the man said.

Brooks was fast, Frank had to give him that much. He pulled and shot the older man before the man could clear leather. The gut-shot gunslick staggered back and fell against the bar, his pistol still in leather.

Brooks giggled like a girl, and Frank concluded then that the young man was possibly about half crazy.

"Damn punk," the dying man said.

Brooks shot him again, then put another slug into the man's chest. The older man fell to the floor, dead.

Brooks slobbered down his chin and giggled.

Seven

The kid is fast, Frank thought. And crazy as a lizard.

Bad combination.

One of the gunslingers that Frank knew casually, name of Fargo, turned and looked at Frank for a few seconds. Frank shrugged slightly, and Fargo nodded, then turned back to the bar.

"You got him good, Brooks!" Martin said. "Man, did you drill him proper."

"I did, didn't I?" Brooks said as he holstered his six-gun.

He didn't reload, Frank noted. *That's a real bad move, kid. You popped three caps, and now you've got at the most three rounds left in that hogleg . . . two if you're smart. You're an amateur, boy.*

"Is the skunk dead?" Martin asked.

"Sure, he's dead. Hell, I put three slugs in him."

"Let's get out of here," Martin suggested.

"Naw. I like it in here. Let's have a drink. We got room at the bar now."

Martin looked around at the room full of hostile faces, then reluctantly joined his cousin at the bar.

Frank finished his coffee and stood. Immediately all eyes in the room turned to him. He slowly brushed back his coat, exposing the butt of his second six-gun. A dozen pairs of eyes were quickly averted. Frank began the slow walk toward the front door.

"Turn around, Morgan," a voice behind him shouted. "I feel lucky today and I got me a need for that money that I'll get when I plug you."

Frank paused and slowly turned. He did not know the man who was facing him. The other men on both sides had made room. No one wanted to be caught in a cross fire.

"You sure the hunt has started?" Frank asked calmly.

"Now's as good a time as any to begin it," the man said.

"You got a name?"

"Why?"

"I need to know what to put on your tombstone, that's why?"

"The name is Tyler. And I ain't figuring on bein' planted any time soon, Morgan. I'm figurin' on bein' a rich man in about a minute."

"Here now!" a voice called from the hotel entrance to the saloon.

Frank cut his eyes for an instant. It was the man who had been pointed out to him as Horace Vanderhoot.

"The hunt has not yet begun," Vanderhoot announced. "Good afternoon, Mr. Morgan. I don't believe we have been formally introduced. I am Horace Vanderhoot. And these two men standing behind me, holding sawed-off shotguns, are my bodyguards."

"You mean those two with shotguns pointed at me?" Frank asked with a half smile playing on his lips.

"Very astute of you, Mr. Morgan."

"You must be very afraid of me, Vanderhoot," Frank said.

"Let's just say I believe in taking precautions."

"When does this here hunt get started?" a man tossed out.

"In a few days," Vanderhoot said. "I want to wait until the weather clears."

"Why?" another gunslick asked.

"Mr. Morgan might want to run, and I want to give him the opportunity to do so."

"Morgan don't run," a familiar voice called from a darkened corner of the saloon.

Frank cut his eyes. It was Dolan.

"He might," Vanderhoot replied.

"Not Morgan," Dolan persisted. "You don't know him. I do. He ain't gonna run."

Vanderhoot waved a hand in a very effeminate gesture. It was not lost on the room filled with hard-bitten men. Many of them smiled. Including Frank. "Whatever," Vanderhoot said. He smiled. "Besides, the longer we wait, the more the tension will heighten. And when it reaches its zenith, the fun will really begin."

"Who the hell is zenith?" a man asked.

"I ain't got no idee," another said. "I ain't never heard of him."

A very pained look crossed Vanderhoot's face. "No money will be paid for Frank Morgan's death until I officially announce the start of the hunt."

"You can be charged for this," Frank said. "It's against the law."

"Perhaps," Vanderhoot acknowledged. "If there was any law out here. But the nearest sheriff is a week's ride away . . . in good weather. And you're a murderer, Mr. Morgan. Besides, there are others who have placed a bounty on your head, and you know it."

Frank looked at the man and remained silent. Vanderhoot had done his homework, for a fact.

Frank shifted his gaze to Tyler. "Still want to lock horns with me, Tyler?"

"I'll wait for a spell, I reckon," the gunhawk said.

"Then get out of my way."

Tyler stepped aside and Frank walked past him. He stepped out into the cool and rainy night to stand under the boardwalk awning.

Doc Raven appeared out of the darkness. "I was standing just outside the door, listening. Care for a few words of advice?"

"Speak your piece, Doc."

"Saddle up and get the hell gone from here, Frank."

"Can't do it."

"You mean you won't."

"I reckon."

"You are a very stubborn man."

"I been told that before."

"Where is the body from the second shooting?"

"Still on the floor. Somebody will probably get tired of stepping over him and drag him out before long."

"Did you know either dead man?"

"No. But I discovered one thing: Brooks is insane."

"Yes. I've suspected that for several years. Martin is not much better."

"Brooks is kill-crazy. If you've got any unsolved gunshot murders around here, I'd sure look hard at him."

"I can't think of any." Raven checked his watch, then snapped it shut. "I've got to ride out in the country a few miles to check on a patient, Frank. I'll see you tonight."

"I reckon I'll be here."

Frank checked on Dog and Horse, and then went back to his room and stretched out on the bed. Within minutes, he was deep in sleep.

* * *

When Frank stepped out onto the boardwalk, it was full dark and pouring rain. He walked to the cafe and had supper, then took a packet of scraps to Dog and sat with him for a time after the big cur ate.

"The doc's right, Dog. We ought to pack up and pull out. But I just don't have it in me to run. I've made it through some hard times, though, so I reckon I'll make it through this mess."

His quiet speaking to Dog was shattered by a couple of gunshots from up the street. Frank paused, waiting for more shots, but none came. A few minutes later, Bob came stomping and muttering into the livery. Frank stepped out of the stall, and Bob pulled up short when he spotted him.

"Damn crazy gunhands," the liveryman said. "They keep shootin' each other, your problem's gonna be solved. There won't be none left."

"That'll suit me just fine, Bob. Who got shot?"

"I don't know his name. Some gunslick from New Mexico Territory. But this one wasn't as slick as he thought. Took two slugs in the belly. He's still alive, but not for long."

"Doc make it back?"

"Not yet."

"Fellow's gonna die hard gut-shot."

"That trouble you?"

"Not really. Who shot him?"

"Don't know him neither. Man ain't been in town more'un two hours. Just rode in. Someone called him Vickers."

"I know him. He's mean as a rattlesnake and just as quick. He must have just made it through before the slides closed the road."

"He's here. That's all I know. And walkin' round trouble-huntin'. That ain't all neither."

"What else?"

"That bodyguard you hit on the noggin with the coffeepot?"

"Sonny. Yes. What about him?"

"He's in the saloon makin' all kinds of mouth 'bout what he's gonna do to you."

Frank smiled. "He doesn't worry me near as much as all these hard cases gathering in town. Sonny will do what his employers tell him to do."

"That's just it, Frank. He quit them city folks."

"He's got the bounty money on his mind, Bob. I can't worry about him any more than I worry about the others. Bob, I may decide to sleep here tonight. I'll make me a pallet in the loft. That all right with you?"

"Sure. Help yourself. I'm going to my shack. See you in the mornin'."

"I hope so," Frank replied with a smile.

Bob returned the smile and walked out the rear of the livery; his "shack" was in the back of the stable.

In the glow of lamplight, Frank checked his pistols, loading up the sixth chambers. He usually kept the hammer over an empty chamber. But considering the circumstances in the town, he might need all the firepower he could muster at any time. Telling Dog to stay put, Frank stepped out of the livery and headed for the saloon. He could not show fear. The instant he did that, he would be dead, and he knew it.

He was a man alone, but had to behave as if he had an army behind him.

He did not pass a single local citizen on his walk to the saloon. Apparently they had all settled in their homes for the night.

"And I sure don't blame them," he muttered a

few seconds after lightning licked across the dark skies and thunder rumbled ominously. "A town full of bounty hunters and the weather is lousy."

A man stepped out of a building stoop and stood silently in the center of the boardwalk, blocking Frank's way.

"Howdy," Frank said.

"You're Frank Morgan, right?"

"That's me. And your name is . . . ?"

"Hill. Dan Hill. That ring a bell with you?"

"No. Can't say that does. Is it supposed to?"

"You don't remember my pa, Daniel Hill?"

"No. Don't think I've ever had the pleasure."

"Well, you damn sure ought to!"

"Why?"

"You killed him, you son of a bitch!"

Frank peered through the darkness, trying to make out the man's face. He could not. But he did sense the man was no kid. "If I did kill him, he was trying to kill me."

"That's a damn lie! My pa never tried to kill nobody. He was a farmer in Texas."

"And I'm supposed to have killed him because he was a farmer?"

"Damn right. You hired your gun out to a big rancher."

"Wrong, mister. I've never done that."

"Enough talk, Morgan. I promised my ma on her deathbed I'd hunt you down and kill you. Now I'm gonna do it."

"You got the wrong man, Hill. I swear to you you have."

"You're a liar as well as a killer. Now . . . draw!"
Hill grabbed for his pistol.

Eight

Frank acted instinctively. Hill had just cleared leather when Frank's bullet tore into the man and knocked him back. Hill grabbed for a support post, missed it, and fell off the boardwalk, into the mud, between a hitch rail and the boardwalk.

Doc Raven came running across the street, carrying his black bag. "I just got back into town," he panted. "Mrs. Perkins delivered twins. Two fine boys, although it was a hard delivery. Who is this man you just shot?"

"Says his name is Hill. Claims I killed his pa down in Texas."

"Did you?"

"Not to my knowledge. Certainly not under the circumstances he described."

Doc Raven knelt down beside the man. "He's dead. Your bullet drilled him right through the heart."

Frank cleared the spent brass and reloaded. "I didn't want to kill him, Doc."

"I believe you. Well, I'll get some men to carry him over to the undertaker's. Then I'm going to wash up and go to bed. I'm tired."

"See you in the morning, Doc."

Frank waited in the shadows until the body of Hill was carried off; then he walked to the saloon. The rain was still coming down: a light drizzle.

None of the gunslicks had bothered to come outside to check on the shooting. Heads turned when
Frank entered the crowded saloon. He ignored the
hard looks and walked to the far end of the bar
and ordered coffee.

"Somebody jump the gun on the hunt and brace
you, Morgan?" a gunslinger standing close by
asked.

"No, this was personal, so he said."

"You know his name?"

"Said his name was Hill. From Texas."

"Don't know that one. He dead?"

"They'll plant him in the morning, I reckon."

The gunhand grunted and took a sip of his beer.
"I done made up my mind 'bout this stupid hunt,
Morgan."

"Oh?"

"Yeah. I'm out of it. I'll stick around till the road
is open, then I'm gone."

"What changed your mind?"

"A number of things. Mainly, though, 'cause this
whole thing is sick. I've hired my gun out many
times, for a lot of reasons. But never for nothin'
like this here. It's stupid. And I just flat don't like
them damn Easterners."

Frank smiled. "Neither do I."

The gunslick laughed softly. "I reckon you
don't." He looked down at his drink. "I know a
way through the mountains. It's a tough ride, but
it's passable. I'm headin' out come first light. You
want to come along?"

Frank met the gunny's eyes. "I should, I know
that. But I just can't. Do you understand?"

The gunslinger slowly nodded his head. "I
reckon I do, Frank. I shore do. I ain't much for
runnin' myself. Just the thought of runnin' away
from a fracas sorta sticks in my craw."

"That's the way I feel about it."

The gunfighter lifted his glass. "Luck to you, Frank."

"Thanks." Frank watched the man drain his glass and then walk away.

Through the front glass of the saloon, Frank watched lightning dart across the skies, listened as thunder rumbled, and then heard the rain increase in intensity.

"When the hell are we gonna get this show goin'?" a man yelled out. "I'm gettin' damn tired of waitin'."

"Patience, patience!" Horace Vanderhoot shouted from the doorway leading from the hotel to the saloon. "As soon as the rain ceases, the hunt will begin. Fifty thousand dollars will go to the man who kills the notorious murderer and gunfighter Frank Morgan. But if Frank Morgan is killed before I officially announce the start of the hunt, not one penny will go to that man. Here is something that might peak your interest. With the exception of Frank Morgan, the last man standing will be declared the winner of the hunt. At last count, there were almost sixty of you men in town. Only one will ride out fifty thousand dollars richer. Think about that and act accordingly. For now, I bid you all a very pleasant good night."

You bloodthirsty son of a bitch! Frank thought as he watched the foyer door close behind Vanderhoot. *You have just opened the gates to hell.*

"Well, now," a gunny said, stepping away from the bar. "Ain't that a kick in the butt?"

"Do that mean what I think it means?" another asked.

"Damn shore does, Jimmy," a redheaded gunhawk said, stepping away from the bar to face the speaker. "And I'm gettin' tarred of lookin' at your ugly mug."

Frank quickly glanced around the saloon. There

was not a local in sight. They had all quietly left the watering hole. Three soiled doves were standing together, pressed up against a far wall. Fear was evident in their faces.

"You're callin' *me* ugly, Steve?" Jimmy asked. "Why . . . when you was a little boy you was so damn ugly, your momma had to tie a piece of salt pork around your neck so's the dogs would play with you."

The saloon rocked with rough and profane laughter.

Frank waited and watched, his coffee turning cold in the cup. The laughter slowly faded and the situation turned tense as the two men backed up a few steps, their hands poised for a hook and draw.

"You leave my ma out of this, you piece of coyote crap!" Steve responded.

"Sure will," Jimmy replied. " 'Cause you didn't have no human ma. You was borned in a travelin' circus in the monkey cage."

"I'll kill you!" Steve shouted.

"You got it to do."

"You're enjoyin' this, ain't you, Morgan?" a gunhand standing close to Frank asked in a soft voice.

"Not really," Frank whispered. "But I'm glad it's them facing a bullet and not me."

"Your time is comin'."

"I'm sure it is. And I'm also sure I'll be here." Or close by, Frank thought. Like waiting in an old deserted town called Red Rock. Frank had given the old town a lot of thought, and the more he thought, the better it sounded for a showdown.

The violent cursing of Steve broke into Frank's thinking. The man was really working himself into a lather. It wouldn't be long now.

Jimmy laughed at the man. "You cuss real good, Steve. But then, I've heard for years that you always did have a big mouth with no guts to back it up."

"That does it for me, you butt-ugly pecker-wood!" Steve grabbed for his gun.

Jimmy cleared leather first and got off the first shot. The bullet missed Steve and blew a hole through one of the front windows.

Steve fired, the bullet hitting Jimmy in the leg and knocking him back against the bar. Jimmy grunted in shock and sudden pain and lifted his .44. He squeezed the trigger. The slug hit Steve in the left shoulder and spun him around, throwing him against a table. Cards and chips were scattered all over the floor.

Jimmy cocked and fired again. The bullet missed its mark and blew a leg off a wooden chair.

Down on one knee, Steve leveled his six-gun and fired. His shot was true, the bullet slamming into Jimmy's belly and doubling him over.

Gasping in pain, Jimmy slowly raised his pistol and fired. The slug hit Steve in the center of his face, disintegrating his nose as the bullet ripped into his brain. Steve dropped to the floor like a heavy rock and did not move.

Jimmy slowly sank down to his knees as the pain in his belly intensified. "Oh, God, I hurt!" he hollered.

"I bet he do," a gunny said.

"Somebody get the doc," another gunslick suggested.

"Why?" another gun-handler asked. "Steve's dead as a rock and Jimmy ain't gonna be long for this world."

"That's a damn lie!" Jimmy yelled, one hand covering the bloody hole in his belly. "I ain't gonna die. I'm gonna collect that bounty money."

"No, you ain't," a man told him. "So why don't you just do us all a favor? Shut your mouth, lay down and close your eyes, and die."

"You black-hearted son of a bitch!" Jimmy said.

Frank stood at the end of the bar and watched in silence. It was nothing new to him; he'd seen it all before, many times.

"Did somebody go for the doc?" Jimmy asked.

"Nope," he was told.

"It's rainin' outside," another said. "And cold."

"You bastard!" Jimmy said.

"Well, now, that just might be true. I can't take no offense at that. My pa was a man with a wanderin' eye, for sure."

Hard waves of pain hit the man, and he trembled at the shock of it, then screamed, "Oh, God, I hurt so bad!"

"That's what you get when you play with guns, Jimmy," a gunny said in hard, rough humor, and the others laughed.

"Damn y'all to the hellfires!" Jimmy said.

The front door opened and a very irritated and rumpled Doc Raven walked in.

"The one stretched out on the floor with half a head is dead, Doc," a man said. "The one on his knees probably ain't long for this world."

"Thank you," Doc Raven said very sarcastically, pushing his way through the crowd. He knelt down beside Jimmy and tried to pull the wounded man's hands away from his bloody stomach. He could not. "I can't help you if you won't let me look at the wound."

"Give me somethin' for the pain, Doc!" Jimmy begged.

"Let me look at the wound."

"No!" Jimmy screamed. "If I move my hands my guts will fall out."

"That's ridiculous!" Raven snapped. "Your intestines are not going to fall out." He looked up at the men gathered around. "Some of you grab him and stretch him out on the floor. I've got to see about this wound."

Jimmy was forcefully laid out on the floor and his hands moved away from the bullet wound. Doc Raven looked at the wound and grunted softly.

"It's bad, ain't it, Doc?" Jimmy moaned.

"It isn't good."

"Am I going to die?"

"Probably."

"Ah . . . hell, Doc!" Jimmy cried out. "I'm too young to die."

There was really nothing Raven could do. He'd seen men gut-shot live, but they were the exception, not the rule. The entry wound in Jimmy's stomach was huge and the bleeding was copious. There was no way of knowing what other damage the bullet had done, and no real way of telling for sure. Raven cleaned the wound and packed it closed, then stood up.

"Is that all you're gonna do?" Jimmy asked.

"There is nothing else I can do," Raven told him. "I'm sure the lining of your stomach has been perforated."

"What does that mean?" Jimmy asked with a groan.

"It has a big hole in it."

"Oh, Lord. I'm really gonna die, ain't I?"

"You want me to get a minister for you?"

"Can he fix the hole in my gut?"

"No. But he can comfort you with prayer."

Jimmy very graphically told Doc Raven where he could stick his suggestion.

Raven shook his head and stood up, disgust on his face and in his eyes. He looked down the bar at Frank, then turned his attention to the bartender. "Get me a cup of coffee, please."

"Comin' right up, Doc."

Doc Raven joined Frank at the bar. "What a mess."

"And it'll get worse, Doc. Bet on it."

"Horace Vanderhoot has opened Pandora's box, Frank."

"I've read about that, Doc. Yes. You're right. The undertaker is going to be very busy for a time."

"I'll suggest this one more time, Frank. Get clear of here."

"Doc, you're the man who runs this town. If you order me to leave, I'll do so. But not until then."

"I won't order you out, Frank. I've told you that."

"What if locals start getting hurt, or killed?"

"The people will handle it then." Raven smiled at Frank's expression of doubt. "Frank, this town is filled with veterans of the War Between the States, ex-buffalo hunters, Indian fighters, and early settlers. Believe me, when the locals get enough, they'll handle it. Have you ever heard of a Western town being totally buffaloed?"

"Not many, for a fact."

"This one won't be either."

The gut-shot Jimmy began moaning and hollering in pain. "Doc! It's hurtin' real bad. Help me."

"Can you do anything for him?" Frank asked.

Doc Raven shook his head. "No. Nothing. Probing for the bullet would be useless, even if I could locate and remove it. I can't cut him open and repair his stomach."

"Somebody get that crybaby out of here," a gunslick said. "I'm gettin' tarred of listenin' to him holler."

"You know that insensitive lout?" Raven asked in a whisper.

"Jack Miller," Frank replied. "Back-shooter out of Arkansas. I thought he was long dead."

"Somethin's wrong with me, Doc!" Jimmy yelled. "It's gettin' hard for me to breathe and the light is fadin'."

"Good," the Arkansas back-shooter said in a too-loud voice. "Go on and die."

"Shut up, Jack," another gun-handler said. "Let the man die in peace."

"You want to try to shut me up?" Jack challenged.

"Doc!" Jimmy yelled.

"Blood's a-pourin' out of his mouth, Doc," a man standing close to Jimmy said. "I don't think he's long for this world."

Raven left Frank's side and knelt down beside Jimmy for a moment. Jimmy began to convulse on the floor.

"What the hell's he doin' now, Doc?" a man asked.

"Losing consciousness," Raven replied.

"Why?"

Raven's sigh was evident even where Frank stood. "The bullet probably traveled upward and nicked a lung . . . or both lungs."

Jimmy's legs began jerking, his boot heels drumming on the dirty floor.

"What a horrible way to die," one of the bar's soiled doves said, moving closer to where Jimmy lay.

"How much for a good hump?" a man asked her.

She leaned down and whispered in his ear.

"It better be a good one for that price," the man said, standing up.

She led him toward the rear of the saloon, and they disappeared into the darkness of a hall.

Jimmy yelled once more and then was silent, his body ceasing its jerking and convulsing. His head lolled to one side.

"That's all," Raven said. "He's gone."

" 'Bout damn time," Jack Miller said. "Gimmie another beer," he told the barkeep.

"Some of you men carry these bodies out of here and over to the undertaker's," Raven said. The bodies were dragged outside, sawdust was sprinkled over the blood spots, and the card games and talking resumed.

Doc Raven finished his coffee and picked up his black bag. "See you in the morning, Frank."

"I sure hope so, Doc."

Frank stood at the bar for a few moments, then pushed his way through the crowd and walked out of the bar. He stood for a moment on the boardwalk, breathing in the cold wet air of fall and mulling over his situation. What had Vanderhoot said? As soon as the rain ceased the hunt would begin.

Frank walked down the boardwalk toward the barn. He'd sleep in the loft this night. He was sure the saloon would be noisy until the wee hours. There were few lamplights shining; the locals had gone to bed.

"Good idea," Frank muttered. In the livery, he got his blanket roll and climbed up into the loft. He was asleep in the hay a few minutes after closing his eyes.

Nine

Frank awakened at Dog's low, almost inaudible growl in the stall beneath where he slept in the loft. He lay still, listening, his right hand silently closing around the butt of his Peacemaker. Dog did not repeat his growl.

Then Frank heard the very faint scrape of a boot. It sounded as though it came from just outside the livery. Frank eared back the hammer of the .45 and waited.

After a few quiet moments, he heard boot steps moving away from the livery, slowly fading into the night. Frank did not know what time it was, but he had awakened feeling refreshed, so he knew it must be close to his normal getting-up time. He pulled on his boots and silently climbed down to the floor of the livery. He let Dog out back to do his morning business, and without lighting the lantern, slipped out the front of the stable and stood for a time in the early morning darkness, listening. The rain had slackened off to an irritating drizzle. He could hear no sound except the soft sighing of the cold wind.

Frank stepped back into the huge livery, silently closing the door, and popped a match into light, checking his watch. The hands read 3:30. He let Dog back in, and the big cur immediately went to the stall with Horse and lay down in a corner.

"You stay put," Frank told him.

Frank walked to the cafe. It was dark. Frank guessed the cook probably wouldn't show up for another hour. He glanced at the saloon. It too was dark and silent. He turned up the collar of his coat against the chill and walked on until he reached the edge of the short business district, then crossed over and began walking down the other side. He walked slowly, pausing often to listen. He heard nothing out of the ordinary. It appeared he was the only one awake at this hour.

He wondered where all the hired guns had found shelter to sleep. Then he recalled overhearing one of the gunslicks in the saloon the past night talking about them renting several empty houses in town.

"I hope the roofs leak and they all catch pneumonia," he muttered, then smiled at his remark.

He stopped and stepped back into the darkness of a door stoop at the sounds of several riders coming from the east. He watched as the three men rode up the street, all of them wearing slickers. Their horses looked very tired.

"My God," Frank muttered under his breath. "More bounty hunters. Maybe it is time for me to give some serious thought to pulling out."

The trio of riders rode down to the livery stable and out of earshot. Frank waited in the darkness. A few minutes later, he saw the faint glow of a lantern. They had rousted Old Bob out of his warm bed. Bob would not be in a very good mood, Frank thought with a grin. He decided to walk down to the livery and see if Bob would put the coffeepot on.

The men who had just ridden in were stripping the saddles from their horses when Frank walked in. Bob was standing off to one side, looking very unhappy about being rousted out of bed. The trio of riders turned and stared at Frank.

"Morgan," one of them said.

"Roberts," Frank replied. "Been a long time."

"Ten years, I reckon. Down in Louisiana, wasn't it?"

"New Orleans, yes. I believe you were beating a woman, weren't you?"

Sudden anger flushed Roberts's face. He momentarily tensed, then smiled and relaxed. "You stepped into a situation you didn't understand and should have stayed out of."

"No woman deserves a beating like that, Roberts."

"Whatever happened to that French bitch?" Roberts asked.

"She died about a week after the beating."

Roberts shrugged. "I had a headache for a week after you hit me with that rifle butt. I owe you for that, Morgan."

"And now you're here to collect, right?"

"That's about it."

"Any more guns riding in?"

"A few more. Small-time gun-handlers. They should be here later on today."

"Well, it promises to be quite a show."

"You don't seem to be too worried about it, Morgan."

"Last man standing gets the money. And you boys are late getting into the game."

"I heard some boys came out of retirement for this hunt."

"A few. Lonesome Howard. Vickers. Olmstead. Dolan is here."

"No kidding? Well, that's quite a crew. Lots of old friends around here for a while, right, Morgan?"

"That's one way of looking at it, I reckon."

"I aim to collect that money, Frank. Me and the boys here."

"Who are your friends?"

"This here is Don Blanchard from West Texas way." He jerked a thumb. "And that's Russ Temple. He's a Wyoming boy."

"You ain't as old as I thought you'd be, Morgan," Don said. "All the stories told about you, I figured you'd be near'bouts a hundred or so."

Bob stepped in and said, "I don't know where you boys is gonna sleep, but you ain't sleeping in my livery. I'll stable your horses, and that's it."

"You a feisty old fart, ain't you?" Russ said.

"Keep runnin' that mouth, boy," Bob replied, "and you and your horse can sleep under a tree."

Roberts held up a hand. "We'll find us a place to sleep, old man. You just take care of our horses."

"I can do that."

"When's the cafe open for business?"

"Five-thirty or so."

Roberts looked at Frank. "You gonna be there?"

"I plan on it."

"We'll see you there then."

"I can hardly wait," Frank replied sarcastically.

"Hey!" Russ called from the huge front doors of the livery. "It's rainin' again."

Roberts cussed and said, "Is this crap ever gonna stop?"

"Maybe it's God's will," Bob said.

"What the hell are you talkin' 'bout, old man?" Don asked.

"He destroyed the earth once by a flood, didn't He?" Bob replied. "Maybe He's gonna do it again."

"Why would God do that?" Russ asked, moving back toward the group.

"Sin," Bob answered.

"Ahh!" Roberts said, slashing the air with a hand. "I don't believe that crap."

"You don't believe in God?" Bob asked.

"I didn't say that," Roberts replied quickly. "Course I believe in God. I was baptized when I was a boy."

"In a river?" Bob asked.

"In a crick behind the church."

Bob smiled. "Is the water fit to drink yet?"

Roberts stared at the liveryman for a few seconds. "I don't like you, old man. I don't like you a-tall."

"I can live with it," Bob replied.

Roberts wheeled around. "Come on, boys. We'll go sit in front of the cafe. Stinks in this place."

Bob muttered something under his breath.

Roberts turned. "What'd you say, old man?"

"I said, 'You probably smellin' your own butt.' That's what I said."

"I'll deal with you later," Roberts said. "After I deal with Morgan."

"Want to deal with me now?" Frank challenged.

Dog was sitting just inside Horse's stall, taking it all in. He had not barked or snarled, just sat watching and listening very intently. Russ had moved away from Roberts, angling for a clear shot at Frank should it come to that. He had moved very close to Dog, which was not the smartest move he could have made.

"I put lead in you now," Roberts said, "I don't get to collect no money. That's the way I heard the game is played."

"Now or later," Frank said. "Either way you're a dead man."

Russ's hand dropped to the butt of his pistol. Dog silently stood up on all four paws, the hair on his back rising.

Bob moved back a few steps.

"Do it now or shut your damn mouth," Frank told Roberts.

"You're forcin' me to kill you, Morgan," Roberts said. "What's with you anyways? You lost your mind, or somethin'?" He cut his eyes to Russ.

Russ's hand closed around the butt of his six-gun, and Dog leaped and nailed him, his jaws closing around the man's arm. Russ hollered and lost his balance as he tried to shake Dog loose. He fell to the livery floor, Dog's powerful jaws tearing at his arm.

"I'll kill that damn dog!" Don yelled, grabbing for his pistol.

Frank shot him, the bullet ripping into his chest and dropping the man, mortally wounded.

Dog was busy ripping at Russ's arm.

Frank turned to face Roberts. His eyes burned at the man while a small smile played at his mouth.

Roberts held his hands up and away from his gunbelt. "That's it, Morgan. I'm out of it for now. Call off your damn dog!"

Frank spoke one sharp command, and Dog turned loose of Russ's arm and backed up, his teeth bared in a terrible snarl. Russ lay on the floor and moaned, blood leaking from the multiple wounds on his arm.

"You're crazy, Morgan," Roberts blurted out. "You've gone nuts on me."

Frank holstered his Peacemaker. "Drag your partners out of here, Roberts. And remember this: The next time you brace me, be ready to die."

"What the hell am I 'posed to do with a dead body at four o'clock in the mornin'!"

"Prop him up and look at him," Frank told him. "I don't give a damn what you do with him. Just drag him out of here."

"Russ is hurt bad."

"That's his problem. 'Sides, I don't think he's hurt too bad. The doc's will be open about dawn. He'll live till then."

Roberts helped Russ to his feet, and together they dragged the body of the dead man outside into the rain.

"This ain't right," Russ said. "It ain't decent."

"What the hell do you know about anything decent?" Frank asked, following the men to the front of the livery. "If there was a ounce of decency in you, you wouldn't be hanging around scum like Roberts."

"My arm is tore up bad," Russ griped. "And it's hurtin' something fierce. That damn dog probably give me hydrophoby, or somethin'."

"No, he didn't. But I've got to be sure and wash his mouth out good. I don't want him getting sick after chewing on you."

The hired guns dumped the body of Don by the side of the livery and walked away, up the boardwalk.

"Man, you are quick," Bob said. "I never even seen that hook and draw. God blessed you with a gift, for a fact."

"God?" Morgan asked, punching out the brass and reloading. "You think God gave me the ability to kill people?"

"The Good Book says God works in mysterious ways, Frank."

Morgan had no reply to that as he found a rag and wiped the blood from Dog's mouth. Bob forked hay into the stall for Horse. Morgan combed his thick brown hair with his fingers, using a piece of broken mirror to gaze into. Was there a bit more gray in his hair? Sure looked that way.

"You studying 'bout how handsome you are?" Bob asked with a grin, returning from his shack out back, now dressed for the day.

"Yeah, I'm a real lady-killer for sure," Frank replied sourly, settling his hat on his head. "Women just can't keep their hands off me," he added with a smile to soften the acid reply.

"You probably ain't been lookin' too hard for a good woman to settle down with," Bob told him. "I know for a fact they's hard to find."

"You told me you were married once. What happened?"

"Didn't work out. She took the young'uns and went back East. I ain't heard a word from her since. Probably never will."

"I'm sorry."

"No need to be. I ain't. Things usually work out for the best. I put on the coffeepot. Should be ready to swaller in a few minutes. I got some biscuits makin' too."

"Sounds good to me."

They both turned as Doc Raven strolled into the livery. "Morning, boys," he said.

"What are you doin' up so early, Doc?" Bob asked.

"Couldn't sleep. Did I hear you say you've got coffee, Bob?"

"For a fact, you did. Come on, we'll have us a . . ."

Half a dozen gunshots ripped the early morning and cut off Bob's statement.

Doc Raven sighed. "I guess I'd better get my bag. The day's starting off bloody."

Ten

Doc Raven paused at the door and looked back at Frank. "Oh, I almost forgot. I have something for you, Frank. Stop by my office sometime this morning, will you?"

"Sure, Doc."

The doctor walked out of the livery into the rain.

"Wonder what that was all about?" Frank mused aloud.

"Beats me," Bob said. "You want to have that coffee now?"

"I better tag along behind the doc. He might run into trouble. Thanks, though. A cup would have tasted mighty fine."

"I'll think about you whilst I'm eatin' them biscuits."

Frank grinned and stepped out into the wet predawn darkness, quickly catching up with the doctor.

"What do you want?" Raven said, hurrying toward his office.

"Keeping you out of trouble."

"You keeping *me* out of trouble! That's a laugh. Here we are. Come on in while I find my bag. Damn, I sure wanted some coffee."

"We'll get some at the cafe. It should be open by the time we see what those shots were all about."

A moment later they were slopping across the

street to where a group of men were gathered around two bodies sprawled face-down in the mud.

"They're both dead, Doc," a local dressed in his nightshirt called from the boardwalk. "They killed each other, I reckon."

"What a pity," Doc Raven muttered, kneeling down to check the bodies. "Bring that lantern closer," he said to a man. "That's it. Thanks." It didn't take him long to check the men for signs of life. He stood up and wiped his hands on a towel he took from his bag. "They're dead, all right. Both of them belly-shot and one with a bullet in his chest, the other with a bullet hole between his eyes."

Frank picked up the six-shooters and checked the cylinders. Three shots had been fired from each weapon. "I guess they fired at the same time while they were going down."

"You know them, Frank?"

"No."

"Any of you men know them?"

"I seen them ride in 'bout sundown," a gunslick said, his voice slurry from whiskey. "I never laid eyes on 'em 'fore then." He ended that with a loud belch.

"Go sleep it off," Raven told him.

"Somebody gimme a drink," the hired gun responded.

"Come on, Frank," Doc Raven said. "I want to talk to you."

"What about these bodies?" a man questioned.

"Put them behind the undertaker's office," the doctor said. "And get that body by the side of the livery too. They'll keep in this weather."

Frank accompanied Doc Raven back to his office, and was waved to a seat. Raven built up the fire in the stove and put on a pot of water to boil. "We'll have us some coffee in a little while. Frank, do you find anything odd about this constant delay in starting off this so-called hunt?"

"Well, other than the obvious, no. Vanderhoot has said the hunt will begin as soon as the rain stops."

"He changed his mind again."

"When?"

"Late last evening. Now he says the hunt will begin when the roads are open."

"I hadn't heard. Hell, Doc, that might be two or three weeks."

"Yes. Something is very queer about this entire matter."

"I reckon so, now that you bring it up."

The doctor pulled open a drawer on his desk and tossed a badge to Frank. "I've had that thing for a long time. Never wore it. Didn't want anyone to know I had it."

Frank looked at the badge. A deputy U.S. marshal's badge. "I don't understand, Doc."

"I can appoint anyone I choose to help me in time of emergency. That's why I was given two badges. That's the law as I understand it. Well, I'm appointing you, Frank. Stand up and raise your right hand."

"Are you serious?"

"I sure as hell am. You've carried a badge before. Now you're going to carry another one. Stand up."

Frank stood up and Doc Raven swore him in, then pinned the badge to his vest, under his jacket.

"This may not be legal, Doc."

"It is as far as I'm concerned."

"When were you appointed a deputy U.S. marshal?"

"About ten years ago. I told the federal judge then I wasn't qualified to have the badge. He said I could swear someone in to help should the need ever present itself. The commission has never been revoked. Now go find out what this damn hunt is all about."

"How about some coffee first?"

"Good idea. With thinking like that you'll make a fine U.S. marshal."

Frank and Doc Raven enjoyed a pot of coffee and some good conversation until daybreak. Then they walked over to the cafe to get some breakfast. The place was crowded with Vanderhoot and his Eastern friends and their wives. Frank and Raven took the only table left in the cafe and sat down.

"Take off your heavy jacket, Frank," Raven whispered. "Let them see the badge. Let's see what reaction we get from those people."

"Should be interesting," Frank replied, removing his winter coat and standing up to hang it on a hook.

When he turned around to stand for a moment facing the front, the cafe patrons fell silent, all eyes on the badge pinned to his vest.

Horace Vanderhoot's face flushed a deep red. He opened his mouth to speak, then closed it when he could find no words.

"You people suddenly run out of things to talk about?" Frank asked, staring at the crowd of Easterners.

"Where did you get that badge?" Maxwell Crawford asked. "I don't believe it's real."

"It's real," Doc Raven said. "Frank Morgan is a legally appointed deputy U.S. marshal." He smiled. "You people should have done a bit more checking before you embarked on this barbaric hunt."

"You weren't wearing it before," Jackson Mills said. "Why did you wait until now to pin it on?"

"Maybe I wanted to see if this so-called hunt of

yours was real," Frank answered, "or if you were just playing some sort of silly game."

At that remark, Vanderhoot suddenly looked very startled. His hands gripped the edge of the table until his knuckles turned white.

Odd, Frank thought, taking in the man's reaction. Now what brought that on?

Vanderhoot suddenly stood up, took his wife's hand, and together they left the cafe.

"Must not have liked the way his eggs were cooked," Doc Raven said, smiling.

"I guess so," Frank replied, sitting down. He whispered, "What the hell is going on, Doc?"

"I really don't know for sure," Raven whispered in return. "But I have some strong suspicions."

"Want to share them with me?"

"Not yet, Frank. Give me a little while."

"All right."

They watched as the Easterners left the cafe en masse, their food uneaten. The waitress set their own food on the table before them. It smelled delicious.

"It's coming together in my mind," Doc Raven said. "I'm going to have a chat with Horace after I eat. I think the man set a very dangerous game into motion. And if I'm correct, the man is a damned fool."

"I could have told you that on the first day you told me about the hunt," Frank said, buttering a biscuit and taking a bite.

Doc Raven nodded his head and glanced outside. It was raining again.

When Frank walked into the saloon later that day, one could have heard a pin drop, even though the place was filled with gunslicks. Horace Vanderhoot and his Eastern cohorts were nowhere to be seen. Not a word was spoken as Frank made his way to the far end of the bar and told Phil to bring him a cup of coffee.

"Coming right up, Marshal," Phil said with a smile and a twinkle in his eyes. Obviously, the word had spread very quickly throughout the town.

"I never knowed you was a federal marshal, Morgan," a gunny called from across the room.

"Now you do," Frank replied.

"And that's supposed to make a difference to us?" another asked.

"Only if you're smart."

"Well, it don't make a damn to me," Fargo said from the other end of the bar where he was nursing a mug of beer.

"That's your option, Fargo," Frank told him. "This town's still got a nice big jail, right, Phil?"

"Sure does. Got four big cells in it."

"You ain't puttin' me in no damn jail!" Fargo said.

"Keep runnin' that mouth and I just might."

"By God, I'll stand up to this tin badge if none of the rest of you ain't got the guts!" a man said, pushing back his chair and standing up.

"Who are you?" Frank asked.

"I'm called Utah Slim."

"Never heard of you," Frank said, and using his left hand, lifted his cup and took a sip of coffee.

"Folks is gonna hear about me plenty after I put lead in you, Morgan."

"You ain't gonna get no money, Slim," a gunhandler reminded him.

"Hell with the money! I want the reputation. The man who kills Frank Morgan can write his own ticket anywheres in the West."

"That there is a natural fact," a man Frank knew

as Nils Finley said. "Slim's shore enough got a point."

"You kill a federal marshal and they ain't never gonna stop lookin' for you," another gunny said.

"The West is a big place," Slim replied. " 'Sides, my mind is made up. Step out here and face me, Morgan."

"You mind if I finish my coffee first?" Frank asked. "I'm a coffee-drinking man and this is fresh brewed."

"Step out here, badge-toter!" Slim yelled. "I ain't in no damn mood for a mess of jawin'—"

"In a minute," Frank said softly.

"Now!" Slim yelled.

"Are you in that big a hurry to die, Slim?" Frank asked.

"Hell with you, Morgan. I think you've gone yeller on me. I think I'll just shoot you right now and listen to you beg."

Frank stepped away from the bar just as Doc Raven and Bob walked into the saloon. They saw what was happening and immediately stepped to one side, out of the way of any stray bullets.

"I don't beg for anything to any man, Slim," Frank said, ice in his tone. "Never have, never will. So either make your play or shut your damn mouth and get out of here . . . while you're still able to walk."

Utah Slim grabbed for his six-gun. Just as his hand closed around the butt, he heard the boom of Frank's Peacemaker and felt a hammerlike blow slam into his belly. He doubled over and grabbed for the bar. He held on and tried to clear leather, finally managing to fumble his Colt from leather. He eared back the hammer and raised the pistol.

"Now die, Morgan," he gasped.

Frank's second shot hit the Utah gunfighter in the chest and knocked him away from the bar. Slim dropped his pistol and fell against a table. "I got kin who'll git you, Morgan," he said. "They'll track you down and kill you."

"Not if they're no better than you were," Frank said. "And I stress *were.*"

"Damn, Morgan," a gunhawk said, being careful to keep his hands away from his guns. "You're a cold-hearted man."

"You want to find out how really cold I am?"

"Nope."

"Wise of you."

Utah Slim lost his grip on the table and fell hard to the saloon floor.

"You want to look at him, Doc?" a bounty hunter asked.

"Not really," Raven said. "But I suppose I should."

"Gimme something for the pain," Slim said.

"You probably won't be hurting much longer," Raven said, pushing through the crowd. He called to Bob. "Get my bag for me, will you, Bob?"

"Comin' right up, Doc," the liveryman said, heading for the door.

Doc Raven knelt down beside the fallen gunman and opened the man's shirt. He looked at the wounds and grunted softly. Already, pink froth was forming on Utah Slim's lips. A sure sign that the man had been lung-shot.

"How's it look, Doc?" Slim asked. "I'm a-feared to look."

"Bad," Raven told him. "You're hard hit."

"I'm I gonna die?"

"Let's just say if I were you, I wouldn't be worried about lunch today."

"Oh, Lord!" Utah Slim hollered.

"You want me to get a minister for you?" Raven asked.

"What the hell good would he do?" Slim questioned.

"He could pray for your soul."

"The preacher is stuck on the other side of the slides," a local said. "Might get Sister Clarabelle to call on the Good Lord for him."

"Clarabelle wouldn't set her feet in a saloon," another local said. "She don't hold with drinkin'."

"Well, so much for that," Raven said, standing up.

"Do somethin', Doc!" Slim yelled weakly.

"Nothing I can do. Make your own peace with God." He looked at the bartender. "Pour me a cup of coffee, Phil."

"Comin' right up, Doc."

Raven joined Frank at the bar.

"You a sorry excuse for a doctor, you are," Slim said.

Raven looked at the gunfighter. "You're gut-shot and lung-shot, boy. There is nothing I can do."

"I hear the angels' chariots comin' for me!" Slim said.

"Naw," a gunslinger told him. "That's just the rain comin' down."

"I can hear the beatin' of heavenly wings!" Slim insisted.

"That's the sounds of Sam pokin' one of the bar women in the back room," another gunslick said. "She's gruntin' like a hog."

Frank had reloaded his Peacemaker, and Phil had poured another cup of coffee for him. He leaned against the bar, saying nothing.

"Hi, Mama!" Utah Slim suddenly yelled. He closed his eyes and died.

"Some of you men tote him over to the undertaker's," Raven said. "It'll be a couple of days before he can be buried, unless you want to plant him as is."

"I ain't diggin' no damn hole in the rain," a man said.

"Throw him in a ditch at the edge of town," another suggested.

"So much for the brotherhood of the gun," Raven muttered.

"Yee-haw!" the soiled dove servicing Sam in the back room yelled.

"Lucille ought to give Sam ten dollars for that pokin'," Phil said to Frank and Doc Raven.

Eleven

Bob came in with Doc's medical bag. He looked at Utah Slim and shrugged his shoulders. "You want me to take this back to your office, Doc?"

"No, Bob. But thank you. Bring it over to me. Hell, I might need it yet."

Bob walked over to his friends, carefully stepping over the body of Utah Slim, and waved for Phil to bring him some coffee. He leaned close to Frank and Doc Raven. "Something mighty queer goin' on in town, boys. Seems them hoity-toity Easterners all of a sudden got into a sweat about pullin' out."

"What do you mean?" Frank asked.

"Seems like they sent a man out to the Lassiter Ranch to buy a bunch of horses and to see about a guide to take them over the mountains out of here. And everything is supposed to be on the hush-hush."

"How'd you hear about it?" Raven asked.

"The schoolboy who does some work for me down at the livery—Able Stover—overheered them talkin' early this mornin'. He just now told me 'bout it."

"Well, now, it's slowly coming into place," Raven said. "My suspicions were quite correct, I'm thinking."

"What suspicions?" Bob asked.

Doc Raven shook his head. "Let me prowl

around some. I want to talk with Maxwell about this. For some reason, he's been avoiding me since they got here. It might be on account of Wilma. But I'll force a conversation with him."

"Maybe then you'll get around to telling me what this is all about," Frank said, a sarcastic edge to his voice.

"Oh, I will, Frank," Doc Raven said with a smile. "You can be assured of that."

"Thanks so much, Doc."

"You're certainly welcome." He picked up his cup and took a sip. "Good coffee."

"I like it a mite stronger than this," Bob said.

"I'm gettin' damn tarred of steppin' over Slim," a man said. "Come on, some of you boys give me a hand and we'll toss him out the back."

"Oh, hell, I'll hep you," another gunny said. "We can't leave him there for long. He'll commence to stinkin'. You grab one end, I'll git the other. One of you boys open the back door for us, will you?"

"What lovely people," Doc Raven muttered.

"In a different way, them damn rich Easterners ain't no better," Bob opined.

"I have to concur with that," Doc Raven said. "In fact, I'll add they're worse. Maxwell and his friends all have fine educations that, in the end, seem to have been wasted."

"We got some families here in town that's moving out for the time bein'," Bob said. "They're goin' to visit friends in the country till this mess in town is straightened out."

"To hell with you, Nichols!" a gunslick yelled, silencing the conversation in the saloon. "I've had your damn smart mouth!"

"Then do something 'bout it, Jake!" Nichols yelled back, pushing back his chair and standing up. "Git up and fill your hand."

"Settle down, boys," another gunhand said. "This damn waitin' is gettin' to us all."

"You go right straight to hell, Quinn," Jake said.

"Don't tell me to go to hell, you two-bit horse thief," Quinn responded.

"Take it easy, boys," Dolan said from a table in the rear of the saloon. "All of you. We didn't come here to shoot each other."

"Well, shootin' Morgan seems to be out of the question," another gun-handler piped up. "I ain't gonna be the one to put lead in no damn federal marshal. So what do we do now?"

That question settled in the brains of all the men in the saloon. Quinn, Jake, and Nichols looked sheepishly at each other and sat down. Dolan stood up and walked over to stand at the bar beside Morgan.

"How do you want to play this, Morgan?" he asked.

"I don't think it's up to me to decide that," Frank replied. "That's a decision you men will have to make."

"I think this was a mess from the git-go," Dolan said. "I thought about it long and hard 'fore I saddled up for the ride."

"You think you should have stayed at home?"

"I do, for a fact."

"But now you believe it's too late?"

"I didn't say that, Morgan. But I'll tell you this. That badge you're wearin' don't mean squat to me. If that thousands of dollars of bounty money is really up for your head, I'll take my chances on collectin' it."

"But you have doubts about it being real?"

"I'm beginnin' to, yeah. Somethin' smells funny about this deal. And I just flat don't like them damn Easterners."

"They seem to be laying low, don't they?"

"Yeah, that's for sure. I'm gonna nose around and find out 'bout this thing, Morgan. And if it's on the up and up, I'm comin' for you."

"I'll be here, Dolan. You got any kin you want me to notify after we plant you?"

Dolan's smile was hard, devoid of any humor. "You can't outdraw me, Morgan. I've had too many people tell me that."

"You'll be betting your life on it."

"So I will. See you around, Morgan."

The gunfighter walked away, out the front door of the saloon.

"Can he take you, Frank?" Bob asked.

"He's fast," Frank conceded. And that was all he had to say about it.

Frank stood on the boardwalk as night wrapped her dark arms around the countryside. It was a wet darkness, for the rain continued without any signs of abating. Frank had seen nothing of the Easterners that day, and had no idea where they were or what they might be doing. Neither had he seen Doc Raven since the shooting in the saloon. There were lamps on in the doctor's office, but Frank didn't want to disturb him, figuring he might be busy with patients.

Just as Frank started to pop a match into flame, to light a fresh-rolled cigarette, he caught a glint of light off something in the alley across the muddy street . . . something that appeared to be about shoulder high. Frank quickly stepped back into the shadows and stuck the unlit cigarette and match into his jacket pocket.

He silently made his way down the boardwalk, keeping close to the buildings. He stepped off and ducked into an alley, then made his way behind a couple of buildings and dashed across the street, working his way up to the rear of the alley where he'd seen the flash of light off of metal. He cautiously looked around the corner of the building, and could just make out the dark shape of a man standing near the mouth of the alley, facing the street.

The man was holding a rifle.

Frank eased his way up the alley, the rain covering any small sound he might make. When he was close enough to the man to touch him, Frank said, "You looking for me?"

The man spun around, the muzzle of the rifle coming up. Frank hit him on the side of the jaw with a gloved right fist, and the man dropped to the littered ground. Frank dragged him out of the alley and up onto the boardwalk, then dragged him to the marshal's office and unlocked the door, using the key Doc Raven had given him earlier in the day. Frank had spent some time in the office that afternoon, sweeping it out and building a fire in the potbellied stove. There were living quarters in the jail, and Frank had moved his gear into the small room. Dog came out of the living quarters and sniffed suspiciously at the unconscious man.

Frank slapped the man awake and stood over him. He did not think he had ever seen the man before. "Do I know you?" he asked.

"Hell with you, Morgan."

"Well, obviously you know me. I hate to tell you but the hunt hasn't started yet. It's doubtful it ever will."

"Damn the hunt! I didn't come here to collect no money. I been looking for you for months. I aim to kill you."

"Why?"

" 'Cause you killed a buddy of mine, that's why."

"You sure I did it?"

"Damn right."

"Where and when and why?"

"Huh?"

Frank sighed. "The man's name and where did it happen and why did it happen."

"Barney Hampton was his name. It happened in Missouri and you called him out into the street and gunned him down."

"Wrong on all counts, partner. You've been tracking the wrong man."

"You say!"

"That's right. I say. Now, if I turn you loose, what are you going to do?"

"Git me another rifle and shoot you."

Frank walked over to the stove, poured a cup of coffee, and sat down in a wooden swivel chair at the battered old desk. He stared at the man sitting on the floor. "That's unacceptable, partner."

"Then you're gonna put me in jail?"

"I don't see where I have a choice."

"I'll kill you when I get out."

Frank sighed, wondering how in the world he had allowed his life to become so complicated. He pointed toward a row of cells in the back. "Get in that front cell and close the door. I've got to lock you up until I can decide what to do with you."

"You gonna feed me supper?"

"Get in the damn cell and be quiet!"

Surprisingly, the man obliged without another word. Frank locked the door, and went back into the office and stood for a moment. He put the man's rifle in a rack and his gunbelt and pistol in a desk drawer. Then he shook his head in disgust and walked out into the rainy night. "Incredible," he muttered. "This is the damnest situation I believe I have ever been in. Fifty people wanting to kill me for bounty money and more showing up trying to avenge a killing I didn't do . . ."

"Who are you talking to, Frank?" Doc Raven asked, walking up and breaking into his thoughts.

"Myself, Doc." He quickly and briefly brought the doctor up to date.

"Did you kill this Barney Hampton?"

"I never heard of any man called Barney Hampton. And I never called any man out into the street in Missouri."

"The price of fame, Frank."

"I guess. What did you learn from your college friend?"

"Nothing substantive. He carefully avoided directly answering any question I asked."

"So he's hiding something."

"Yes. Without a doubt."

"I got all the bodies carried over to the undertaker," Frank said. "The streets and alleys are clear of dead men—for the time being, that is."

"That will certainly please Sister Clarabelle. She came to see me today, complaining about the drinking and cussing and immoral behavior of the gunmen in town. She plans to lead a march up and down the boardwalks tomorrow. In the street if it stops raining."

"A march for what?"

"To protest the gunmen being in town . . . among other matters. The church has a band . . . of sorts: a man who beats the bass drum, a tuba player, a trumpeter, a trombonist, and a chorus of ladies. Very ample ladies," Doc Raven added drily.

"Sounds wonderful and, ah, spiritually uplifting," Frank said, trying to keep the sarcasm out of his voice.

Doc Raven smiled. "If the boardwalk doesn't collapse. Yes, it will be entertaining, I assure you."

"I'm sure it will be. Doc, does the town have a budget for feeding prisoners?"

"Sure. Get the food at the cafe and keep a record."

"I'd better do that now."

"All right, Frank. I'll try to speak with Maxwell again in the morning. For all the good it will do."

"Let me know if you find out anything."

"I certainly will, Frank. Good night."

"Night, Doc."

Frank walked the streets of town as the rain continued to fall. He went to the cafe and got a plate of food for his prisoner and a sack of scraps for Dog, carrying the food back to the jail.

"Morgan," the man in the cell called. "I want to talk to you."

"We'll talk while you eat. You want a cup of coffee?"

"I'd 'preciate it."

Frank pulled a chair over to the cell and sat down.

"There never was no shoot-out in Missouri," the prisoner said.

"I know."

"And I ain't got no kin named Barney Hampton."

"Then why were you laying in ambush for me?"

"Money. A man give me two hundred and fifty dollars to kill you."

"What man?"

"I don't know his name. He never told me. He talked to me whilst stayin' in the shadders. I couldn't see him."

"Was there anything unusual in his voice?"

"What do you mean?"

"Just that. Did he stutter or have a foreign accent? Anything like that."

"No. But he talked kinda funny."

"How do you mean?"

"I don't rightly know how to say it. He talked, well, real prissy, sort of. If you know what I mean."

"Prissy?"

"Not like no Western man."

"Like maybe he was well educated, a big-city man?"

"Yeah, that's it!"

"Thanks. You've been a help."

"You gonna keep me in jail?"

"What do you think?"

"I think you'd better. I sort of like it. It's warm and dry in here and the grub ain't bad."

Frank nodded and left the cell area. He let Dog out in the back for a few minutes while he locked up and turned down the lamps. Then he went to bed.

"Just gets more and more curious," he muttered.

Twelve

Leaving the prisoner to sleep, Frank walked over to the cafe for breakfast. The place had just opened and the local crowd had not yet showed up. Only Doc Raven was in the cafe, sitting alone at a table sipping coffee. The doctor waved Frank over.

"The coffee's hot and fresh and good, Frank. But I guess you've already had a pot or two this morning."

"I didn't make any at the office. Just got dressed and sat outside for a time, watching it rain."

"It's slowly tapering off. Another day and it'll move out of here, I'm thinking. That's the way it usually happens."

"Then the excitement will start," Frank said after thanking the waitress for the pot of coffee she placed on the table. He poured a cup and sugared it.

"Maybe, maybe not. If it does, it might not be directed toward you."

"Oh?"

"I had a visitor last night. Just after I left you on the boardwalk. Clerk at the general store stopped by and told me the Olsen cousins bought a lot of supplies at the store late yesterday. Half a wagon load. Said he overheard them whispering about heading out today. Seems they've been hired by someone as guides."

"The Easterners?"

"That would be my guess."

"I guess they succeeded in buying horses."

"Looks like it."

"Where were the supplies delivered?"

"He didn't know. The cousins drove up in the wagon and hauled it off, keeping away from the main street."

"You know what those cousins are likely to do, don't you?"

"They'd have to get the hired bodyguards to go along with them, Frank."

"You think that would take a lot of persuading?"

Doc Raven grunted. "Probably not. Hell, Frank, I never thought of that. They'd rob them all, then kill the men, have their way with the women, and leave whoever was left to die in the big wilderness."

"That's my thinking. Brooks is not totin' a full load, Doc. I think he's capable of doing just about anything."

"Wilma will be leaving with them, Frank."

"She made her choice a long time ago."

Doc Raven's eyes betrayed him when a faraway light suddenly appeared. "Yes, I suppose that's true."

"You still have feelings for her, don't you?"

The doctor smiled. "Yes, Frank. I do."

Frank's eyes were as sad as his voice when he said, "I reckon that sometimes real love never dies."

"Sounds as though you've been there, Frank."

Frank sighed. "I have, Doc."

Both were silent with their own thoughts for a moment. Then Doc Raven asked, "What do you plan to do about the Easterners?"

"Not a thing, Doc. At least not until I see what really happens. After that, well, they're grown-up folks and there are no children involved. If they

want to try their luck by riding off into the Big
Empty, let them go."

Doc Raven slowly nodded. "You're right. It's
their choice."

Bob entered the cafe and sat down at the table.
"The Easterners slipped out of town last night. Left
their fancy wagons. What'd y'all make of that?"

"Where are all the gunslingers?" Doc Raven
asked.

"Sleepin' off last night's drunk. All over town."

"It's doubtful they'll be up 'fore noon," Frank
said. "Most of them anyway. After that . . ." He
shrugged. "The word will spread pretty quick, I'm
thinking. Then it's going to get real interesting
around town."

"I better check my bag," Doc Raven said. "And
restock my operating room."

"That might be a real good idea," Frank replied.

"Sister Clarabelle is set to crank up the band
about noon," Bob said, a very mischievous twinkle
in his eyes. "Just about the time them gunslicks hit
the street all headachy and bleary-eyed. Them
churchgoers will be marchin' up and down the
boardwalks, tootin' their horns and beatin' on the
drums and singin' to the high heavens. Should be
right interestin'."

Doc Raven glanced at his longtime friend for a
few seconds. "Bob, you've got a real vicious streak
in you."

"I know it," the liveryman said. "I can't help it.
I think I was borned this way. But it didn't really
come out till after I got married." He shook his
head sorrowfully. "That woman would try the patience of a saint."

"Did she ever remarry, Bob?" Frank asked.

"Damned if I know. I doubt it. Who the hell
would have her?"

"I was told she was a really fine woman," Doc Raven said after a hidden wink at Frank.

"Whoever said that told you a bald-faced lie!" Bob said. "That woman nagged and ragged me so bad, the chickens quit layin' and the cow stopped givin' milk. My good dog run off and joined up with a coyote pack on account of her."

"Did your dog ever come back home?" Frank asked.

"The very day that damn woman left. I was glad to see him too."

"I've got to go after listening to that big whopper," Doc Raven said. "I'll see you boys later."

"I'm right behind you, Doc," Frank said, standing up and reaching for his hat.

"It's the truth, I swear it is," Bob insisted. "Well, most of it."

Laughing, the doctor and the gunfighter left the cafe and walked out onto the boardwalk. While Frank rolled a smoke, Doc Raven said, "Every town has its character. Bob is ours. See you after a while, Frank."

Frank stood in front of the cafe for a time, smoking and watching the town wake up. Then he decided to walk around and check out the wagons of the Easterners. Just as Bob had said, the wagons were uninhabited. Frank looked inside several. The interiors were plush, with carpet on the floor and fancy curtains on the small windows. And devoid of people.

"These wagons must have cost plenty to build and outfit," Frank muttered. "And the dudes just ride off and leave them."

Frank turned as a boy of about ten or eleven walked up. "Them fancy people left in the night, Mr. Morgan," he said. "Something woke me up and I watched 'em ride out."

"Did you see which way they went?"

"Sure did. I slipped out of bed and followed 'em a ways. They headed due north up the old road that leads to Red Rock."

"The road ends there, doesn't it?"

"Yes, sir. Ain't nothin' beyond that 'ceptin' empty."

"The women riding sidesaddle?"

"Yes, sir. Proper-like."

"I wonder where they got the sidesaddle rigs."

"Maybe they brung 'em with 'em."

"Maybe they did," Frank said. "Thanks, boy."

"You're welcome, sir.

The boy walked off and Frank whispered, "They had it all planned out. They never intended to pay any bounty for killing me. It was all some sort of crazy joke. Well, folks, the joke backfired on you. And now you're in trouble and on your own as far as I'm concerned."

At mid-morning, the bleary-eyed gunslicks and bounty hunters began staggering and lurching out into the streets of town, all of them badly hungover, with aching and throbbing heads. All of them searching for some hot coffee.

Doc Raven, Bob, and Frank sat on a bench outside the marshal's office, watching the pitiful-looking assemblage.

"Ain't that about the sorriest-lookin' bunch you ever laid eyes on?" Bob said.

"They're rough-looking, for a fact," Frank acknowledged.

One of the hungover gunslicks staggered up to the trio. "Gimme something, Doc!" he asked in a slurry voice. "I think I'm dyin'."

"You'll live," Doc Raven told him. "Get some coffee and something to eat."

"Eat?" the still-half-drunk gunhand gasped. "Oh, God!" Then he fell off the boardwalk and lay puking by the side of the main street.

"Well, I damn shore don't want no lunch now," Bob said. "That's plumb disgustin'. Why don't you toss him in jail, Frank?"

Before Frank could reply to that, Sister Clarabelle's band struck up in a practice session.

"My God," Frank said. "Someone's being tortured."

Doc Raven laughed. "No, Frank. That's the Mission Church Band warming up in practice. Something they never quite get enough of, as you can tell."

"Yeah," Bob said. "Just wait until Clarabelle starts singin'. Then you'll really think someone's being tortured."

"That bad?" Frank asked.

"Bad?" the liveryman said, shaking his head. "Clarabelle used to claim she was trained for the opera. 'Bout ten years ago this travelin' group of musicians from back East was forced to spend a week here due to the rain. They decided to give us a show for our hospitality—"

Doc Raven started laughing in remembrance, cutting off Bob's telling.

"The music was that bad?" Frank asked.

"The music was fine," Bob said. "But Clarabelle had somehow got herself invited to sing some famous opera piece . . ."

The doctor started laughing again, and Bob waited for a moment.

"Well, sir, Clarabelle hoisted herself up on that stage—she's sort of a large woman; right ample, you might say. The song was 'posed to be sung in I-talian. Clarabelle has sort of a deep voice for a woman, you see. Everybody in the place braced themselves. Me, I had edged myself close to the door so's I could get out right quick. The conductor pecked his little stick on the music stand, the orchestry begun playin', and Clarabelle let out a couple of bellers that got every cat in town squallin'. Sounded like a entar herd of constipated moose backed up and all farted at once. Scared that conductor so bad he fell off the platform. The band got all out of tune. But that didn't stop Clarabelle. She kept right on a-bellerin' and a-snortin' in I-talian. She's got a right powerful voice, that woman does. I mean to tell you, winders was crackin' and kids was cryin' and dogs was howlin'. Clarabelle throwed out her arms and commenced to really give it her all. It was a love song, we was all told 'fore it began. But that song writer must have had a grudge against women when he wrote that piece. I never heard nothin' so awful in all my life. I mean, folks was leavin' that place fast as they could get to the door. Clarabelle had her eyes closed and was lettin' it rip. She throwed herself into the piece. Started jumpin' up and down and a-bellerin'. Entar buildin' was a-shakin'. Stage broke and Clarabelle disappeared in a cloud of dust. But that didn't stop her. She was coughin' and singin' and the band was playin' all out of key amidst a cloud of dust so thick somebody on the other end of town thought the place was on far and rung the far bell. A bucket brigade was formed up and folks started throwin' water where the stage used to be. Hell, even when the band quit playin' that didn't shut up Clarabelle. She was determined to finish that love song." Bob paused to take a deep breath.

Doc Raven was laughing so hard, tears were running down his face and he was clutching his sides.

"Someone finally was brave enough to get close enough to toss a bucket of water on Clarabelle, and that seemed to bring her to her senses," Bob said.

"She stopped her squallin'. I mean to tell you it was a hell of a night here in town. That bunch of musicians all said later they hadn't never heard nothin' like it and hoped they never would again."

Frank wiped his eyes with a bandanna. "Bob, how much of that tale is really true?"

"Almost all of it," Doc Raven answered. "I was there. I had never heard Clarabelle sing before, and was looking forward to her performance." He shook his head. "We all make mistakes. I should have left town before the band tuned up."

"And she still sings?" Frank asked.

"You gonna hear her in a few minutes," Bob said. "She ain't bad until she starts gettin' all carried away . . . and she will. She always does. If I was you, Frank, I'd put my dog in the barn till it's over. This is likely to affect him forever."

"It can't be that bad!"

"You wanna bet?"

Frank listened to the out of tune and out of time band practicing and shook his head. "No, I don't think so."

"I didn't figure you would," Bob replied.

The drunk gunslinger lying on the ground raised his head at the sounds of the band practicing. He moaned and grimaced. "What in the name of God is that awful sound? Have I died and gone to hell?"

"You should have stayed passed out," Doc Raven told him. "In a few minutes you're going be very sorry you woke up."

"I think I need a drink," the gunslick said.

"That's not a bad idea," Bob said. "Why don't we all go have a drink?"

"Can we get clear of that terrible band?" Frank asked.

"Not entirely," Doc Raven said. "But it'll be bearable."

Frank stood up. "Let's go."

Thirteen

The saloon was filled with sullen, hungover, and bad-tempered gunfighters. Doc Raven, Bob, and Frank made their way to a table in the rear and ordered drinks. Whiskey for Bob and the doctor, beer for Frank.

The barkeep had just placed the drinks on the table when Dolan walked in and up to the bar. He ordered coffee and then turned to face the crowd. "Well, boys, have you heard the news?" he asked in a loud voice.

"What news?" Jack Miller asked. Miller needed a shave and a haircut and most especially, a bath. The man's body odor was offensive to those sitting several tables away.

"The Eastern dudes pulled out last night," Dolan said. "They slipped away like a pack of damn coyotes."

"What the hell do you mean?" Miller said.

"Are you deaf?" Dolan challenged. "They're gone. Pulled out. Left here. There ain't gonna be no money for no hunt. It's over. Them damn dudes pulled a fast one on us."

"Why would they do that?" the gunslick called Fargo asked. "That don't make no sense."

"Here it comes," Doc Raven whispered.

"I think it was all a joke," Dolan said. "I think them damn slick Easterners wanted to see us go at each other and kill each other off in some sort of wild shoot-out . . . right down to the very last man left standin'. When we didn't, they got nervous about all that money they promised and snuck out."

"That's close enough to the truth," Doc Raven whispered.

"That's crazy, Doc," Frank said in a low voice. "Stupid. Didn't they realize what kind of a dangerous game they were playing?"

"No, Frank. They didn't. None of them have ever been west of Pennsylvania. They grew up and have lived their lives in a society that had police officers on call and strictly enforced laws. They didn't know what they were getting into."

"They still don't," Bob added. "With them damn crazy Olsen boys within spittin' distance, they're in a hell of a lot more danger than they would have been stayin' right here in town."

"Well, where the hell did they go?" a bounty hunter yelled.

"I don't know, Max," Dolan told the man. "All I know is they pulled out. Left them fancy wagons and hauled their ashes out of here."

The saloon was suddenly filled with cussing and vile threats. A burly man called Nick stood up and said, "By God, we can all read sign. Let's go find 'em."

"I got things to do first," Dolan said. "They'll be travelin' slow. We got plenty of time to find them and collect our due."

"What things?" Lonesome Howard asked.

"Dealin' with Morgan yonder."

"You ain't gonna get paid for it," Moses Gunther called from a table.

"That don't make no nevermind to me," Dolan said. "I can take him, and that's what I aim to do."

"Bringing in the sheaves, bringing in the sheaves."

The sounds of the hymn drifted to those in the saloon.

"What the hell is that?" a hired gun named Ballard asked.

"That's a very beautiful hymn, you damned heathen!" Lonesome Howard told him.

"We shall come rejoicing, bringing in the sheaves."

The singing was getting closer and louder. The band began playing: drums, tuba, trombone, and trumpet. The sound of many footsteps marching in unison on the boardwalk rattled the windows of the saloon.

"Onward, Christian Soldiers, marching as to war . . ."

"I think them women and the band is gonna come in here!" a gunslick standing close to the front door said.

"I hope to hell not," another said. "My head is hurtin' some fierce."

"Your time has come, Morgan," Dolan said. "I'm gonna kill you just for the hell of it."

"Don't be a fool, Dolan," Frank told him, still sitting at the table. "I don't have any quarrel with you."

"I got a bone to pick clean with you, Morgan. You're alive and that bothers me. I aim to bury that bone this day. Now stand up and face me."

"You better give that some serious thought, Dolan. 'Cause if I stand up, I'm going to kill you."

"Big talk, Morgan. You talk mighty big. Stand up, you bastard."

Frank had started to push back his chair when the door banged open and Sister Clarabelle marched in, the band and the singers right behind her.

"Sing, ladies!" Clarabelle bellowed. "Lips that taste whiskey will never touch mine."

"Lips that taste whiskey will never touch mine."

"Oh, for a Christian man my heart pines."

"Oh, for a Christian man my heart pines."

"Them gals ain't half bad," Bob said. "As long as Clarabelle don't start tryin' to sing."

"I'm not familiar with that song," Doc Raven said.

"Me neither," Frank said as the marchers got between Frank and Dolan.

"Git out of the way, goddamnit!" Dolan yelled.

"You watch that filthy mouth!" Lonesome Howard hollered. "Them's good Christian ladies, you damn scum!"

"Beer and whiskey are tools of the devil," Clarabelle shouted.

"Beer and whiskey are tools of the devil."

"Imbibing in either is the path to evil."

"Imbibing in either is the path to evil."

"Kinda hard to pat your foot to that song, though," Bob opined.

"Stand up, Morgan!" Dolan shouted over the singing and chanting and band-playing. "You son of a bitch!"

Clarabelle pushed her considerable bulk through a knot of gunfighters who were trying, unsuccessfully, to get out of her way. One man who was slower than his compadres got a hard shove from Clarabelle that sent him reeling into Dolan.

"Get out of my way, you drunken oaf!" Clarabelle yelled.

Dolan and the man went down on the floor in a tangle of arms and legs, both men losing their hats.

Dolan really let the obscenities rip and roar as he hit the floor, coloring the air with violent expletives.

"How dare you talk to me using such filth!" Clarabelle shouted.

"Stand up, stand up, for Jesus," the singers sang.

Omp-pa-pa went the tuba. *Rat-a-tat-tat* replied the snare drummer.

"Goddamnit!" Dolan yelled.

"This day, the noise of battle."

Clarabelle grabbed the mallet from the bass drum player's hand and conked Dolan on the head.

"Rock of ages, cleft for me," the singers solemnly harmonized.

"You lard-assed heifer!" Dolan yelled, trying to get to his feet. "Stop hittin' me on the head with that damn club!"

"Lard-assed!" Clarabelle yelled.

"Let me hide myself in thee."

Dolan got to his feet just as Clarabelle swung the mallet again. This time it impacted solidly on Dolan's nose. Dolan went down again, the blood dripping from his busted beak.

"That woman's dangerous," a gunslick said. "I'm gettin' the hell outta here."

"I think she's wonderful," Lonesome Howard said, his eyes shining as he was caught up in the moment. "Magnificent."

"I think you're crazy as a road lizard eatin' loco weed," the gunslick told him.

Frank, Doc, and Bob were laughing so hard, tears were welling up in their eyes.

"My nose is busted!" Dolan hollered.

"I'll break your head," Clarabelle hollered as she swung the mallet again, conking Dolan on the top of his head.

"Somebody get this ton of lard away from me!" Dolan yelled.

"Ton of lard!" Clarabelle screamed, her voice rattling the beer mugs behind the bar. She grabbed up a bottle of whiskey from a table and swung it with all her might. The bottle smashed against Dolan's head. His eyes rolled back and he hit the floor, out like a candle at dawn.

"Praise the Lord!" the singers yelled.

"Amen!" Lonesome Howard shouted, his Bible in one hand and a shot glass of rye whiskey in the other.

"Hallelujah, brother!" one of the band members shouted, while the snare drummer beat a tattoo and the bass drummer pounded away.

"Who are you?" Sister Clarabelle demanded.

"They call me Lonesome Howard, Sister."

"How quaint. Are you a gunfighter?"

"Well, yes, sort of. But I'm a good Christian man who reads the Good Book every day."

"How can you be a Christian and be a gunfighter?"

"I kill for the Lord."

"Nonsense. Get down on your knees and pray for His wonderful forgiveness."

"Forgiveness for what?"

"For being a killer and for consorting with trash."

"I got one more man to kill, Sister. Then I'll drop on my knees onto a pile of sharp stones and pray all day."

"Who are you going to kill, Howard?"

Lonesome Howard turned to look at Frank. He pointed a finger. "That godless heathen right over there, Sister?"

"Don't be absurd! That man is a United States marshal. He put his hand on a Bible and took a oath."

Lonesome Howard shook his head. "Don't make no difference if he did. He's evil, Sister. And he's got to be killed."

Jack Miller stood up, his hands hovering near his guns. "That's so, Lonesome. But you ain't gonna be the one who does the killin'. That job is mine."

"The hell you say!" Lonesome cut his eyes to Clarabelle. "Kindly excuse my language, Sister. I backslid for a moment."

"Shet your blowhole, Lonesome," Jack told him. "And git outta my way. I got me a job to do."

"Here, now!" Clarabelle shouted. "Stop this."

"Shet up, Lard ass," Jack told her.

"Lard ass!" Clarabelle shrieked. "How dare you speak to me in such a manner?"

"That's easy," Jack told her. " 'Cause you draggin' a hell of a big caboose, that's why."

"I think he means to kill you, Frank," Doc Raven whispered.

Frank didn't reply, just nodded his head.

"Don't you insult that fine woman!" Lonesome said, his hand dropping to the butt of his six-gun. "You'll answer to me for that."

"Then hook and draw, you Bible-readin' son of a bitch!" Jack yelled.

Frank slowly stood up, shoving his chair back, and stepping away from the table. "Get out of the way, Howard."

"I don't need you to fight my battles, Morgan," Lonesome replied without taking his eyes from Miller. "I'll deal with this loudmouth and then we'll settle our business."

"You're both fools," Frank told them. "I have no quarrel with either of you. This is what those damn Easterners wanted. Can't you see that?"

"What are you talkin' 'bout, Morgan?" Miller asked, his eyes never leaving Lonesome. "Them dudes is gone."

"And you're still playing their stupid game," Frank insisted. "With no chance of ever collecting any money. Personally, I don't think they ever intended to pay any money. It was all a cruel joke."

"On who?" a gunhawk called Lucky Luke asked.

"On all of you," Doc Raven said, pushing back

his chair and standing up. "I think they wanted to see a bloody show—a number of killings until the last man was standing."

"And then they'd have to pay that man," Red Henson said.

"No," Doc Raven replied. "Then they'd just ride out under the protection of their bodyguards. They would have seen a so-called Wild West drama played out to their satisfaction. It was a joke, and the joke was on you men."

"I don't believe that," Nils Finley said. "No one would do somethin' that stupid. None of it makes any sense."

"Shore as hell don't," Vic Pressman said. "That there is a story, that's all. You make it all up, Doc. To try an' protect your friend Morgan."

"I give up," the doctor said. "I can't get through to these men." He shook his head and sat down.

Clarabelle was unusually quiet, standing in the midst of the West's most dangerous gunfighters, listening. The band was silent, as were the singers.

"It's over, boys," Bob said. "The dudes is gone. Pulled out. The show is over 'fore it ever got started good."

"He's right," Phil the bartender said. "Any gunplay now would be for naught."

Jack Miller shook his head. "Maybe so, maybe not. But I still aim to kill Frank Morgan. So get out of the way, Lonesome."

Frank tensed. He felt Miller was all through talking. The man was ready to kill. There was nothing to do now except kill or be killed.

"Make your play, Miller," Frank said.

Jack Miller moved his hand closer to the butt of his gun.

Fourteen

Miller was either so angry, nervous, or hungover that he was shaking as Frank faced him. Clarabelle and her group had backed up against a far wall. They all stood silent, mesmerized by the scene. Lonesome Howard had stepped back, carefully moving his hand away from the butt of his pistol. Those men who had lined the bar had backed away, dragging Dolan with them. Dolan was conscious, but still addled from the blow on the head.

"Pull, Morgan!" Miller yelled.

"After you, Miller," Frank calmly told him. "I won't draw first."

"I knowed it all along. You done lost your stomach for a fight. You've turned yeller, Morgan. You're a damn coward."

"There's one way to prove that, Miller. And you know what it is. So why don't you stop running your mouth and pull iron?"

"I will!" Miller yelled.

"I'm waiting," Frank replied.

Miller suddenly yelled like a deranged person and grabbed for his gun. Frank cleared leather as fast as a rattler's strike and fired, the bullet hitting Miller in the chest and knocking him stumbling backward. He held onto his pistol and managed to cock it and bring it level. He was grinning as Frank's .45 boomed again, the heavy slug taking

Miller in the side and turning him around, the bullet blowing out the man's back. Miller dropped his six-gun and it went off as it hit the floor, the bullet slamming into the side of the bar. Jack Miller sank to his knees and stayed there.

"Fast as he ever was," Red Henson said in a low tone.

"Too damn fast for me," another bounty hunter said. "I just quit this game."

"Me too," another said.

"Help me," Miller said. "I can't get up."

"Ain't no point in you doin' that, Jack," Lonesome Howard said. "You best just stay where you is and go on and ex-pire."

"Hell with you, Lonesome!" Miller gasped.

"You want me to say some words over you?" Lonesome asked. "I can read from the Good Book. That might make your passin' a tad easier."

"Take your words and the Good Book and stick 'em up your . . ."

"Oh, my heavens!" Clarabelle said, as Jack finished his suggestion.

"You ain't no fittin' man for no words of the Lord," Lonesome said. "Your soul is on the way to the hellfires."

"I'll see you there too, you bastard!" Miller told him. "Doc! Come over here and patch me up."

"I can tell from here no amount of patching will do you any good, Jack," Doc Raven told the man.

Miller suddenly fell forward on his face. "I can't . . ." Whatever it was he couldn't do was left unsaid as Miller lapsed into unconsciousness.

Clarabelle and her followers began quietly exiting the saloon. Few of the hardened gunslicks even took note of their departing.

Frank sat back down at the table. "Bring me some coffee, will you, Phil?"

"Comin' right up, Frank."

"What the hell is goin' on?" Dolan asked, sitting up on the floor. He shook his head. "Where am I?"

He was ignored.

"I smell gun smoke," Dolan said. "Have I been shot?"

"No, you ain't been shot," a gunny named Nick Bell told him. "But Jack Miller damn shore was."

"Who shot him?"

"Morgan."

Dolan's eyes cleared and he looked at Miller, lying on the barroom floor a few feet away. "Damn, boy, you look bad," Dolan said.

Miller did not reply. His soul was reaching out to shake hands with the Grim Reaper. The Reaper is always a heartbeat away from all of us.

Frank sipped his coffee.

"You want some of us to tote Miller over to your office, Doc?" a gunhawk known only as Stoner asked.

"No point in that," Doc Raven replied. "He's about dead."

"How in the hell can you tell that from where you're sittin'?" Red Henson asked.

"From years of experience." The doctor pushed away his empty glass. "Phil? Bring me a cup of that coffee, will you?"

"You got to be the sorriest doctor I ever had the misfortune to run into," Red said. "You didn't even git up to look at Miller."

Miller jerked once and would never move again . . . at least not on this earth and not under his own power.

"I believe Miller just passed," Lonesome said. "Praise the Lord. Barkeep, bring me a fresh bottle, will you?"

"Let's some of us get him out of here and over to the undertaker," Fargo suggested. "He smelt bad enough livin'. He'll really be stinkin' in a little while."

"That there is a natural fact," a gunslinger said. "Come on, boys. Let's tote him out of here."

Several men got up and carried Miller outside.

Lonesome Howard turned slowly to stare at Frank. "Someday, Morgan, it'll be me and you. Then we'll settle this thing."

"Nothing between us to settle, Howard. Nothing at all."

"I think there is, Morgan."

"What?"

"You're an evil man and you got to be stopped."

"That'll be my job, Lonesome," Dolan said, straightening up and setting his hat gingerly on his head.

"Why don't you men stop this?" Doc Raven questioned. "My God! What has Frank done to either of you?"

"He don't have to have done nothin', Doc," Lonesome said.

"Then I don't understand."

"He's who he is, and we're who we are," Dolan said. "That's 'bout the onliest way I know to say it."

"You men really want this . . . foolishness to happen, don't you?" Doc Raven questioned. "This last man standing nonsense?"

"It's somethin' to do," Red Henson said.

"Now that is no reason for killing!"

Red shrugged that off and signaled for Phil to bring him another beer.

Frank finished his coffee and pushed back his chair. "I think I'll turn the prisoner loose and tell him to get out of town. The money men are gone; he can't get paid now for shooting me."

"He might decide to shoot you just for the hell of it," Bob said.

"I don't think so. Anyway, I'm going to cut him loose. See you men later." Frank walked out of the saloon, conscious of a lot of hostile eyes on him. But he was accustomed to that sensation and ignored the hot glares.

Frank turned the prisoner loose and told him to get his horse and head out of town.

"I'm gone, Marshal," the man said. "You'll not see me again."

"Good."

Frank emptied the chamber pot and cleaned up the man's cell. Then he washed up a bit and headed for the cafe to get Dog some scraps to eat. That done, he walked back to the saloon and leaned against the bar, drinking coffee and listening to the low murmur of voices around him. He covertly counted heads and realized that about half a dozen of the men were gone. Most of those gunslicks that he knew, or at least whose names he knew, were all present in the saloon. He motioned to Phil.

"Who left, Phil?"

"I know the names of three of them, Frank. Carl Repp, Jimmy Deggins, and Hamp Jennings. Something else too. That gunhawk called Roberts and his buddy with the chewed-up arm, Russ Temple? They pulled out early this morning, so I was just told."

"Going after the Easterners?"

"Damned if I know. But that would be a good guess."

"Thanks, Phil."

"You going after them?"

"I don't know. Far as I'm concerned, the Eastern folks got themselves into this mess, they can get themselves out of it."

"That sounds good to me."

Phil left to go wait on another customer and Frank

walked out to stand on the boardwalk. "Yeah," he muttered. "It sounds real good except for what's probably going to happen to the women traveling with those arrogant men. Damn!" Frank tossed his cigarette into a mud hole in the street and paced up and down the boardwalk for a couple of minutes. Then he made up his mind.

Frank walked over to Doc Raven's office. The doctor was sitting in his office reading a medical book. "What's on your mind, Frank?"

Frank told the doctor what the bartender had told him. "I'm going after those men, Doc."

Doc Raven laid the medical book aside. "You don't know that they've gone after the Easterners, Frank."

"I will as soon as I've picked up their tracks."

"You know, of course, that as soon as that mob of gunslicks in the saloon realize you're gone, they'll be coming after you?"

"That's probably very true."

"Counting the bodyguards with Maxwell and the others, you'll be facing odds of about fifty to one."

"You don't want me to go after your old college friends?"

Doc Raven grimaced at that question. "Please, they're not my friends, Frank. Far from it. As far as the women with them . . . well, in a way they're just as guilty as their husbands. Probably in a lot of ways," he added softly, then fell silent, except for drumming his fingertips on the desk. He opened his mouth to add something, then shook his head.

"But you're worried about Wilma?"

The doctor turned his gaze to Frank and stared at him for a few seconds. "She's married to Maxwell, Frank."

"But you're still in love with her."

"I suppose I do still have some sort of . . . ah, affection for her."

Frank smiled. "Sure, Doc. Some sort of affection. That's a very interesting way of putting it."

"We have had no communication for years, Frank. Not since just after the War of Northern Aggression."

"I saw the way you two looked at each other."

Doc Raven said nothing.

"I don't think she's very happy married to Maxwell."

"Perhaps not."

"Did they have any children, Doc?"

"Two. A boy and a girl. The boy is in business in New York City. The girl is married and living"— he waved a hand—"somewhere."

"So you've spoken with Wilma since her arrival here." It was not put as a question.

"A couple of times. Briefly."

"Will you take care of Dog for me, Doc?"

"Of course I will. But will he stay with me if you ride out?"

"If I tell him to. Especially if I don't take Horse with me."

Doc Raven sighed and smiled. "Dog and Horse." He laughed softly. "Couldn't you have come up with something a bit more original?"

"It fits them."

"I have a big mountain-bred Appaloosa. You saw him in the stable."

"Yes, I did. A beautiful animal."

"You can take him. He'll go all day and he certainly needs the exercise. His name is Stormy."

"I appreciate that."

"A bit of warning, Frank. He'll try you when you first swing into the saddle. Just to show you who's boss."

"I wouldn't have it any other way."

"When do you plan on pulling out?"

"Just as soon as I supply up."

Doc Raven was silent for a few seconds. "If you stay on the road, you'll find plenty of deserted cabins to spent the night. Most of them are in pretty good shape. Red Rock itself is deserted. Past Red Rock, the way is rough. It will be very slow going for Vanderhoot and his party."

"I'm counting on that, Doc."

"I'll have Bob put your rig on Stormy. Then I'll meet you behind the general store. How long do you plan on being gone?"

"As long as it takes, Doc." Frank turned and headed for the door. Raven's voice stopped him. "Yes, Doc?"

"Bring Wilma back to me, Frank."

Frank nodded his head and walked out of the office.

Fifteen

Frank waited until the store was empty of customers, then bought several boxes of cartridges for pistol and rifle, and bacon, beans, coffee, flour, and salt. He took the supplies out to the rear of the store and waited for Doc to show up. He did not have a long wait.

Stormy was a big Appaloosa, about seventeen hands high, which is somewhat larger than the average Ap. He had the typical markings for that breed: light gray in color with dark gray spots on his hips. And Stormy was a stepper with a lot of spirit; Frank could tell that just by looking at him. And he was young. The Ap cut his eyes to Frank as Frank approached him. But Frank had a way with horses; a gift, some would call it. After a few moments of gently talking with the big Ap, stroking the horse's nose, Frank swung into the saddle.

"He likes you, Frank," Doc Raven said. "He doesn't like many people. Sort of like your horse. And your horse is getting along in years too."

"He isn't a colt, that's for sure."

"Oh, I agree with you on that. He needs riding. However, there are a lot of trails Stormy would like to see. It's a shame I can't ride him more than I do. I just don't have the time."

"What are you getting at, Doc?"

"Horse likes me."

"Horse doesn't like anybody," Frank said.

"He likes me. I can assure you of that. I've been going down there when I could and feeding him bits of apple."

"He took it out of your hand?"

"Sure did. After I talked to him a bit."

"Damn wonder he didn't take your hand off."

"I've still got both hands," Doc Raven said with a smile.

"Again I ask, what are you getting at?"

"You want to trade horses, Frank?"

"Are you serious?"

"I sure am. You're a man who knows horses and you like horses. You're sitting on Stormy as though you two have known each other for years. Now . . . before you say no, I understand that Horse is not old; he's got a lot of years left in him. But he's also seen a lot of trails. He needs a good rest. Surely you'll agree with that."

"I will for a fact."

"You try Stormy on the trail. See how you two get along. Then make up your mind."

"I'll do that, Doc. See you when I get back. And"—he smiled—"I'll do my best to bring Wilma back with me."

"I hope so, Frank."

Frank lifted a hand and rode out of town. He had ridden only a few miles before his mind was made up. Horse was going to get himself the rest he so richly deserved. Stormy was born to the trail. The rain had stopped and the sun was finally shining after days of rain and drizzle and gloomy skies. Frank came to a spot in the old road that was not a mud pile and let Stormy have his head. The big Ap could almost fly, and loved strutting his stuff. Frank reined him in and swung down from the saddle, letting Stormy blow for a moment.

"You and me, Stormy, are going to get along just fine."

Stormy turned to look at Frank, and a bond was formed between the horse and Frank. After a few minutes, Frank stepped back into the saddle and headed for the ghost town of Red Rock. He didn't figure on making the town before dark, so after several hours on the trail, he began looking for a place to make camp for the night. He found some old wagon ruts deeply embedded in the almost indiscernible old road that led off to the east, and took it. About a quarter of a mile later he came to an old cabin in the timber, with a lean-to-type stable built off to one side. The roof looked to be in good shape, so Frank decided this was as good as he was apt to find and dismounted to check out the place.

Looking around, he could find no signs that anyone had visited the place recently. He put Stormy in the old stable and went inside the cabin.

Whoever had vacated the place had pulled out in a hurry, leaving some of the furniture behind. There was a rocking chair that looked to be in good shape. A table and three chairs. A bed frame with no mattress and a chest of drawers and a trunk. There were ample signs that small animals had frequented the place.

"It'll do for a home for the night," Frank said.

He looked around for a broom, found a piece of one with a broken handle, and used that to sweep out the place as best he could. He found some old boards and sticks in one side of the lean-to, and used that to build a fire, then put on water to boil for coffee. He'd bought some crackers and tins of beef and some pickles at the general store; he'd have those for supper.

Frank let Stormy out and hobbled him so he could graze and not go far from the cabin. He tried the water in the well and it tasted sweet. He filled up his canteen with that. The water was boiling when he got back to the cabin, and the day was getting colder. "Well, it's time for that," Frank said. "I just hope it doesn't snow."

Frank drank a cup of coffee and had supper. He went out and gathered up enough wood to last him the night, then went back to the cabin. He poured another cup of coffee, then rolled a smoke and enjoyed the quiet of late afternoon.

He heard Stormy whinny and stamp his feet and snort. Frank grabbed up his rifle and went out the back door. Stormy had not moved far from where Frank had hobbled him at the rear of the cabin. Frank led him close to the house and tied him there, so he would be safe from any bullets coming from the front.

"You stay here and be safe," Frank told the big Ap, stroking his nose. "I'll be back."

Frank headed for the timber and circled around, moving swiftly and soundlessly through the timber. There was just enough light left for him to see, but he knew that would not last for long. He reached the edge of the clearing, far in front of the old cabin, and squatted down, his eyes moving, scanning all around him.

He caught a glimpse of red across the clearing and lifted his rifle, easing back the hammer.

"You see anything, Charlie?" a voice called.

Frank froze; the voice couldn't be more than a dozen yards away from him, to his right.

"Nothing, Rich. But somebody's in there, they's smoke a-comin' from the chimley."

Chimley? Frank thought. Man either has a speech defect or he's ignorant.

"But is it Morgan?"

"How the hell does I know?" Rich called. "Them guys we met comin' from town said he would prob'ly be headin' thisaway. Mayhaps it is, mayhaps it ain't."

"Where's his damn horse, I wonder."

"I dasn't know that neither. But I heared him whinny."

"They's big bounty money on Morgan's head, Rich. And not from them uppity Easterners, neither. I heard about another bounty when I was over in Wyoming. Big money too. I never thought I'd get me a chance to collect it. But here it is."

"I wants me some of that money," Charlie called softly. "I shorely does. Hell, let's just shoot up the cabin. There ain't nobody gonna hear us."

"What if that ain't Morgan yonder?"

"You really give a damn?"

"No. But we ain't got no money to buy no more shells with."

"So we'll kill this traveler and take his gear and horse and sell it."

"That there's good thinkin', Rich. Mighty good thinkin'. Let's do it."

"You do it, Charlie. I'm out of cartridges for my rifle. All I got's my pistol."

Nice folks, Frank thought. He lifted his rifle and drilled the spot of red across the way, then before the sound of the rifle had stopped echoing, Frank had hit the ground and bellied down.

"Oh, Lordy, Rich!" Charlie called. "I'm hit. Oh, hell, Rich. I'm hit hard. I'm a-bleedin' something fierce, I is."

The air above Frank's head was filled with hot lead for a few seconds as Rich emptied his pistol. Frank counted six. Then he returned the rifle as fast as he could lever his Winchester. He rolled away and quickly reloaded.

"Rich!" Charlie called. "Is you hit?"

There was no reply.

"Rich?" Charlie called. "I got to have me some help, Rich. I'm bleedin' real bad."

Frank bellied his way through the brush and peered through a bush. But there was no need for being careful. Rich was sitting up, his back to a tree. He was very still. He had taken a round in the center of his face.

"Rich?" Charlie called. "My guts is on far, Rich. I'm hurt bad."

Frank made his way through the timber back to the cabin, then around to the wounded man, being careful not to expose himself. Charlie was probably badly wounded, but the man could still pull a trigger.

Frank approached the man slowly and silently. Charlie was stretched out on the ground, his rifle a few feet away from him. Frank walked over and kicked the rifle away, then looked down into Charlie's pain-filled eyes.

"Is you Morgan?" Charlie asked.

"Yes," Frank said, noticing that the man's front teeth were missing.

"You a son of a bitch," Charlie said.

"I've been called worse."

"Help me."

"Where'd you come from?"

"Huh? I was borned in Arkansas."

"Where did you come from today?"

"The ghost town up the road a few miles."

"Red Rock?"

"I reckon."

"Did you see a group of men and women up that way?"

"Shore did. Fancy men and women. All duded up to the nines." Charlie paused for a few seconds as intense pain hit him. He clutched at his belly with bloody hands. "You carryin' anything for pain?"

"No. How about a group of men, all traveling together?"

"I seen them. Seemed like they had all joined up with the fancy people. Hard-lookin' bunch of people. The fancy people didn't look like they liked it none a-tall."

"Did you talk to them?"

"Rich did most of the talkin'. They didn't want nothin' to do with us, so we lef' right quick." Charlie groaned. "Can you git me to a doctor?"

"No. The nearest doctor is miles away. Can you ride?"

"I don't think so. It hurts to move. My guts is on far."

"You want me to say I'm sorry?"

"To hell with you, Morgan. You ain't a damn bit sorry you shot me, is you?"

"Not a bit."

Charlie cussed Frank until he was out of breath. "Is Rich dead?"

"He took a bullet in the center of his face."

"He's got kin back in Fort Smith. They'll git you, Morgan."

"They'll be at the end of a long line."

"Huh?"

Frank concluded that Charlie was a bit on the slow side. "Forget it. Can you walk?"

"I ain't gonna move. If I stand up my guts will fall out."

"If you don't try, you can die alone right here in the timber."

"One place is as good as any, I reckon." Charlie's voice was weak and his eyes held a strange, faraway light.

Frank squatted down, staying a few feet away from the man. "Do you want me to get a bedroll from your horse?"

Charlie could not reply. He opened his mouth

to speak, but his tongue could not form the words. He looked at Frank for a moment, then closed his eyes and was still. Frank watched him for a couple of minutes, then stood up.

It was too dark to try and bury the men, so Frank left them where they had fallen and walked over to the road and up to the main road. He found the men's horses and shook his head at their condition. They had not been cared for and were in bad shape. He stripped saddles and bridles from them, turning the horses loose. He took the hobbles off Stormy and stabled him, then took the saddlebags back to the cabin and lit a couple of candles. He poured a cup of coffee and then went through the saddlebags. He could not find a thing that would tell him anything about any relatives of the men. The saddlebags contained nothing except wads of filthy clothing and a handful of gold teeth. Obviously the men had been robbing graves, knocking out the gold teeth of the dead to sell later.

In disgust and revulsion, Frank threw the gold teeth into the shadows of the cabin. "Sorry damn bastards," he swore. "A couple of worthless lowlifes."

Frank rolled a smoke and leaned back in the rocking chair. He made up his mind then and there that he would not bury the two come morning. He would leave them for the animals.

"They don't deserve any better," he muttered. "Trash and scum."

He tossed the filthy clothing into the fire and sat and watched it burn. He missed the company of Dog, but the animal was better off staying in town with Horse. Doc would make sure the dog was well fed and loved.

He smiled, hoping Dog would not get too attached to Doc Raven.

Frank lifted his head. What was that sound? Or was it a noise at all? Yes. He was sure he'd heard something. Something that was not a normal sound of the night.

He listened intently. There it was again. A human sound, he was certain of that.

He picked up his rifle and went out the back of the cabin, standing for a moment, listening.

"Help!" The night carried the cry for help. "Help me, please."

"What the hell?" Frank muttered, just as the cry came again. Frank stepped around the corner and began walking toward the sound.

The night closed around him.

Sixteen

The pleas for help changed into a low moaning in the night. Frank cautiously followed the sounds, staying on the road, but close to the timber. When he was close to the main road leading to Red Rock, he spotted the figure of a man lying in the middle of the cabin road. Frank stopped, stepping into the timber and surveying everything around him, listening intently. He could neither see, hear, nor sense anything hostile awaiting him. He walked up to the man and knelt down.

It was Maxwell Crawford. The man's clothing was ripped and torn and he had been badly beaten, his face swollen and covered with dried blood.

"My God," Maxwell whispered. "I'm badly hurt. Please help me."

"Can you walk?" Frank asked.

"Yes, I think so."

"Come on. I'll help you up. That's good. Now lean on me. The cabin isn't far."

Frank managed to get Maxwell to the cabin and into a chair by the table. He put on water to boil, lit several candles for more light, built up the fire, and then turned his attention to Maxwell.

The man had been savagely beaten. Frank could tell the man's nose was broken and several teeth had been knocked out.

"My ribs are broken," Maxwell said. "And I'm

coughing up blood. My chest hurts terribly. I believe a lung has been punctured."

"Water will be hot in a few minutes. Then I'll clean you up. Tell me what happened to you, Maxwell."

"The men we hired as guides, the Olsen cousins, turned on us. They were in league with our bodyguards. I don't know how they arranged that, but they did. I think it had been planned with the assistance of some of those who had gathered in town . . ."

Maxwell paused to take a ragged breath, and Frank asked, "Roberts, Russ Temple, Hamp Jennings, that bunch?"

"Yes. They helped take us prisoner. They were, are, holding us for ransom. I fought them and they beat me until I was unconscious. When they weren't looking, I crawled away and got onto a horse and slipped away. About a mile from here, the horse was startled by something and threw me. I walked and crawled until I smelled smoke, and then began yelling for help. Thank God you found me."

"The women?"

"They haven't been . . . raped. At least not when I left. But they're going to be. I overheard the hoodlums talking about it."

"Are any more men from town a part of this? The bounty hunters, I mean. Not locals."

"I . . . think so. Not sure."

Maxwell slipped into unconsciousness, and Frank took that time to bathe the man's face with hot water and take his coat and shirt off. As gently as possible, Frank probed the man's bare chest and sides. He had several ribs broken, probably by savage kicks. Maxwell coughed up a pink froth several times. A sure indication that a lung had been punctured, maybe both lungs. His breathing was very ragged.

Frank covered the man with a blanket and stepped back. There was little else he could do for Maxwell Crawford. There was a terrible swelling knot on the side of the man's head. It was possible, probably even likely, the man's skull had been busted and there was bleeding inside.

"Damn!" Frank muttered.

"The manhunt was all a joke," Maxwell mumbled, becoming conscious for a moment. "Just something for us to do; a little excitement for our wives. It was stupid. We misjudged the caliber of Western men. Sorry about any inconvenience we caused you, Mr. Morgan. I am truly sorry."

"Forget it. Get some rest."

"I'm going to have plenty of time to rest," Maxwell said, his voice firming. "I'm dying and I know it. My skull has been fractured and lungs punctured. Even if you got me to a doctor, there is nothing he could do."

"You want to lie down? I can fix you a pallet on the floor."

Maxwell shook his head and moaned from the pain that caused. "No. I don't want to move, Mr. Morgan. It just hurts too much."

"Frank. My name is Frank."

"Thank you, Frank. The hoodlums, Frank, they're going to take the hostages to another old ghost town in the mountains."

"Does it have a name?"

"Freetown, I heard one of them say. Do you know where it is?"

"I've heard of it. It was built by ex-slaves right after the war. It isn't far from Red Rock. Just a few miles east of there. But I didn't know it was a ghost town."

"They said it would be fifteen minutes after they got there."

"I see. Nice bunch of people."

"They're all trash and scum. Right down to the last man." He coughed up blood and his body trembled from the pain. "I have to rest a minute, Frank. All right?"

"Sure, Maxwell. You rest for a few minutes. I'll get us some coffee."

"I would like some coffee. It would taste good."

Frank left the man's side and fixed coffee, then dumped in some cold water and waited for the grounds to settle. He poured two cups and returned to the table. Maxwell was unconscious. Frank was doubtful the man would ever wake up. He sat in a chair and drank his coffee and smoked. Just as he drained the last of his coffee, Maxwell shivered once and died peacefully.

"What a mess," Frank said, looking at the body of Maxwell, sitting in the old kitchen chair, his chin resting on his chest. "What a completely unnecessary mess."

Frank carried the body outside and laid it by the side of the cabin, covering it with a blanket. He hoped there was a shovel around the place. If not, he would have to cover Maxwell with rocks until someone could get the body for transport back East. Or maybe the family would leave him here. Frank had no way of knowing. And really, he thought, why the hell should I care?

Frank went back into the cabin, built up the fire, and tried to sleep, managing to sleep only fitfully. He was up before dawn and made coffee. He sat by the fire and drank coffee and smoked until it became light enough to see. He prowled around the place, but could find no shovel, not even a piece of one. He carried the body of Maxwell to a spot away from the cabin and began gathering rocks, piling them on the body. The rocks would not keep any large determined animal from the body, but it was the best Frank could do under the circumstances.

Back in the cabin, Frank heated water and washed up as best he could. He did not bother to shave. He doused the fire and rolled up his kit, then saddled up Stormy. In the saddle, Frank paused once on his way to the road to look back at the spot where he'd covered Maxwell.

"Sorry, Maxwell," he whispered. "You folks should have stayed in the big city. And found some other way to amuse yourselves."

Frank lifted the reins and rode away. He figured he would make the old town of Red Rock in a few hours. After that? He would handle whatever situation confronted him in the best way he could.

Frank reined up a few hundred yards from the old town and studied the place for a few seconds, then turned Stormy into the timber. The weather had turned decidedly colder, but he could see no signs of smoke from the ghost town. If anyone was in town, they must be awfully cold. Frank felt the place was deserted, the outlaws and their hostages having moved on toward Freetown.

Staying in the timber, Frank rode slowly toward the town, coming up behind the town proper, amid a small gathering of houses. He could see no smoke coming from any of the houses or the row of abandoned stores.

"Gone," Frank muttered. He stepped down from the saddle and pulled his rifle from the saddle scabbard. He left Stormy and began prowling the ghost town on foot, staying behind the row of stores, pausing every few seconds to listen.

He could hear nothing except the sighing of the cold late fall wind.

When he reached the last of the stores on the east side, he tried the back door. It was unlocked. He pushed the door open and stepped into the dimness of an old storeroom. He could see light coming in from what remained of the storefront windows. He cautiously made his way to the front and looked out onto the single main street. He saw recent horse droppings in the street, but no signs of human life. And could smell no smoke.

Somewhere in the town something—human, he hoped—began moaning.

He had never heard any animal moan like that. But there had been reports of strange, manlike, hairy beasts roaming in this area. Frank had heard the rumors, but had never seen any of the beasts, and sincerely hoped he never would.

The moaning began anew and Frank shivered, not entirely due to the cold winds that were blowing.

"Get hold of yourself, Frank," he whispered. "What you're thinking about is old Indian rumors, that's all."

Or was it?

"Ah, hell!" Frank said, and stepped out of cover, walking toward the sounds of moaning, which were getting louder.

Frank located the building where the moaning seemed to be coming from, and slowly pushed open the warped old door.

"Don't hurt me no more!" a man screamed from a pile of bloody rags in a dark corner of the room.

"I'm not going to hurt you," Frank said, walking toward the man and kneeling down. "Who are you and what happened here?"

"Waylon." The man shoved the word past swollen and bloody lips. "I was driftin' and come up on this old town; decided to spend the night here. Las' night, no, night 'fore las', I guess it was, a whole bunch of people showed up. Mean bunch, as it turned out. Outlaws, I reckon they was. Had some folks prisoners. Men and women. They was beatin' up on the men and manhandlin' the womenfolk." The badly beaten man paused for several breaths.

"Take it easy," Frank told him. "Let me get my horse and I'll get you some water. Hang on."

" 'Preciate it, partner. I'm hurt bad, I think."

Frank walked swiftly back to Stormy and rode back into town, reining up behind the building where he'd found the man. He got his canteen and entered through the back door. He wet a bandanna and mopped Waylon's swollen and battered face, then gave the canteen to the man. Waylon drank deeply and sighed.

"Man, that's good. Better than rye. Thanks."

"Feel like finishing what you were telling me?"

"Yeah. Ain't that much more to tell." Waylon took another pull from the canteen. "I seen what was happenin' and tried to leave. Some of them no-counts hung a loop over me and dragged me off my horse. Then they commenced to beatin' on me for the fun of it. I don't know how many times they whupped on me. More'un once, I can tell you that."

"What about the women? Have they been raped?"

"Not yet, I don't think. But that's comin' for shore. All the men done been beat on some. One got away, though, I think."

"He's dead. I found him a few miles down the road."

A whinny sounded out in the street and the cowboy's eyes widened. "That's my horse. I thought they'd stole him."

Frank stood up. "I'll see about him."

"That's mighty good of you, mister."

Frank found the horse and took him to the old livery barn. He stripped saddle and bridle from the horse and stabled him, then went back to the injured man.

"Let me gather up some wood and I'll build a fire and make us some coffee," Frank said. "And I have some bacon I can fry up."

"All that would taste fine, mister. I ain't et in a couple of days, not since them outlaws grabbed me. I had some grub in my saddlebags. Did you look in there?"

"No, I didn't. Don't worry about it. I have plenty of food."

"I . . . I guess I had give up till you come along. That ain't like me a-tall. I ain't no quitter. Let me try to stand up."

"No. Lay still, until I get back and try to check for broken ribs and such. Okay?"

"All right. Say! What's your name, anyways?"

"Morgan. Frank Morgan."

Waylon's mouth dropped open, and he was still stuttering and sputtering as Frank walked out to his horse.

Waylon ate a little bit and drank a cup of coffee, then went to sleep. Frank didn't think the man had any life-threatening injuries; he had just had the crap beat out of him and probably felt he was going to die.

When Waylon woke up, he stood and walked slowly around the room for a moment, then sat back down. "I reckon I'll live," he said.

Frank poured him another cup of coffee and

asked, "Did you overhear where this bunch of outlaws were heading?"

"They talked about Freetown."

"People still live there, don't they?"

"I don't think so, Frank. I think the last bunch of colored folks pulled out about a year ago. I don't know where they went."

"I hope you're right about that."

"They's still colored families live in that area. Nice folks. I've et with them a couple of times. They pretty much keep to themselves. Don't never bother no one."

"I hope they keep to themselves while this bunch of no-goods is around."

"Yeah. They mean as a basket full of rattlesnakes, for a fact." He frowned. "And I got the marks to prove that. They left me to die, Frank. Just rode out a-laughin' 'bout what they done. I feel sorry for them women. I really do."

"They'll probably kill the men."

"After they have some sport with them."

"Sport?"

"Makin' 'em beg and plead for their lives. If they beg hard and long enough, them outlaws said they'd let them live. But I don't believe it."

"Neither do I. Listen, Waylon. When you get to South Raven, go to Doc Raven's office. Tell him what happened and tell him about me. Will you do that?"

"Shore will."

"But try not to tell anyone else you saw me up here. Okay?"

"I got you, Frank. I won't."

"You going to be all right if I leave?"

"Sure. You go on. I'll rest here till morning, then I'll head into town. Frank? I do 'preciate all you done for me."

"No problem, Waylon. I'm heading out. See you, partner."

"Frank? Take care, you hear? That's a mean damn bunch."

"I know," Frank said softly. "Believe me, I know."

Seventeen

Frank left the old road to Freetown about two miles from the village and headed into the timber, circling wide around so he would approach the town from the east side out of the timber. The narrow road ended at Freetown. Frank felt the outlaws would be less vigilant toward the east. He pulled saddle and bridle from the horse, left Stormy in a hastily built brush corral, and proceeded through the timber on foot. If he didn't return, Stormy could easily bust out of the corral. Frank stuffed his pockets with cartridges for rifle and pistols. He left his spurs in his saddlebags before he headed out.

"The odds sure aren't good," he muttered as he carefully made his way through the timber and brush. "How come I always get myself into these pickles?"

There was no ready answer for that, and Frank didn't push it.

At the extreme Eastern edge of the village, Frank found his first body: A negro man who had been shot in the back.

"So much for the town being deserted," Frank muttered. There was nothing in the dead man's pockets. Frank left him and moved cautiously toward the small town.

The corral at the old livery barn was full of

horses. Frank skirted the corral so as not to spook the horses, and eased up to the rear of the barn. He pressed his ear to the cold wood and listened. He could hear the faint protestations of a woman. She was begging for someone to stop doing whatever they were doing.

Frank had a pretty good idea what that was.

He peeked through a crack in the building, but could see nothing. The attack was taking place near the front of the barn. The woman was begging and crying, the man was panting and laughing. Frank carefully opened the back door and slipped into the barn, ducking into an empty stall.

"Please stop!" the woman begged. "For God's sake, what kind of man are you?"

The sounds of a blow followed that.

"Damnit, Claude, you done knocked her out," a man said. "I don't wanna poke no unconscious woman."

"Shut up, Jeff," Claude said. "She'll come around in a minute. I'm done anyways."

"Well, pull up your britches and get the hell out of here. I don't like no spectators."

Claude laughed. "All right, all right. See . . . she's comin' around like I tole you she would. Get to pokin'. I'm goin' out back for a smoke."

"Don't set the damn barn on fire."

"Idiot! I said I was goin' out back."

"Oh, God!" the woman cried weakly. "Please, no more. Please!"

"Shut up!" Jeff told her. "As long as you can stand a humpin', you'll stay alive. You bes' remember that."

Claude walked up to the stall, and Frank clubbed him on the back of the head with the butt of his rifle, catching the man before he could fall to the barn floor. Frank dragged him into the stall and tied his hands behind his back with the man's own belt. He stuffed a dirty piece of cloth left in the stall into the man's mouth and took Claude's pistol.

Frank picked up a piece of what appeared to have been part of a singletree and slipped up behind Jeff, who was busy grunting away, and popped him on the head. Jeff abruptly ceased his grunting and collapsed on top of the woman. Her dress was shoved up to her waist and her bodice was ripped open.

"Marshal Morgan!" the woman gasped. "Turn your head, sir. I am shamefully exposed."

"You don't have a thing showing I haven't seen before, lady. Get your dress straightened up and let's get the hell out of here."

"Sir!" the woman protested, hurriedly pulling her dress down to her ankles. Her bodice was still wide open, and the lady was amply endowed in that area.

Frank sighed. "Your, ah . . ." He pointed.

She turned red and hastily closed her dress.

"Thank you," Frank said, hauling the woman up to her feet and gently guiding her toward the rear of the livery. "Can you ride?"

"If the mount is gentle and I have the proper saddle."

"I don't know about the mount and you're going to have to ride astraddle."

"Impossible!"

"You want to stay here, lady?"

"Hell, no!" the lady blurted out.

"Then come on."

"I'm Mrs. Dunbar," she said, finding and struggling into her winter coat.

"I know who you are now. I didn't recognize you at first with most of your clothes off." Colette flushed and opened her mouth to speak. Frank shushed her. "Be quiet, Colette."

She ignored that. "Are those . . . my attackers, dead?"

"One of them isn't." Frank pointed to the tied-up man in the horse stall they were passing. "That one. The one I busted on the head might have a broken skull. I don't know for sure and don't really give a damn."

"Neither do I."

"I'm sure." Frank pushed open the back door and motioned Colette out. "Head to the right and stay as low as possible. And be quiet, if you want to live."

Colette did as she was told and at the edge of the corral, Frank motioned her on into the timber. "Wait for me. I've got to get you a horse."

"I refuse to leave here without my friends," she said stubbornly.

"Don't be a fool, Colette. I can't take on thirty or forty men single-handed."

"There are only thirty-four of them, Marshal," she whispered. "I counted them."

"*Only* thirty-four of them?"

"You're a famed shootist, Marshal. Go dispose of them."

Before Frank could respond to that, a man let out a yell from the front of the barn. "Hey! Claude and Jeff are down and the woman's gone!"

"Down?" another man hollered on the run toward the barn. "How in the hell could one woman do that?"

"I don't know. But she damn shore did it. Look for yourself."

"Run toward the timber, Colette," Frank said. "Wait for me at the top of that first rise. You see it?"

"Yes."

"Move!"

Colette turned away, paused, and looked back at Frank. "We're in real trouble, aren't we, Marshal?"

"Yeah, lady. We are."

"I'm sorry. About everything."

"We'll talk later. Move, lady."

Colette made the timber unseen, and Frank waited by the old corral, listening to the outlaws talk.

"She might have gone into the timber," another man hollered.

"City folks? No way. You've heard them talk. They're all lost as sheep. Even the men. They've been lost ever since we grabbed 'em. Search the town and the edges of the timber."

"Maxwell might have made South Raven," a third man said. "We better get the hell out of here."

"I don't think so. He was bad hurt when he got away. I think he died 'fore he got there. If there ain't nobody here in a few hours, we're home free. 'Sides, we got enough firepower to hold off the Army. Find that damn woman. Move!"

Frank edged back into the timber and watched as men hurriedly blocked the road leading out of town, while others began a building-to-building search of the town.

He tensed as one man returned to the corral and walked around it, counting the horses. Frank relaxed as the man finished his count and walked away, satisfied that no horses had been taken.

"I got into this," Frank muttered. "Now how the hell am I going to get out of it?" Shaking his head at the predicaments he could get into, Frank eased his way up the rise to where Colette was waiting.

"I'm freezing to death!" the woman said.

"Doubtful," Frank told her. "But tonight's going to be a different story. We've got to find a place to hole up and build a fire or we will be in trouble."

"Maxwell got away," Colette said. "Help is on the way."

"Maxwell is dead. I buried him early this morning."

"Oh, my God! Wilma will be devastated."

"Have all the women been assaulted?"

"No. Not yet. Only two of us so far. But the outlaws are getting impatient about that. It won't be long before a mass rape will occur."

"Your getting away might have delayed that," Frank said. "Colette . . . if I could get you a horse, do you think you could make it back to South Raven?"

"I . . . don't know, Marshal," she replied honestly. "I don't even know where I am. You see, we were all blindfolded. But I suppose I could try."

Frank shook his head. "No. Forget it." He looked up at the now-sullen skies. The day was very cloudy and cold. The nights would be below freezing. Frank figured there were maybe five hours of good daylight left.

Six hours at the most.

He made up his mind. It was going to be a bloody afternoon.

Eighteen

Frank quickly led the way back to Stormy. "Can you saddle a horse?" he asked.

"No," Colette said. "We always had people to do that for us. And certainly not one of those large Western saddles. I couldn't even lift the thing."

Looking at the woman, very pale and slender, Frank didn't doubt her for a moment. She had probably never picked up anything heavier than a teapot in years. And she was probably very near the end of her emotional rope. "All right. You'll be cold, but you'll be alive."

"What do you mean?" she demanded.

"I'm going to rig you up a lean-to using my groundsheet. I'll leave you my blankets to bundle up in. Then I'm going back to the town and start this ball rolling."

"You're going to leave me alone?"

"No. Stormy will be here with you. You can talk to him."

"Don't be insulting, Marshal!"

"Then don't ask stupid questions, lady."

"As you wish, Marshal."

While Frank was rigging up a lean-to, he asked, "Can you shoot a pistol?"

"Certainly not!"

Muttering about women in general, and spoiled,

uppity city women in particular, Frank finished the
lean-to and pointed to it. "You get in there and
stay put, Colette. There is my canteen and you'll
find food in my saddlebags. I probably won't be
back until tomorrow. If I'm not back by noon tomorrow, you somehow get on that horse and give
him his head. He'll get you back to town. It might
take him a day or two, but he'll get you back. Understood?"

"Yes. You're really going to do battle with all
those thugs?"

"I don't have much of a choice, Colette. Now do
I?"

"I suppose you don't."

Frank went to a nearby creek and filled his hat
with water, taking it back for Stormy to drink. He
patted the animal's neck and stroked his nose for
a moment, then turned to Colette. "If I don't come
back, Colette, take good care of Stormy, will you?
He's a good horse."

"You are a very strange and complex man, Marshal. Not at all as you are portrayed in dime novels
and in many newspaper articles. I think you are a
study in contradiction."

"Whatever that means," Frank said, checking
one of the pistols he'd taken from the men in the
barn.

"We all owe you an apology."

"You owe me nothing, lady. Now watch carefully." He showed her the workings of the .45: how
to load it, cock it, aim it, and pull the trigger. He
then loaded it full and gave her a handful of cartridges. "If you are approached by any of the outlaws, aim for the thickest part of the body, between
the waist and the neck. Understood?"

"Yes. And I believe I could actually shoot those
hoodlums."

"I hope so. I'll be going now, Colette."

"I wish you success, Marshal."

Frank nodded and stepped out of the brush corral, walking away. He did not look back.

Frank stayed in the timber and took his time, circling the town, coming up at the far end, a block away from the livery. Some of the hostages were, he believed, being held in the center of the short block of buildings, others in the town's only church building. Probably the men and women were separated.

Wonderful, Frank thought. I've figured that out. Now if I could just come up with a successful plan of attack.

"She ain't in town!" a man hollered from across the street. "We've searched everywhere."

"She didn't take no horse neither," another yelled.

Frank watched from his hiding place as Sonny, the big-city bodyguard who had worked for the rich folks, stepped out of a building to stand on the boardwalk, about a dozen yards from where Frank was crouched in the brush.

That bastard, Frank thought. I bet he's behind all this treachery.

That theory was confirmed when Sonny yelled, "Then she's on foot in the timber and lost. Forget her. She'll die out there."

"When you reckon we'll get our money, Sonny?" Frank recognized a bounty hunter from town.

Sonny waved the man over to him. "By now the kids have opened the ransom letter and have set the wheels in motion. My man in Boise will get word to the telegraph agent in South Raven as soon as the lines are up. For now, we just have to wait."

So you've a man in town waiting for the word, Frank thought. But who is he? And how about the man in Boise? Damn! This plan was carefully thought out by somebody, and Frank didn't believe Sonny was the mastermind behind it all.

Then . . . who could it be?

"Hell, Sonny," Brooks Olsen said, walking out of the building next to Sonny. "That might be weeks from now."

"Could be," Sonny said. "But that's the way it was all set up. And it's damn sure too late to change it now."

"What's gonna keep them from sending the Army in here after us?" another outlaw asked, stepping out of the building where Frank was sure some of the hostages were being held.

"The kids won't tell anyone," Sonny replied. "We warned them in the letter that if they did, they'd never see their parents alive."

So I was right, Frank mused. Sonny isn't alone in this kidnapping.

"Purty slick, Sonny," the outlaw said. "So all we got to do is sit tight, right?"

"For a while. In another three or four days, we'll move again. We . . ." His words were cut off by the sound of a single shot. Sonny froze for a couple of seconds, then whirled around and shouted, "What the hell was that?"

"I got me a nigger, Sonny," a man shouted from the other end of the short block of town. "He was snoopin' around and tried to run when I spotted him. He won't run no more."

"Well, that's two we got," Brooks said with a smile.

"Double the guards on the road," Sonny said. "I don't want any of these darky families living around here to slip through and warn anyone. Do it, Red."

"Done," the outlaw acknowledged, and turned away, disappearing into a building.

"Where will we move to, Sonny?" Brooks asked.

"There's an old Army fort that's been deserted for years. We'll move there."

But he didn't say where it's located, Frank thought. Smart of him. That way none of the outlaws would dare try to kill him and take over. Sonny is slicker than I figured.

Frank sensed someone moving up behind him, and his hands tightened on his rifle as he prepared to whirl around and fire.

"Mister," the girl's voice called in a whisper. "I ain't part of them outlaws. I promise you I ain't."

Frank turned around to face the voice. It was a young Negro girl, maybe thirteen or fourteen years old, peering at him from the brush in back of the line of stores. He left his hiding place and moved to her.

"My name's Bessie," she whispered. "I live with my grandmother about a mile and a quarter from here. I seen it all."

"Let's move further back into the brush," Frank said.

"Them's a bad bunch," Bessie said as they slipped deeper into the thick brush. "I seen 'em kill Cassius. Shot him down right after they got here."

Frank pointed toward where he had found the first Negro body. "Over there?"

"Yes, sir."

"He a relative of yours?"

"No, sir. Jes' a friend. Been knowin' him since I was borned. I been talkin' to that white lady you hid out in the woods. You want me to take her to my cabin?"

"Exactly where is your cabin?"

"Come on. I'll show you the path. It's hard to find if you don't know what you're lookin' for."

About a half mile from the town, Bessie pointed out a narrow gap through the woods. "Right through there will take you to the cabin. Cassius was gonna help me and my grandmother move from here. Now he's dead and we ain't got nobody else to help us."

"You help me, Bessie, and I'll help you and your grandmother move. That's a promise."

The girl looked at him through eyes that were not quite trusting. "Lots of white people say that. Don't none of them mean it."

"I do."

"We'll see, I reckon."

"I thought there were other families living around here."

"There was until last spring. The last families moved away then. Can't grow no crops here; too hilly and rocky. My grandmother says it was a mistake to come here in the first place. But she did 'cause my mother and father did. My folks died last year of the fever."

"Does your grandmother know about these outlaws?"

"Sure. I told her after I spied on 'em and seen how they been treatin' them folks they got prisoner. They an evil bunch."

"Yes, they are. Come on, let's go back to my horse and get Colette."

"You comin' with us to the cabin?"

"Yes. For a short time. Then I'm going back to town to help the others get away."

"They too many of 'em for just one man."

"That depends on the man."

"I reckon."

An hour later they were sitting in the small warm cabin, drinking coffee and talking with Bessie's grandmother, Marvella. Stormy was stabled in the corral out back of the cabin.

"I know who you are, Frank Morgan," the older woman said. "I been hearin' 'bout you for years."

"Who am I, Marvella?"

"You a pistol man. Did you fight in the war, Frank Morgan?"

"I did. For the Gray."

She nodded her head. "Well, I won't hold that agin you. There was good and bad men on both sides." She peered intently at him. "Did you hold slaves, Frank Morgan?"

"No. I never believed in it."

"Bessie, see about that corn bread, child. You got to have a full belly, Frank Morgan, if you're gonna fight all them men over yonder."

"I could sure do with a bite, Miss Marvella. Smells mighty fine."

"Sure it does. I made it." She smiled. "Tell me, Frank Morgan. You didn't see nor smell no smoke from the fire whilst you were comin' here, did you?"

"No, I didn't. Whoever built this cabin knew what they were doing. All this tall timber around the cabin breaks up the smoke. Very smart."

"My son did it. Died of the fever last year. He and his wife. They're buried on that little rise, lookin' down on the cabin he built. It's sad, though. A mother shouldn't have to bury her child."

Frank nodded in agreement. "How are you folks getting your supplies since the town became deserted?"

"We ain't," Marvella replied. "We're near'bouts out of everything. That's why Cassius was gonna help us move out of here. Don't know what we'll do now."

"I'll make sure you get moved," Colette surprised Frank by saying. "And you get moved into a nice house."

"Right nice of you, ma'am," Marvella said. "But why would you do that for us?"

"Because you helped me . . ." She looked at Frank and smiled. "Us."

"Bessie," the old woman said, "you cut up that corn bread and give half of it to Frank Morgan. He's got to have something to take with him back to Freetown."

"Yes, ma'am."

Frank did not protest; he knew it would do no good.

"You must be a man who's real sure of himself, Frank Morgan," Marvella said. "One man agin all those white trash back in town."

"They're wrong and I'm right, Marvella. You can't stop a man who knows he's right and just keeps on coming at you."

"I reckon that's right." She turned her head for a few seconds. "Bessie, you wrap up that corn bread in some clean cloth now, you hear?"

"Yes, ma'am."

With the wrapped-up corn bread tucked inside his jacket, Frank picked up his rifle and headed for the door. Marvella had given him two heavy quilts to use if he had to spend the night in the lean-to. His hand on the door latch, Frank said, "You know how to use that shotgun I saw over in the corner, Marvella?"

"I surely do, Frank Morgan. And I got me a bag of shells for it too."

"Good," Frank said with a smile. "Just don't shoot me with it."

"You give out a holler when you get back, Mr. Morgan," Bessie said.

"I'll do that for sure. All right then, I'll see you ladies later on."

Frank opened the door and stepped out onto the porch, pausing for a moment. He would head first to the lean-to to cache the food and quilts, and then head for Freetown for a showdown.

Nineteen

It was the middle of the afternoon before Frank once more reached the outskirts of Freetown. Only a couple hours of good daylight left. The two buildings where he had determined the hostages were being held were heavily guarded, front and back. He would not attempt to breech that security . . . not yet. First he would take out any outlaw he could find wandering alone around the edges of town—if any were that stupid.

Frank smiled as his eyes touched several small buildings behind the line of stores on his side of the old town. Single- and double-hole outhouses.

"Why not?" he whispered. "That's a dandy place to start."

Staying in the timber, he shifted positions until he was about a dozen or so yards behind an outhouse in the center of the short block. He knelt down and waited. Sooner or later somebody would have to make a visit to the outhouse. Frank almost laughed aloud at the possible ramifications of his plan. He struggled to contain his laughter and waited.

A few minutes passed in silence before the back door to a building opened and a man walked out and began quick-stepping to the outhouse, obviously in a hurry to get things done. Frank waited until the door had closed before making his move.

He stepped out of the timber and ran to the outhouse. Using a piece of wood he'd picked up in the timber he wedged the stick against the door, one end firmly in the ground.

"Who the hell is that?" the muffled voice of the man in the outhouse asked.

Frank growled ominously and scratched at the door.

"Jesus!" the outlaw said softly, his voice just carrying to Frank. "What is that?"

Frank snarled and then slipped back into the timber and waited.

A few minutes passed and the man tried to open the door. He could not. The door was wedged shut tightly.

"Hey!" the man yelled. "Hey!"

His shouts were muffled and did not carry into the occupied buildings.

"Damnit! Somebody come help me get out of here!" the outlaw yelled. He shouted and squalled his frustration and began beating on the door. "There's a damn bear out here, or something that ain't human. Get me out of here."

The back door opened and two men stepped out. One shouted, "Andy? What the hell's wrong out here?"

"Barlow?" Andy shouted. "Watch it. There's a bear out here."

"A bear?" Barlow asked, looking all around him. "I don't see no damn bear."

"You sure it was a bear?" the other man asked.

"Damn right it was, Caswell," Andy shouted through the door. "An' the door's stuck tight, too. I can't get out of this crapper. An' with that damn animal out there, I don't know that I want to get out."

"I don't see no tracks of any bear, Andy," Barstow said. "Are you sure you didn't fart real loud and scare yourself?"

"You go to hell, Barstow!" Andy yelled.

"Barstow," Caswell said, looking hard at the outhouse door and then all around him. "I'm thinkin' it might have been that damn Morgan, foolin' around out here. No bear drove that stake into the ground and wedged that door shut."

Barstow jerked his pistol out of leather, and Caswell was only a few seconds behind him. "They's still bounty money on Morgan's head, Cas, and I aim to collect it. I want to shoot that bastard in the belly and listen to him holler 'fore he dies."

"What the hell are you two talking about?" Andy hollered.

"Morgan," Caswell said. "He's the one been makin' noises like a bear."

"I don't believe it," Andy said. "I think it was maybe that critter the Injuns talk about. That big hairy creature."

Caswell and Barstow exchanged glances. "He's maybe got something there," Barstow said. "I hadn't thought of that."

"This is his territory for a fact."

"But would he have enough brains to drive a stake into the ground to block a door?" Barstow asked.

"Get me the hell out of this stinkin' place!" Andy yelled. "If that hairy monster is out there, I want to be able to shoot it."

The door was unblocked and Andy stepped out, drawing his six-gun and looking all around him. "That hairy thing is 'posed to be half human," he said. "He'd have enough sense to block a door."

Frank eased down the hammer on his rifle. Why shoot somebody if he could scare them away? He smiled at that thought. Then his smile faded. But would it work? And if it did, would enough of these hard cases be spooked enough to pull out?

He'd never know if he didn't try it.

Frank stayed in the timber and worked his way around to the town's dump. He let his eyes do the searching while he remained in cover. The first search produced nothing he felt he could use. He shifted positions to the rear of the dump, and after a few minutes spotted a rolled-up bundle that looked like ragged old blankets and something else he couldn't determine from where he was. Looking carefully all around him, he ran to the huge pile of discarded trash and grabbed up the bundle, quickly moving back into the thick brush and timber. He unrolled the bundle and smiled at the contents: three old ragged blankets and an old bearskin rug that had probably seen its better days a couple of years before it was finally thrown out.

"Perfect," Frank muttered.

The blankets and quilts and bearskin rug smelled awful and to Frank's mind, that only added to the perfection of his find. Frank bundled them up and carried the stinking articles back to the timber at the rear of the block of stores.

He glanced up at the skies. Maybe an hour of good daylight left. Then Frank would put his plan to the test.

He was looking forward to it. Frank had to stifle his laughter at the thought.

A gunslick who called himself Dakota Dan stepped out of a building after eating his supper and stood for a moment while he rolled a cigarette. The light was fading fast, and Dan was a bit jumpy after listening to the yarns from the other men concerning hairy monsters. Andy was certain that a hairy monster was prowling the edges of the town, and Caswell and Barstow were leaning toward the same belief. Dan's grandpa had been a mountain man, and Dan clearly remembered the tales the old man had told about great hairy monsters, half man, half beast, that prowled the Northwest. Huge beasts about six and a half feet tall, incredibly strong and with a powerful body odor. Dan inhaled deeply and looked all around him. He needed to visit the outhouse, but was reluctant to do so. He'd forgotten to bring a candle with him.

Dan's innards grumbled and he headed for the outhouse. Monster or not, he had to go to the crapper.

A few minutes later, Dakota Dan had done his business and stepped out into the darkness, hitching up his britches. Suddenly, Dan was knocked to the ground by a large hairy beast with a terrible body odor. The beast snarled and growled and scratched Dan's neck with what appeared to be long fingernails. Dan was so terrified he fainted. The great hairy beast slipped away into the darkness of the timber . . . on moccasined feet. Frank had changed back at the lean-to.

Just as the "beast" was slipping away into the timber, two men stepped out of the building, one of them holding a lantern, and spotted Dan sprawled on the ground. "Sonny!" one of them yelled. "Dan's down!"

The building emptied of men, all quickly gathering around Dan. Sonny waved his hand under his nose and said, "Whew! Damn, what a foul odor. What the hell is that stinking?"

"Dan," a gunfighter called Ot said. "And it looks like bits of hair all over him."

Sonny squatted down and poked at Dan. Dan didn't move.

"Is he dead?" someone asked.

Sonny picked off some of the hair from Dan and looked at it. "What the hell caused all this?"

"Monster," Caswell said. "The beast is amongst us, boys."

Frank didn't hear any of this conversation. He had slipped deep into the timber, fearful that the foul odor of the bearskin would betray his presence. Besides, the stinking old skin was about to make him sick.

"There is no such thing!" Sonny said. "That is a native myth, nothing more than that."

"You a city boy, Sonny," Carl Depp told him. "You might have been borned in a small town, but you told us you've lived in New Yawk City all your life; that your daddy and mommy took you and your sister to the city when youse was chilen."

"That's right, Sonny," a gunhawk called Idaho said. "We're all Western borned and raised. We growed up hearin' stories about this here critter."

"And there ain't none of them very nice neither," Russ added. "Why . . . them things has been known to haul off and eat folks. I think maybe that's what run all them darkies from this town."

"Yeah, and they a little spooked to begin with," Sandy said.

"They shore as hell ain't no more spooked than I is!" Miller said. "This damn thing—whatever the hell is it, and I ain't sayin' it's one o' them things— has got me as jumpy as a one legged man in an ass-kickin' contest."

Frank had cached the stinking bearskin a few hundred yards from the town and slipped back to listen.

"And I heard tell of a time when some men was held trapped in a cabin for hours by about a dozen of them hairy things. Why, they was a-howlin' and a-throwin' big rocks and tryin' to break into the roof and all sorts of turrible things."

Grinning, Frank picked up a couple of rocks.

"Are you men serious?" Sonny demanded. "This . . . monster thing is a myth, that's all. There is no truth to it."

"Then you tell me this," Hamp Jennings said. "If it was a human man, how come he didn't take Dan's gun. It's still in leather."

The growing group of hard cases pressed closer, several of them holding lanterns. No one said anything for a moment, but everyone looked around them, doubt and some fear slowly developing in their eyes.

A rock suddenly arced downward, hitting a gunslick on the side of his head and dropping him like a brick.

"What the hell was that?" Jimmy Deggins shouted. Another rock sailed through the air and slammed into a man's shoulder, bringing a grunt of pain from the impact.

Frank let out a roar from the timber, and while the animal-like roar was still echoing around the night, quickly changed positions.

"I tole you!" a man shouted. "I said they throwed rocks. Them creatures is out there. I tole you they was."

Frank hurled a piece of thick branch he'd found on the ground into the tightly gathered group, the rotten wood striking a man on the back and nearly knocking him to his knees. Frank again changed positions.

Sonny jerked out his pistol and fired into the dark brush and timber, emptying the six-gun. Other outlaws followed suit, splitting the night with muzzle flashes and hot lead. Frank had bellied down on the ground, behind a tree.

"I bet we got him!" Ot shouted. "Ain't nothin' gonna live through that."

Frank closed his hand around another rock and

let it fly. The rock hit a just-awakening Dan on the knee and brought a howl of pain.

"Think agin!" a gunny called Blane said, quickly reloading. "You cain't kill them creatures. The Injuns say they're spirits!"

"Nonsense!" Sonny said, reloading his pistol. "All that is pure nonsense. Nothing more. You men get ahold of yourselves."

Frank left his hiding place and made his way to the far edge of town. He ran across a clearing and eased up to a dark building. Pressing his ear to the wood, he listened. He could detect no signs of life inside the building. No whispers, no breathing, no moving around. He picked up a chunk of rotting firewood and threw it through a window, then took off at a run, making his way unseen to the other side of the rutted street.

"What the hell was that?" Barstow yelled, stepping away from the group. "Dick, raise that lantern up high, will you?"

Frank found an empty whiskey bottle in a pile of trash and hurled it with all his strength. The bottle smashed through a storefront window across the street.

"They's more than one of them things!" Dick said. "I think they's a entar pack of 'em."

"Now, just wait a damn minute!" Sonny yelled, silencing the group of hard cases. "That's probably the same bunch who attacked Jeff and Claude. Think about that before you all get hysterical."

"Well, who could it be?" Jake asked.

"A bunch of niggers probably," another said.

"Aw, hell." Depp waved that off. "They ain't got the sand and grit to attack us. They're all a bunch of cowards."

"Don't you believe that for a second," Sonny said. "That's crap. I spent some time with a colored unit during the war. They're just as brave as any of us."

"It ain't nothin' human," Barstow insisted. "Them's monsters out there. I bet you all it is."

Frank tossed another rock, arcing it high in the air just as a guard stepped out of a building and onto the boardwalk for a smoke. The rock landed on the boardwalk about a foot from the man and bounced high and hard, hitting him on the knee.

"I been shot!" the man hollered, sitting down to try to relieve the pain. "Oh, damn, boys. Somebody shot me."

Sonny led the group around to the front. "Nobody shot you, Devon," he said, holding up a lantern. "It was a rock."

"A rock!" Devon said. "Who the hell is throwin' rocks?"

"Monsters," Dan said. "Them creatures that attacked me."

"Monsters?" Devon asked. "I don't believe in them things."

"I didn't used to," a gunfighter called Teddy said. "But I damn shore do now."

Frank began howling and roaring and throwing whatever he could find against the rear of the buildings on his side of the street.

"You still think that ain't a monster now, Sonny?" Crump asked.

Sonny did not respond to that. He didn't know exactly what to make of it all.

Frank ceased his howling and roaring and moved to the old church building. He peeked into a side window. Bessie had told him the women were being held in the church, the men in a building in the center of town, and she had been correct about the women, at least. They were all huddled together on benches in the center of the room. A couple of them looked as though they'd just been manhandled, and were crying. Their hair was all disheveled and their clothing very rumpled.

Raped, Frank thought.

He moved to the building where the men were being held, and chanced a look through a crack in a boarded-up window. The men were not in good shape. They had all been beaten, some of them savagely.

The time for fun was over, Frank concluded. It had been fun playing a monster, but the men and women being held hostage were not enjoying any of it. It was time to deal the cards and play the hand dealt.

But where and how to start?

Frank moved back into the timber. He was amazed that Sonny had not posted more guards around the town. He could only conclude that Sonny was too sure of himself without the experience to back up that self-assurance.

But Frank knew the odds were still very strong against him succeeding in this plan . . . whatever his plan might be.

He carefully made his way back to the church and crouched in the timber behind the building. He had to get the women out first and get them to safety. He could not let the raping continue. He tensed as the back door to the church opened and a man with a lantern stepped out, heading for the outhouse.

"Don't let no monster get you, Jones!" a man called out from inside the church.

"I don't believe in them things," Jones said. "And don't you touch that redhead whilst I'm gone. I want me another taste of that one."

You won't get another taste, you bastard! Frank thought, as the back door closed. Your time on this earth is over!

Twenty

Frank's hand closed around a chunk of wood he'd picked up. Jones opened the door to the outhouse and set the lantern inside, on the floor. Frank quickly and silently moved up behind the man and smacked the outlaw on the head. He caught him before he could tumble to the ground. Stretching the outlaw on the ground, he jerked Jones's six-gun from leather, stuck it behind his own gunbelt, then quickly pulled the man's belt from his britches and secured his hands behind his back. He closed the door, then dragged Jones a dozen yards behind the outhouse and left him. He didn't know if he'd fractured Jones's skull and if the man might be dying . . . and he didn't care. Kidnappers and rapists and murderers were among those who deserved no mercy, and Frank sure as hell wasn't going to give them any.

One down, Frank thought. Thirty or so to go.

He figured he had maybe fifteen minutes at the most before somebody would get curious about Jones and come outside to check on him.

Frank once more slipped up to the boarded-up window and looked through the crack. He could see four guards, widely separated, one on each side of the large room. There was no way he could shoot them all and get the women into the timber.

The other gunhands in the town would be all over him before he could accomplish that.

Frank was stymied as to what to do next.

He listened as the bootsteps of several men struck the wood of the old boardwalk, then faded as the men stepped off the boardwalk. He could faintly hear the sounds of talking. Then the conversation grew louder. The men were approaching the church.

Damn! Frank thought. Now what?

He slipped back into the darkness, circled around to the far side of the church, crouched beneath another boarded-up window, and waited and listened. He heard the front door open.

"Everything all right here, Woolsey?" a man asked.

"Okay," Woolsey replied.

"Where's Jones?"

"In the crapper. Did y'all find the monster?"

Brief cussing followed that, then a moment of laughter. "There ain't no monsters, Woolsey. But a few boys damn shore believe it. They're talkin' 'bout pullin' out come mornin'. Sonny's tryin' to talk some sense into 'em now."

"How's Claude and Jeff?"

"Claude is all right. Looks like Jeff ain't gonna make it. His head is all busted and swole up. He's talkin' crazy stuff."

"No creature did that to them boys."

"No. Sonny figures it's Morgan."

"Morgan! Here?"

"Yeah."

"That ain't good news," another man said. "Morgan ain't afraid to tackle a tornader."

"He can't fight thirty of us. Sonny's thinkin' up a plan now if he tries it."

"If that is Morgan out there slippin' around, he ain't tryin' it, Brownie, he's doin' it!"

"Relax, Davis. Just take it easy . . ."

"Easy, hell!" Davis came right back. "I don't like the idea of Frank Morgan slippin' around in the dark. I'd rather it was a monster."

"None of you will get away with this," a woman said, her voice firm and strong. "You'll all hang."

"Shut up, lady," Brownie said. "Just keep your mouth shut and you'll live through this. Keep flappin' your gums and we'll bury you out yonder in the dump."

"You are a vile, disgusting man!" the woman said. "All of you. What have you done with my husband?"

"He's alive," Brownie told her. "He begs right good." Brownie laughed. "He's more concerned with his own hide than with yours. He said we could have you if we'd just turn him loose."

"I don't believe that!"

"Then you don't know your husband a-tall, lady. He's been beggin' and a-sobbin' and a-carryin' on like a baby."

"Fuller has never begged for anything in his life," Mavis Ross said haughtily.

"Teddy, you and Burke bring her husband over here and have him say to her face what he done tole us," Brownie said.

Mavis hissed her fear and loathing at the man.

"That'll be fun," Teddy said. "Then he can watch us strip her down and have a poke at her."

"That's the idea," Brownie replied.

Frank sighed, his breath steaming in the cold air. He could not wait any longer. The situation was getting out of hand. He didn't think he had a chance of getting all the women free, but he sure had to try.

Frank moved around to the front of the church and waited by the side of the steps. The door opened and Teddy and Burke stepped out, closing the door behind them. Frank waited until they had stepped down to ground level before he eared back the hammer on his .45. "You boys stand real still and I'll let you live," Frank told them softly. "Make any loud noises and you'll both be dead before you hit the ground."

"Morgan?" Teddy asked.

"That's me. And you boys know I will kill you."

"We ain't movin' nothin' but our mouths, Morgan. What do you want?"

"You boys walk back up the steps. I'll be a step behind you. You open the door when I tell you to. Understood?" They nodded their understanding. "And when you're inside, you step to one side. You make a try for your guns and I'll kill you first."

"You're crazy, Morgan," Burke said. "You can't buffalo ever'body in that church. Somebody is gonna make a play for their guns, and if you shoot, this place will be surrounded by men in two minutes . . . or less."

"You're already in trouble, Morgan," Teddy said with a quiet laugh. "Yonder comes Sonny. Now what are you gonna do?"

Frank cut his eyes. Sonny was walking toward the church, for a fact, carrying a lantern. "We'll just wait for him, boys. This is either going to go real smooth, or it's going to get real bloody real fast."

"I ain't lookin' to die, Morgan," Burke said. "Keep that in mind."

"Whether you live or die is all up to you," Frank told him.

"I feel the same way about dyin', Morgan," Burke said.

"Just stay cool and collected, boys."

Sonny walked up and before he could raise the lantern to see who it was on the steps, Frank shoved the muzzle of his .45 under the man's chin.

"Stand easy, Sonny," Frank warned him. "And don't make a sound."

"Morgan!" Sonny whispered. "You son of a bitch!"

"We're all going into the church, Sonny," Frank said softly. "And if you behave, you'll live. You get my meaning?"

"I got it."

"Good. Move!"

Sonny stepped up the steps, behind Teddy and Burke. When they reached the door, Burke whispered, "Openin' the door, Morgan."

"Go ahead."

The outlaws pushed open the door and stepped in, Morgan crowding in close behind them. As Teddy and Burke moved to one side, Frank again stuck the muzzle of his pistol under Sonny's chin and pulled him to one side.

"What the hell?" Brownie said.

"Shut up," Frank told him. "Tell them, Sonny."

"You boys keep your hands away from your weapons," Sonny said, a definite edge to his voice. "Do what Morgan tells you to do."

"And if we don't?" Woolsey demanded.

"Sonny dies and you boys never know who your contacts are in Boise and South Raven," Frank said. "You get no ransom money. Think about it."

"If you take the rich folks out of here," Davis said, "we get no money no way. Right?"

"I'm taking the women," Frank said. "And leaving the men. So your glass is still half full, or half empty. Depends on your point of view."

"I reckon that's so," Davis said. "Now what, Morgan?"

"You boys shuck those guns. And do it real careful-like. Put them on the floor and back away from them. All of you get over there in the corner at the far end of the building." He moved his head, indicating the corner. "Start moving, right now."

When the outlaws hesitated, Frank again eared back the hammer of his .45 and Sonny said, "Goddamnit, move, boys. Don't do anything stupid or we're all in trouble."

"He can't take us all, Sonny," Woolsey said.

"He can take me," Sonny said. "And I'm the only one who knows all the details about this kidnapping. If I die, you're all leaving here broke as the day you were born."

The outlaws put their guns on the floor and slowly moved to the corner of the building. Frank still held Sonny under his gun. "You ladies," Frank said. "Get into your coats and move over to the wall to my left. But stay clear of me. Don't get between me and the outlaws. Move."

The women quickly obeyed.

"You men get out of your winter coats," Frank said. "Throw them into the center of the room. Do it!"

"What the hell are you up to, Morgan," Davis asked, tossing his coat on the floor.

"Getting clear of here," Frank said. "Without killing anyone else. You want to be the one who spoils my plan?"

"I didn't say that," Davis blurted out quickly. "I just axed a question, that's all I done."

"I answered it."

"Shut up, Davis," Burke said. "For God's sake, close your mouth."

"Some of you women pick up those coats," Frank said. "Do it carefully. Rest of you gather up those pistols."

The heavy coats and pistols were quickly collected.

"Now what, Morgan?" Sonny asked.

"Strip," Frank told the outlaws. "Peel it all off right down to your skin."

"What?" Woolsey demanded.

Several of the women smiled.

"Strip, damnit!" Frank said. "Right now. Boots and clothing in the center of the room." He pushed Sonny a few feet away. "You too, big man. Do it."

Frank chanced a glance at a couple of the women. "You ladies get their boots and clothing. Bundle it up tight and secure it with their belts and galluses. Do it quickly, ladies."

The outlaws were soon naked and shivering, doing their best to cover their privates with their hands.

"You son of a bitch!" Sonny cussed Frank. "I'll cut your balls off for this."

"Yours have shriveled up to the size of peanuts," Wilma Crawford told the leader of the outlaws.

Sonny cussed her.

"That's enough," Frank said. "You ladies, out the back door. Move it, ladies. Let's get the hell gone from here."

Outside, Frank closed the door and paused for a few seconds, just long enough to say, "We've got about three or four minutes, ladies. At the most. Follow me and don't say a word. Try not to break off any twigs or low-hanging branches. Let's go."

Frank led the women into the timber, and they were well away from the old town before the shouting began. Frank led them first to the lean-to and let the women rest for a time.

"Where are you taking us, Mr. Morgan?" Eudora Edmonds asked.

"To where I have Colette hidden."

"She's unhurt?"

"Yes."

"Our husbands?" Nellie Vanderhoot asked. "What about them?"

"After I get you to safety, I'll go back and try to free them. But I can't promise anything. I've got to be honest about that."

"What you did for us was very brave, Mr. Morgan," Ethel Steele said. "You risked your own life when you certainly didn't have to. Not after the way we have behaved toward you. I shall see you are compensated quite handsomely."

Frank chuckled in the darkness.

"Does that amuse you, Mr. Morgan?" Clovis Knox asked.

"In a way, yes. I didn't do this for money. I assure you, I have enough money to last me several lifetimes."

"Then the rumors about you and Mrs. Browning are true?"

"I don't know what all the rumors say, ma'am. But Vivian and I were married right after the War Between the States. Conrad is my son."

"I knew Vivian," Nora Greene said. "Most of us here did. She was a fine woman, and Conrad is a very handsome young man."

"Then you came to rescue us because you are a United States marshal?" Margaret Harrison asked.

"I guess so, ma'am."

"You still risked your life."

"I reckon so." Frank stood up. "Come on, ladies. Let's move out. We've got a ways to go before you can relax and get really warm."

Frank sat before the fireplace drinking coffee, and smoking. The women were sprawled all over the cabin, all of them sleeping very heavily. Marvella came over and sat down. She whispered, "You had the Good Lord with you this day, Frank Morgan."

"I reckon I did, Miss Marvella."

"But you ain't got a chance in hell of gettin' these ladies' husbands free from them white trash and you know it, don't you?"

"I reckon that's so. I 'spect time I get back to the town tomorrow, they'll all be long gone to that old fort. And I don't know where that is."

"I do."

Frank lifted his eyes and smiled at the old woman. "I had me a hunch you did."

"I'll draw you a map. It's on the north fork of the Boise River. Halfway 'tween the north fork and the middle fork."

"That's a ways from South Raven."

"It is for a fact."

So Sonny is probably planning a double cross, Frank thought. He doesn't have a man in South Raven. But he has one in Boise. And he'll be the one to ride in and collect the money, and that will be the last any of the outlaws will ever see of him. Very cute.

But there will be one person who'll damn sure see you again, Sonny.

Me!

Twenty-one

Frank left the cabin long before dawn to return to Freetown, young Bessie with him. His suspicions a few hours back proved correct. The town was devoid of human life. The outlaws had pulled out in a hurry, leaving behind many articles of clothing, food, and more importantly, a corral full of horses, the saddles in the old barn.

"How come they left the horses, Mr. Frank?" Bessie asked.

"Good question, Bessie. One guess is they didn't want to be slowed down by herding them along. I'll saddle up a horse for you. You ride back to your cabin and get the others. Let your grandmother ride on the way back here. Will you do that?"

"Sure, I will."

"I'll have the horses saddled up and ready to go by the time you get back. Don't let the others tarry, Bessie."

"I won't. I'll make them hurry."

Moments after Bessie had ridden off, Frank was prowling the town. He found the outlaw called Jeff in the back room of a building. The man was drifting in and out of consciousness, and Frank did not believe he was long for this world. Frank squatted down beside the dying outlaw and spoke to him.

"Is that you, Claude?" Jeff asked, his voice very weak.

"No. It's Frank Morgan."

"I can't see you, Claude. My eyes has quit workin' and my head is hurtin' something awful. Can you get me somethin' for the pain?"

"I don't have anything, Jeff. Where'd the others go?"

"To the fort, Claude. They said they'd send a doctor back for me."

Sure they will, Frank thought. Right. "I won't leave you, Jeff."

"You a good friend, Claude. . . ." The man's voice trailed off and he once more lapsed into unconsciousness.

Frank left the man and went to saddle the horses. When he returned, Jeff was still unconscious and his breathing was very bad. Frank had doubts as to whether the man would ever wake up. He went outside to smoke a cigarette. The day was sunny and bright, the sky an impossible blue. It was cold, but with no wind, it was not really uncomfortable.

"Claude!" Jeff cried out once.

When Frank reached the man's side, Jeff was dead; blood had leaked out of his nose and mouth, the flow of crimson ceasing when the man's heart stopped. Frank covered the man with a blanket and closed and locked the door. The old building was as good a grave as the ground.

Frank walked the town. The bodies of Cassius and the other Negro the outlaws had shot were gone. Frank had no idea what had happened to them, and a quick search failed to locate them. The outlaws might have hauled the bodies off into the timber or tossed them in the trash dump. Frank called off his search, and began gathering up what food the outlaws had left and filling saddlebags with the canned goods. He rolled the few blankets left behind and tied them behind the saddles. By the time he finished, Bessie was leading the women into the town.

"We can't stop to rest, ladies," Frank told them. "We've got to make time. We're burnin' daylight and we've got a ways to go."

"Our husbands?" Mavis asked.

"Gone." He pulled Colette to one side and asked, "Did you tell Wilma about her husband?"

"Yes. She wants to see his grave."

"We'll be there tomorrow. It's not that far from here. We can spend some time there and Wilma can pay her respects to Maxwell."

"They weren't a very happy couple, Frank."

"So I heard from a friend of hers in town."

"Dr. Raven?"

"Yes."

"I suspect she'll return to this country after the estate is settled."

"Could be. Let's ride."

It was slow going on the trail, for several of the women had been beaten repeatedly, and were bruised and sore and had to stop and rest several times. They spent the night in the ghost town of Red Rock. Prowling around, the women found several old pots and kettles and heated water to wash up in, then set about making some semblance of supper out of the food the outlaws had left behind. They were all sound asleep just after dark. The next morning, Frank was the first one out of his blankets. He stoked up the fire and put on water for coffee, then slipped into his winter coat and stepped outside for an early morning smoke.

He didn't tarry with his cigarette, for the air was

very cold. He was back into the warmth of the old home in a very few minutes, and poured a cup of coffee. He turned as Wilma Crawford walked into the room.

"Good morning, Mrs. Crawford."

"Morning. Please call me Wilma, won't you, Frank?"

"If you would like that, certainly. Coffee?"

"Please." A cup of coffee in her hands, Wilma thanked him, then asked, "Did my husband die well, Frank."

"Yes, he did, Wilma. He conducted himself very well at the end."

"Mavis's husband offered her in exchange for the beatings to stop."

"I heard that. You think it's true?"

"Oh, yes. I have no difficultly at all believing every word of it."

Frank shook his head at the deadly flatness of her tone; it was filled with disgust. "Mrs. Ross . . . Does she believe it?"

"She's maintaining a strong and stoic face, but yes, she believes it."

"Tough way to learn what her husband is made of."

"About half of these men are heirs, Frank. They didn't personally earn their wealth, they inherited it."

"Their daddies gave it to them?"

"Precisely. And they have very skilled men working for them to insure they'll make more money."

"While they play around."

"Yes. Don't misunderstand what I say, Frank. These men are not stupid. They all have fine educations and they understand business. But they have so much money they don't know what to do with it, and they have so much time on their hands."

"And they have never been tested as men." It was not a question.

"They've never been tested as human beings, Frank. Not in my opinion."

Frank smiled as his fingers were busy rolling another cigarette. He held it up. "You mind if I smoke?"

"Not at all."

"Thanks. We need to be thinking of getting the others up if we want to make town today."

"In a little while. I enjoy talking with you."

"Strange that a lady of your standing would say that. I'm not very genteel, Wilma."

"You're real, Frank. And I can't tell you what a relief it is to speak with someone who knows what life is all about."

Frank smiled as he popped a match into flame. "I'd be lost in your city, Wilma."

Wilma ignored that comment and asked, "You're going after the outlaws, Frank?"

"Oh, yes."

"Alone?"

"Probably. I'd rather have it that way really."

A noise in the other room put an end to the conversation. Wilma and Frank looked toward the archway as Nellie Vanderhoot walked into the room, her eyes still puffy from hours of deep sleep. "I must look a fright," she said, running fingers through her hair. She took a deep breath and exclaimed, "Oh, my, is that coffee?"

Wilma smiled at her friend and replied, "It is and it's good and strong. I believe it's called cowboy coffee, isn't it, Frank?"

"I reckon you could call it that. Most Westerners like their coffee strong. Some folks say you could float a horseshoe in it."

As she was pouring a cup for Nellie, Wilma said, "Frank says we'll be back in South Raven today."

"A long hot bath and clean clothing," Nellie said, taking the cup. "I do so look forward to that."

"And then the wait for our . . . your husbands," Wilma said, correcting herself. She sighed heavily.

"I'm sorry, Wilma," Nellie said after taking a sip of coffee. "I know you must be feeling your loss terribly. You've been so brave about it."

"You'd better prepare yourself for the worst, Nellie," Wilma told her.

"I already have," the woman said softly. She looked at Frank. "The chances for all our husbands coming out of this ordeal alive are not very good, are they, Mr. Morgan?"

"Not real good, Mrs. Vanderhoot. I got to be honest about that."

"My name is Nellie, please. May I address you as Frank?"

"I wish you would. Mister sounds sort of stuffy."

"Actually, we're rather stuffy people, Frank," Nellie said, much to Wilma's surprise. "Arrogant might be a better description."

"It's the way you were brought up," Frank said. "But the West has a way of bringing out either the worst or the best in people."

"I've certainly been humbled," Nellie confessed. "I shan't return to my old ways. You can be assured of that." She took another sip of coffee and sat down. "Will we have time to hold a small service for Maxwell, Frank?"

"We'll make time, Nellie. I think Maxwell would rest easier after that." Providing some bear hasn't toted the body off and ate it, he thought.

Marvella and Bessie were the next ones up, and over the protests of Frank and Nellie and Wilma, Marvella set about slicing bacon and frying it, and then made a big skillet of pan bread. Bessie made another pot of coffee.

"I hate to eat anything them damn white trash

had their hands on," Marvella said. "But I ain't one to waste food."

"We'll have you say a breakfast prayer over it, Marvella," Frank said. "That ought to take care of it."

"I plans on doin' that, Frank Morgan," she replied. "I does that 'fore ever' meal. And I'll say me a prayer for you too. Thanks and good huntin'."

"I need it," Frank said with a smile.

"I knows that too," the old woman replied with a laugh. "I allow as to how you needs it in more ways than one."

Frank got a good chuckle out of that. "You're sure right about that, Marvella. You purely are."

Everyone had a good meal to start the day, and Frank went out to saddle the horses while the ladies rolled up bedding and secured and stowed away pots and skillets and the coffeepot. Frank had another cup of coffee, and they were on the road just as the gold was chasing away the last bits of silver from the eastern skyline.

"Will we make town this day?" Ethel Steele asked, wriggling around a little, trying to ease her butt a bit in the Western saddle.

"We should be riding into South Raven by late afternoon," Frank said.

"Thank God," more than one of the ladies whispered.

Marvella smiled as Frank cut his eyes at the old woman. She was as tough as whang leather, and carried her double-barreled shotgun over one shoulder by a sling. Frank had no doubts about her capability and willingness to use the weapon.

Frank led them toward the cabin where he had buried Maxwell Crawford. The day was sunny and cool and they made good time. Wilma rode up beside Frank, and they rode in silence for a few minutes.

"Is it far now, Frank?"

"Just over the next rise. I wrapped him in a blanket and piled rocks over his body."

"I'm . . . glad you warned me about that."

"I figured I'd better. It's the best I could do without a shovel. You can make arrangements to move the body later."

She nodded her head as the tears began trickling silently down her cheeks.

Twenty-two

The service at Maxwell's grave site was brief, with the group backing away afterward, allowing Wilma a few moments alone with Maxwell.

"It's a beautiful spot," Nellie Vanderhoot remarked, looking around her. "So peaceful and quiet."

"You suppose she'll have the body returned to New York?" Eudora asked.

"I don't know," Clovis Knox replied. "But I wouldn't. I'd buy the land and create a permanent memorial."

"That's a good idea," Nellie said. "I'll suggest that to her." She looked at the others. "Do you think that would be an inappropriate suggestion?"

When no one replied, Frank said, "I don't, Nellie. I think it's a good idea. What's under those rocks now is just the shell of the man. The soul has gone on."

"That's lovely, Frank," Nellie replied. "You continue to surprise us all."

Frank did not reply to that. It just made good sense to him.

Wilma walked over to the group, wiping her eyes. "I'm ready to go," she said. "There is nothing more to do or say here."

A few hours later, Frank led the group into the town of South Raven. The residents gathered along the sides of the street and watched in silence. Swinging down from the saddle, Frank motioned to Phil, the bartender at the saloon/hotel.

"Get some rooms ready for the ladies, Phil."

"I already done that, Frank. The Stover boy spotted y'all 'bout a mile out and come at a run to tell us."

Doc Raven helped Wilma down from her horse and stood looking at her for a moment, while local men assisted the other ladies.

"I'd have never been able to pull this off without the help of Marvella and Bessie, Doc," Frank said, indicating the old woman and her granddaughter. "I want them treated right. Anyone in town who doesn't will answer to me."

"There are few prejudices in this town, Frank," Doc Raven replied. "I didn't fight for the Gray because I believed in slavery or that colored folks were inferior."

"I know, Doc. Don't get your hackles up. I just wanted to let you know where I stood, that's all."

"Marvella and Bessie will be provided for," Colette said, walking up. "I will insist on that."

"As will I," Wilma said.

Frank walked over to the boardwalk and sat down. He was beat; weary to the bone. He wanted nothing more than a drink, a hot meal, a bath, and a bed.

Doc Raven walked over and sat down beside him. "You all right, Frank?"

"Just tired, Doc."

"Wilma told me about Maxwell."

"He died well. I can say that much about him for sure."

"When do you go after the others?"

"In the morning. And before you ask, no, I don't want a posse."

"All right, Frank. By the way, many of the bounty

hunters left town the same day you did. Some of them, I believe, went in search of the kidnappers."

"To join with them probably."

"That's my theory, yes. Some just drifted away. But let me warn you about this: Dolan is still in town, making talk about what he's going to do to you."

"I'm easy to find, Doc. And if he tries it today, I'll settle it today. I'm in no mood to be charitable."

Liveryman Bob walked up. "Dolan just stepped out of the saloon," he said. "He's been making a lot of talk about you, Frank."

Frank looked toward the saloon. Dolan was standing on the boardwalk, smoking a cigar and looking in his direction. "He's going to call me out in a couple of minutes," Frank said.

"I'll get the women and kids off the street," Bob said.

"The telegraph wires up yet, Doc?" Frank asked as Bob walked away.

"Not yet."

"Anyone checked on the progress of the road-clearing?"

"Crews are still working on it. It'll be clear in a few days. Wilma says the women don't want any outside interference in this situation."

"That's right. That would be a death sentence for their husbands."

"You believe the outlaws would really kill the hostages?"

"I do."

"As soon as the wires are up and the stage starts running, somebody is going to talk about it. You can't keep something this big quiet."

"Then I'd better not waste any time in finding them," Frank said as he rolled a cigarette and popped a match into flame.

"Dolan just stepped off the boardwalk and into the street."

"I see him."

"What is happening here?" Wilma Crawford asked, walking up to the men. "The street is suddenly deserted."

"A shoot-out," Doc Raven told her. "Get inside, Wilma."

"This is ridiculous!" the woman said. "Why in the world would that man want to start a fight with Frank?"

"To see who is the fastest," Doc Raven replied.

Before Wilma could respond to that, Frank toed out his cigarette and stood up, stepping out into the street. He turned to face Dolan, still more than half a block away.

"I told you I'd call you out, Frank!" Dolan yelled.

Frank said nothing. He stood in the middle of the street and waited.

"Big hero now, huh, Frank?" Dolan shouted. "Rescued all the women. Hell, I could have done that myself. But nobody asked me."

Behind closed doors, the locals waited.

Gunslingers began stepping out of the saloon and the cafe to line the boardwalks. They would not interfere in this matter. That would violate the unwritten code.

"You gonna answer me, Morgan?" Dolan yelled.

Frank made no reply. He knew from long years of facing men in the street that Dolan was working up his courage. What was that line he'd read once when he was trying to wade through some writing by that Shakespeare fellow? Screw your courage to the sticking place . . . Yeah, that was it. Frank never could appreciate that Shakespeare fellow. Everybody else said what a great writer he was. Frank couldn't see what was so damn great about him.

Dolan stopped and cursed Frank.

Frank waited.

Dolan began slowly walking toward Frank. "What's the matter, Morgan? You so scared you forgot how to speak?"

"Why don't you shut that flapping mouth of yours, Dolan?"

"Huh?"

"Make your play or shut the hell up and go away. I'm tired of listening to you flap your gums."

"Are you that anxious to die, Morgan?"

"Shut up," Frank told him, exasperation very clear in his tone. "I'm tired and hungry and want a bath. What I don't want is any more lip from you. Now, either pull iron or shut your mouth."

Dolan screamed his outrage and grabbed for his gun. The locals watching the two-man drama being played out in their street would talk about the brief battle for years to come. Frank Morgan drew and fired his .45 so swiftly and cleanly, it was almost too fast for the human eye to follow. Blink, and you would have missed it.

Frank's bullet hit Dolan in the chest, and the bounty hunter sat down in the dirt of the street, a very startled expression on his face. "Well . . . I'll be damned!" Dolan said. He lifted his six-gun and managed to cock it. But he could not raise the weapon enough to point it at Frank. "You've killed me, you bastard!"

"Sure looks like it," Frank said, walking toward the man.

"It ain't 'posed to be this way," Dolan said as blood filled his mouth and began leaking past his lips.

"It never is, Dolan," Frank told him.

"Somebody's gonna get you, Morgan," Dolan said.

"That's the way it usually plays out," Frank replied very matter-of-factly.

Dolan looked at Frank walking toward him, then fell over in the dirt and gasped, "I . . . can't breathe."

Frank said nothing.

"I'll . . . see you in hell, Morgan!" Dolan said, then closed his eyes and died.

Frank slipped his .45 back into leather and walked away, toward the saloon. He pushed his way past the line of gunslicks that crowded the boardwalk, opened the door, and walked up to the bar. "Coffee," he told the bartender. "And make sure it's hot."

"Yes, sir!" the young man said. "Comin' right up, you betcha!"

The gun-handlers walked back into the saloon and either took seats or lined up at the bar. They were very quiet, none of them making eye contact with Frank.

"I'll get the coffee, Jim," Phil told the young man as he stepped in from the hotel lobby. "You serve the others."

Bob and Doc Raven entered the saloon and came to Frank's side. "Make that coffee for us too, Phil," Doc Raven said. He looked at Frank. "I believe, Frank, you are the fastest gun I have ever seen in all my years out here."

"I'm still alive, Doc," Frank said simply.

"I talked to that fellow you released from jail, Frank," Doc Raven said. "He came back into town to buy some supplies. He made it a point to look me up and tell me it was Jackson Mills who paid him to kill you."

"Why didn't he tell me that when I asked him?"

Doc Raven shrugged, then said, "Maybe he was that afraid of you, Frank."

"Did you believe him? Do you think it was Mills who paid him?"

"I don't have any reason to doubt it . . . or to believe it," Doc added.

"What kind of an answer is that, Doc?"

"The best one I can come up with."

"I think you've got Wilma on what's left of your mind," Frank said with a grin.

"You're right about that. I haven't been able to get her off my mind since the day she arrived."

Frank sugared his coffee and stirred it slowly. When he could get sugar, he enjoyed a bit of it in his coffee. "I was real lucky in getting the women loose, Doc. I won't be that lucky with the men."

"The ladies told me you've already talked to them about that. I believe they're prepared for the worst."

"They better be. Doc, as soon as I finish this coffee, I'm going to go take a bath and then provision up so I can get that out of the way and take off early in the morning. Then I'm going to get something to eat, go visit with Dog for a time, and go to bed."

"I won't see you in the morning?"

"Doubtful. I'll be pulling out long before dawn. Marvella drew me a map. I'm heading cross-country until I cut the old road to the fort."

"You and Stormy get along?"

"He's a fine animal. You still sure you want to trade?"

"Absolutely. I've been exercising Horse every day. We get along just fine. But Dog misses you.

"I'll going to sleep in the barn tonight. Just so he won't think I've run off and deserted him."

"Use the storeroom," Bob suggested. "It's got a little potbellied in it and they's lots of wood behind the barn. You'll be a lot warmer in there."

"Thanks. I'll do that."

"They's a cot in there too."

"Good." Frank paused and took a sip of coffee.

"Let me provision up for you, Frank," Doc Raven suggested. "That'll save you a little time."

"I appreciate that. I need a bath in the worst way. I'm beginning to smell a little rank."

"Now that you mention it . . ." Doc Raven said with a smile.

Frank laughed and finished his coffee. Phil looked at him, and Frank put his hand over his cup and shook his head. Phil went back to polishing glasses.

"Frank?" Bob said. " 'Bout ten or twelve of the hired guns has left town. I don't know for shore, but mayhaps they've left to go join with the kidnappers . . . just to be with their own kind. Look around you, see who's missin'."

"I have, Bob."

"You can't fight all them people at oncest. That'd be suicide."

"I can't see that I have much choice in the matter. If we call the law in on this, the hostages are dead for sure. I don't have a doubt in my mind but what Sonny would kill them. He wouldn't hesitate."

"Wilma told me that several of the women expressed doubts about him from the beginning," Doc Raven said. "Said they just didn't trust him."

"They should have trusted their instincts," Frank replied. "That's one man I'm going to make it a point to kill."

"Put a bullet in him for me, Frank," Raven said. "And one for Wilma."

"I'll do that, Doc. See you boys."

"Good luck, Frank," Bob said.

Frank nodded and smiled. "Take care of Marvella and Bessie. I'd never have made it without them."

"Will do," Doc Raven said. "Good hunting."

Frank walked out without looking back.

Twenty-three

Frank did not know what to expect once he reached he old Army fort for it had been deserted for years. He knew there were no towns anywhere near the place, and he suspected the old road leading to the fort would be overgrown from lack of use. Boise was probably a good fifty miles away from the fort.

Frank traveled light, not taking a packhorse. If he ran out of food, he would kill a deer, or live on rabbits and squirrels. He'd done it many times in the past.

I'm a rich man, he thought as he rode out of South Raven several hours before dawn. How do I get myself into these fixes? More importantly, *why* do I get myself into these fixes? Why don't I move to Canada and live peacefully under a false name? I certainly have the money to do so. Frank sighed as he settled more comfortably in the saddle. Because I'm Frank Morgan, he concluded. I've been Frank Morgan for forty some years. That's my name and I'll be damned if I'm going to run away and live under a name that isn't my own.

Frank headed cross-country, riding north for a time, then cutting almost due west. He couldn't be sure, but he figured he was probably paralleling the outlaws and their hostages, with them being north of the route he was taking.

This was tough, rugged country, inhabited by only a few brave souls. Frank had no idea how they managed to eke out a living. The days were bright and sunny and the nights downright cold. Frank traveled the passes and the valleys, avoiding the high-up country most of the time. Stormy liked the trail, and had a pleasing, comfortable gait that ate up the miles.

On his second day out, Frank smelled smoke and headed toward it. He reined up about fifty yards from the camp and gave out a holler.

"If you're friendly, come on in!" a man shouted. "If you're unfriendly, you bes' ride on."

"I'm friendly," Frank shouted. "Just looking for a place to noon and rest my horse."

"Come on in."

The two men looked to be prospectors, and the meat they were frying up and the coffee they were boiling sure smelled good. Frank said as much.

"Be ready in a few minutes," one of the men said. "Light and sit."

"I've got the fixings for some pan bread, if you'd like some," Frank offered.

"That would be tasty," the other man said. "We run out of flour a couple of days ago." He peered at Frank for several seconds. "You look familiar. We ever crossed trails before?"

"I don't know. Name is Morgan."

"Frank Morgan?"

"That's me."

"Great God Amighty! It is you. I seen your picture on the cover of one of them dime books one time."

"What are you doin' out here in the wilderness, Mr. Morgan?" the other man asked.

"Not that it's any of our business, mind you," his partner added quickly.

"Just wandering, boys. Staying away from people

mostly. You haven't seen any big bunches of people close by, have you?"

"We shore have. Early this morning, we did. I mean to tell you they was some hard cases, for shore."

"We fought shy of 'em, Mr. Morgan. Then about two hours later, here come another bunch of hard cases, ridin' hard in the same direction. 'Bout a dozen or so of them. I don't know what's goin' on or where they was all goin', but we shore didn't want to be nowheres close by."

Frank set the skillet on the rocks by the fire and waited while his cup was filled up with the hot brew. "I wonder where they're heading," he said.

"I wouldn't have no idea. If they headin' for Boise, they need to cut south some and get on the road. Be a lot easier goin'. If they stay due west like they're goin' there ain't nothin' except what's left of that old Army fort."

"Army fort?" Frank asked innocently. "I didn't know there was a fort in this area."

"There ain't no more. The Army pulled out years ago. The stone buildin's still there. That's 'bout all."

"I'll be damned. I never knew about that fort." Frank shook his head.

"Not too many people does. Hell, it was built in the middle of nowheres. I never knew why the Army built it there."

"Must be a road to it."

"Not no more. Just a trace of where it used to be. You couldn't get no wagon down it now. It's all growed up."

"Well, I'll make it a point not to get anywhere near that place," Frank said, holding out his cup for coffee.

"Be smart of you to do that."

**

Frank left the two old prospectors and once more hit the trail. If the gunslicks that left South Raven joined up with the kidnappers, that would bring the total to over forty men. There wasn't one chance in hell Frank could free the hostages.

He didn't know what to do.

"If you had any sense at all," he muttered, "you'd just ride on and forget the whole damned thing."

But he knew he wouldn't, couldn't, do that.

"We're gonna be in for a rough time of it, Stormy," he said to his horse. "I'm just too hard-headed to quit."

Frank stopped a couple of hours before dark and put the hobbles on Stormy. He rigged up a make-shift lean-to, then gathered up several armloads of dry leaves to spread on the ground. He laid his groundsheet over the leaves and then unrolled his blankets. He quickly built a fire, put the coffee water on to boil, and then set about gathering up dry firewood, enough to last him through the cold night.

He fried up some bacon and made some pan bread, using that to sop up the bacon grease. He had another cup of coffee and a cigarette, and sat and smoked while the last rays of sun disappeared and shadows began creeping in. As he smoked and drank his coffee, Frank wondered how far he was from any town. A good long ways, he concluded.

Frank figured he couldn't be more than a day and a half behind the outlaws. He knew that in rough country a lone rider could make better time than a large gathering. Of course, he still did not have the foggiest notion what he was going to do once he did make the fort.

Frank pulled his blankets around him and cussed, his breath steaming the cold evening air.

Frank shot a deer the next afternoon. He hated to do it for most of the meat would go to waste. He didn't have enough time to jerk any. He cut off the backstrap and then a haunch to roast. The cooked meat would keep until he reached the fort. Just as he was stowing the meat, he felt eyes on him and turned around.

A group of Indians was watching him, staying in the timber, well away from him. Frank stood up and made the sign of peace. The Indians returned the sign. Frank rubbed his stomach and pointed to the deer, then pointed to the two males, two females, and several kids. One of the men nodded his head and smiled.

Frank mounted up and rode off, feeling better now that he knew the meat from the deer would not go to waste and a family would eat well that day.

That evening, he put the roast on to cook, and fried up some of the backstrap. He ate his fill, leaned back just under his lean-to, and looked out the front at the canopy of stars that filled the heavens. Everything seemed at peace. But Frank knew it was all an illusion: as long as there were evil men walking the land, there would be no peace.

Frank poured another cup of coffee and shook away the thoughts of peace. He was on his way to make war, not peace. He knew that to talk peace with evil men was a waste of time. Frank knew exactly how to deal with evil men.

You killed them.

* * *

Frank topped the ridge that looked down into the long valley. The old fort was clearly visible. Most of the log walls had rotted away, but many of the buildings were still standing. The stone buildings would be there until someone tore them down.

There wasn't much danger of anyone accidentally stumbling upon the ruins of the old fort. The fort was miles and miles away from any town or established road, and no one lived within at least thirty miles of the place. Frank had spent an entire day doing a wide circle of the place, and had found no sign of human habitation.

Frank rode deeper into the timber and dismounted, walking back to the ridge overlooking the old fort. He began studying the layout with his field glasses. There were four guards: one at each corner of the place.

"Bad move, Sonny," Frank muttered. "If you were in the military, you must have spent your time in an office, 'cause you sure don't know crap about posting guards."

Frank had found at least two easy ways into the ruins without running much risk of being spotted, due to the bad placement of the guards.

"Getting in will be easy," he muttered. "However, if I went in with the notion of causing trouble, getting *out* might be a problem."

Frank studied the ravine running right up to the fort. I'll go in and out that way, he concluded. And I'll do that tonight. Prowl around some. He smiled, thinking, Too bad I can't be the hairy monster again. That was fun.

Somebody, Frank thought, put a lot of thought into this kidnapping plan. Somebody other than Sonny had to transport supplies to this place and store them. So there was more than just one man working on this end of it. Probably staying in Boise.

Well, Frank thought, I'll worry about that end of it later. Right now, I've got plenty to do here.

Although he sure as hell wasn't sure exactly *how* to accomplish what he came to do.

At full dark Frank slipped into the ravine and began slowly making his way toward the ruins of the old fort. He had left his spurs in his saddle-bags, and wore or carried nothing that would rattle. There was lamp and candle lights showing through the cracks in the boarded-up windows of the buildings within the compound, enforcing Frank's belief that someone had done a bit of work to the buildings long before the actual kidnapping took place.

He slipped up to the larger of the stone buildings and listened to the hum of conversation taking place inside.

"Lonesome," someone said, "how come you boys think you can just ride in here and deal yourselves into this game?"

"You don't have a lot of choice in the matter, Stoner," Lonesome Howard replied. "You either deal us in or try to kill us all. And if you try any gunplay, a lot of you are goin' to die. Think about that."

"It ain't fair," another man spoke up. "We done all the work and now you boys want a piece of the cake. It ain't fair."

"Nothin' is fair," Lonesome replied. "Them rich folks got their millions by workin' the poor man to death in their mines and railroads and factories. Think about that."

"You gonna give your share to the poor, Lonesome?"

"In a way, yes, I am. I'm gonna build me a church with my share and preach the gospel to the poor sinners."

"Who in the hell would come to listen to you?" another asked. "That's crazy, Lonesome. 'Course you're crazy, so I guess it makes sense to you."

Lonesome laughed. "Crazy like a fox, Harden. But you go on believin' what you like. Women like for preachers to poke them. Think about that. You'll be spendin' your money on soiled doves and rotgut whiskey. But fine-lookin' country women will be knockin' on my church door all hot to bed down with me. Now who's crazy?"

"The man's got a plan," Carl Depp said. "I got to admit that. That's right good thinkin', Lonesome. Can I be one of your choir members?"

"Absolutely not. Once I get my hands on that money, I ain't havin' no more to do with the likes of you godless heathens!"

The entire roomful of men all burst into laughter. Outside, Frank shook his head at Lonesome's plan. Lonesome was always thinking up some angle to work. The years had not changed him a bit.

Frank slipped around to another of the stone buildings and peeked in through another boarded-up window. Sonny was talking with a couple of men.

"Let Lonesome and that bunch from town think they're in tight with us. We'll gather them all in one building just before I go into town for the money and kill them. That will take care of that little problem."

Damn! Frank thought. That would sure enough take care of the problem.

"How about Morgan? We know he's comin' after us."

"What about him?" Sonny asked. "He's just one man. When he gets here, we'll kill him."

I might have something to say about that, Frank thought as he slipped away from the building. As a matter of fact, I'm going to have a hell of lot to say about it!

Twenty-four

Frank spent about an hour the next morning watching the old fort through his field glasses. He soon tired of it because there wasn't a lot of movement to observe. Before sleep dropped him into rest the previous night, he had given a lot of thought about freeing the hostages. He had thought of a dozen plans and rejected them all. Now, watching the old fort, he was forced to admit that he was stymied. He just didn't know what to do. If he tried to free the men one at a time, that would put the others at risk. He didn't know what to do.

Frank picked up his field glasses as two men walked out of a small building and started swinging at each other. Each got in some pretty good licks before one of the men stepped back and pulled his pistol. The other man held one hand out in front of him and shook his head. The word "No!" was forming on his lips a second before he was shot in the chest.

The man dropped to the cold ground and did not move.

The shooter walked to him and looked down as he holstered his six-gun.

Another man walked out of the building and shot the gunman in the back. The gunslick dropped to his knees, a horrible expression on his face, then fell forward, to die by the body of the man he'd shot. The building emptied of men.

Sonny and several other men ran out of one of the larger stone buildings and confronted the back-shooter and those siding with him. Frank could not, of course, hear any of the words, but he could tell the conversation was heated due to the gestures of the men.

Sonny began pointing to something. The back-shooter jerked his hat off his head and threw it on the ground, shaking his head in a negative way.

A dozen men, including Lonesome Howard and the Olsen cousins, came out of another building, all armed with rifles, and lined up with Sonny.

The back-shooter and the half-dozen men who had sided with him looked around them for a moment as Sonny told them something. They all nodded their heads and turned away, walking back into the building. Frank lowered his field glasses, resting his eyes for a moment from the pull of the heavy magnification.

"Interesting," he said. "Now let's see what happens."

After a few minutes the half-dozen men came outside, carrying their bedrolls and saddlebags. They began walking toward the corral, all under the watchful eyes of Sonny and his men. Frank watched them saddle their horses and mount up. They slowly rode past Sonny and his men. Just as they reached what was left of the gate entrance to the old fort, Sonny and his men lifted their rifles and opened fire.

All but one of the men were knocked out of the saddle. The one man who remained mounted slumped over his horse's neck as the frightened animal bolted, racing out of the ruins. The wounded man hung on.

Sonny and his men continued firing as the horse

turned toward the ridge where Frank was watching, putting some old buildings between the rider and the rifle fire. The rider reached the timber and was out of sight.

Sonny pointed toward a man. The man ran for the corral. Moments later, he was riding out of the ruins, in pursuit of the wounded man.

Frank watched the activity in the old fort for a moment longer. The other men showed no interest in riding after the wounded man and his pursuer.

Frank left his hiding place and slipped through the timber, in the direction the wounded man had taken.

It took Frank only a few minutes to locate him. He was lying unconscious on the ground, his horse standing nearby. Frank slipped behind the scant cover of brush as the gunslick sent out from the fort rode slowly up to the downed man and dismounted. Frank stepped out of cover and swung his rifle, the butt taking the gunhand in the face and dropping him like a rock. He wasn't dead, but he'd be out for a time.

The bulging saddlebags of the wounded man held Frank's attention. He quickly jerked the saddle bags off and opened them. A wide smile creased his face. The saddlebags were stuffed with sticks of dynamite, caps, and fuses.

The wounded man moaned, and Frank's .45 leaped into his hand as he spun around.

"I ain't gonna be no trouble to you, Morgan," the man whispered. "I'm done for and I know it."

Frank holstered his pistol and walked over to him. The man had several bloody holes in his back.

"I was on my way to do a bank job when I joined up with this tumble bunch. That's why I was carryin' the dynamite."

"Must have been a hell of a bank if you were going to use all that explosive," Frank said.

The man pushed a smile past bloody lips. "I believe in bein' prepared."

"Are the hostages still alive?"

"Yeah. So far. But some of them is in bad shape from all the beatin's they've took. Sonny is plannin' on killin' them all once he gets the money. Sonny is a mean son of a bitch, let me tell you he is."

"How about this man who came after you?" Frank pointed to the man he'd smacked with his rifle butt.

"Sorry bastard from Kansas name of Hastings. Brags about killin' and rapin' young girls. No damn good a-tall."

The man said no more as his eyes glazed over. He shivered once, and then died far more peacefully than he had ever lived.

Frank took the heavy saddlebags and slipped back into the timber and brush and waited. It wasn't long before half a dozen mounted men rode up and dismounted.

"What the hell happened here?" one asked.

"Don't make no sense unless Hastings fell off his horse," another said.

"Is he dead?" a third man asked, pointing to Hastings.

"Naw. But he's bad hurt. Head looks like it's busted wide open."

"This one's shore 'nuff dead," another said.

"Leave him. Get the horses and let's tote Hastings back to the fort."

"Yeah. I'm hongry."

Frank watched them ride out. He carefully made his way back to his own horse, and then set about capping and fusing the dynamite, making a dozen tied-together bundles of the explosives. Now he had a plan.

* * *

Frank had pinpointed the location of the hostages, and knew which buildings were occupied by the outlaws. He longed for a cup of coffee, but hadn't dared build a fire or even smoke a cigarette for fear of detection. Now, at full dark, on the ridge overlooking the old fort, Frank rolled a smoke to settle his nerves and carefully lit up.

His plan was foolhardy and chancy at best, but it was the best he could come up with. Frank finished his cigarette and picked up the saddlebags filled with dynamite. He had moved Stormy to a location much closer to the old fort. It was time to get moving.

Frank made his way into the ravine and then cautiously slipped into the edge of the fort. If all the horses stampeded during the explosions, his plan was doomed, for on foot in the cold wilderness, the hostages would surely die—most of them anyway. These were men who were not accustomed to hardship or fending for themselves.

Frank stepped out of the ravine and moved up to the first building housing a group of outlaws. He would set the charges for this building, using long fuses, then move on to the building where the hostages were being held and free them as quickly as possible. Frank knew the chance of his plan succeeding was slim. But it was the only plan he had.

He pressed up against the building as several men walked by.

"Sonny says just a couple more days to go," one said. "If we haven't heard from the relatives of the men, we move again."

"Where to?"

"I don't know. He didn't say."

"I'm gettin' tarred of all this damn waitin'," another said. "I'm thinkin' the relatives don't give a damn about these men."

"I'm gettin' that feelin' myself. But they's too much money involved to quit and pull out now. I'm gonna see it through."

"Morgan not showin' up by now worries me some. Where the hell is he?"

"He don't know where we are. Forget him."

The men walked on. Frank watched as they opened the door to a building and stepped inside, closing the door behind them.

Frank placed the heavy charge of dynamite and lit the fuse, moving quickly away toward the building where the hostages were held. Taking a deep breath, Frank pulled his six-gun and opened the door just as the dynamite blew, the enormous sound shattering the quiet of night.

He shot the first guard, shifted position, and drilled the second man. "Move!" he yelled to the Easterners. "Get to the corral and grab a horse. Ride toward the east. Get into the timber and wait for me."

"We don't have time to saddle them properly!" a man said.

"Then goddamnit, ride them bareback, you ninny!" Frank yelled. "Move or die. It's your choice."

Frank quickly lit another charge and tossed it toward a group of men running toward the building. The short-fused bundle of dynamite landed in the middle of the men and blew, knocking bits and pieces of them in all directions.

"Somebody kill that son of a bitch!" a man yelled.

"Kill who?" another man shouted. "Where is he?"

Frank lit another bundle and tossed it into the night.

"Look out!" a man screamed.

The charge landed in a doorway and exploded, the blast ripping the door off its hinges and sending bits of wood and stone and metal into the interior. The concussion momentarily deafened the men inside the building and knocked them all to the floor, one dead and the others hurt, some seriously.

Frank paused long enough to light another bundle, and then ran to another building, reaching it just as the door was jerked open. He tossed the sputtering charge into the room with just a couple of seconds to spare. The dynamite blew, the concussion sending Frank rolling on the ground. He lost the last bundle of dynamite when he hit the ground. He rolled until coming to a stop against a building.

The last building must have held a store of explosives, for when Frank's charge exploded, whatever was stored in there blew with it. The roof blew off, and bits and pieces of outlaws went flying through the night air, one severed leg landing about a yard from Frank.

"There he is!" someone shouted.

The night was filled with gunfire, but none of it came anywhere near Frank. He got to his feet and jerked out his pistol.

"You crazy bastards!" Sonny yelled. "You've killed Owens."

"Oh, damn!" a man said. "I thought it was Morgan."

"The damn hostages is ridin' off toward the east," a man yelled. "They stole the horses and is gettin' away."

During the confusion, Frank began working his way toward the ravine.

He almost made it.

"There he is!" someone shouted. "By the ravine."

"Somebody kill that bastard!" another yelled.

The night became sparked by muzzle blasts. Frank felt a hard blow in his left leg and his boots flew out from under him. Just before he went down hard, a stray bullet nicked the side of his head and Frank felt a gush of hot blood on his cheek. Then he went sliding on his belly into the deep part of the ravine. He began rolling over and over until he hit the bottom. He banged his head hard on the way down and lost consciousness for a moment. He also lost his spare .45. His holstered .45 somehow remained in leather.

"Where the hell did he go?" The shouted question drifted to Frank as he slipped back into consciousness.

"I don't think he made the ravine," someone yelled. "I think he headed out toward the rear of the fort."

"Split up and search for him," Sonny hollered. "Some of you others get those damn horses. Or we'll all have to walk out of here."

Frank began crawling on his hands and knees, trying to be as quiet as possible. The shock of his wounds was wearing off, and now the pain in his leg and head was coming on hard. It had to happen sooner or later, Frank thought. My luck ran out. I took a chance and it didn't work out. I wonder if the hostages made it clear, and if they did, where are they? What did I tell them to do? I can't remember.

One of the outlaws imagined a sighting of some sort at the far end of the old fort and yelled out, "I seen him! There he goes. He's runnin' out the rear of the fort. Come on, boys."

Imagination hit the others, another shouting,

"Yeah! I see him. He's almost in the timber. Come on, boys. Now we got him."

Yeah, Frank thought, as he slowly drifted back into the darkness and uncertainty of unconsciousness. Go chase shadows, boys.

One last thought entered Frank's head as he lost track of reality: I hope the hostages made it out.

Then Frank dropped into darkness.

Twenty-five

Frank came to in a world of hurt and confusion and silence. His head throbbed with pain and his leg was stiff and sore, his pants leg caked with dried blood and mud. The mud must have acted to help stop the bleeding. But Frank couldn't understand the utter silence. He tried to sit up. The movement hurt him and he gave it up for a couple of minutes, then tried again. This time he made it. But God, his head hurt.

He rested for a time, then groped around until he found his hat. Before putting it on, he gently touched the side of his head with his fingers. There was a gash along the side of his head, all caked over with dried blood. He set his hat on his head very gently. It still fit, so his head wasn't swollen. He guessed that meant his skull wasn't busted.

He rested for another few minutes, then stood up. His head seemed to swim for a few seconds, and he thought he might pass out. He leaned against the side of the ravine for a moment until the dizziness passed.

He slowly and very carefully made his way out of the ravine. He suddenly realized that his second gun was gone, but knew it was useless to look for it in the dark. He stepped out of the ravine and looked back at the old fort. It was totally dark. Not a light showed anywhere. Frank sat down on a log and rested for a moment, trying to make some sense out of things.

The old fort looked and felt deserted.

After a time, curiosity got the better of Frank and he made his way back toward the fort. He walked only a few steps before almost tripping over the body of a man. Frank reached down, pulled off the man's gunbelt, and slung it over his shoulder. All the loops were filled with cartridges and the man's .45 was still in leather.

Frank found two other dead men and stripped them of weapons. He walked on through the night, looking into each building. The moon was up, the night cloudless, and he had ample light to see the damage his dynamite had caused.

God, what a mess!

The fort was devoid of living outlaws, the corrals empty. The outlaws were gone.

Hell with it! Frank thought as he passed by a stone building. I need something to eat and several cups of coffee. He stepped inside and struck a match. There was an old potbellied stove in the center of the room and the exterior was still warm, a coffeepot on the lid. Frank hefted the pot; it was nearly full. He found a tin cup and poured. Then he sat down on the side of a bunk and drank the warm coffee and smoked a cigarette. He stoked up the stove, adding some wood, and put the pot back on to heat the coffee.

Frank found a candle and lit it, then set about looking to his wounds . . . as best he could with what he had. He found a canteen of water someone had left behind in their haste to pull out, and lowered his trousers to look at the wound. The bullet had passed through the fleshy part of his leg about halfway between knee and hip. Frank washed out the wound and used his bandanna to bandage it. He washed the gash in his head, and that got it bleeding again and Frank cussing a bit. Looking around, Frank found some stale bread and ate it. It didn't taste very good, but it filled up an empty spot in his belly. Frank rolled a smoke and relaxed for a few moments. In the faint flickering light of the single candle he thought, Now what?

He checked his watch. It had stopped. Frank recalled then that he had forgotten to wind it. Although his leg ached and his head hurt, Frank knew he had to get going. He could not afford to lollygag about. He found a cloth sack and put the spare weapons in it, then picked up the canteen and blew out the candle. He stepped out into the night and began the painful walk back to where he'd left Stormy, hoping the horse would still be there. If not, Frank would have a lot of walking ahead of him. At this time, he chose not to dwell on that.

Stormy was as glad to see him as Frank was to see the big Appaloosa. Frank quickly saddled up and headed out to try to find the trail of the hostages . . . if they were still free, that is. It was going to be difficult at night, but he felt he had to do it. A bunch of Eastern city folks wandering about in the Big Empty? Frank shook his head at the thought.

He found a lot of sign that told him the freed hostages had reached the horses and made the timber in a group. But a few minutes later, the sign showed that the Eastern men had lost their sense of direction (if they ever had any) and had turned north.

"Damn!" Frank said. "Heading deeper into the wilderness."

But what was puzzling to Frank was the absence

of any pursuit from the kidnappers. They had abandoned the old fort, that was a fact, but where had they gone? The horses could not have wandered far before being caught. The outlaws were all experienced men, with plenty of horse sense, many of them as good with a rope as they were with a gun. Had they panicked and given up on the scheme, just let the hostages go free without pursuit?

Sure looked that way to Frank. But if so, what had panicked them?

Staying with the sign, Frank found no indication that any of the Eastern men had broken with the group and wandered off by himself . . . which was a good thing. They stood a chance of making it if they stayed together.

After a couple of hours of slow riding through the timber, Frank suddenly reined up and sat his saddle, sniffing the air.

Wood smoke! Sure as hell it was. And he didn't believe for a moment it was Sonny and his bunch. He rode slowly on, following the sign of the hostages, the smell of wood smoke growing stronger in the cold night. Finally he spotted the flickering fire through the timber. He dismounted, ground-reined Stormy, and slipped up close.

He had found the Eastern men, and they were a sorry-looking bunch for a fact.

"Hello the camp!" Frank called.

The Easterners froze in panic.

"It's Frank Morgan. Take it easy, boys. I'm coming in."

"Oh, thank God!" one of the men exclaimed as they all stood up as one.

The closer Frank drew to the camp, the more he could tell the men were in bad shape. All of them had been badly beaten . . . probably more than once. Some of them were missing teeth, and all had bruises and cuts on their faces.

"You boys have had quite a time of it, haven't you?" Frank said.

"Yes, we have, Mr. Morgan," a man said. "By the way, my name is Aaron Steele."

"I'm Frank, Aaron. Let's keep it on a first-name basis. It'll be a lot easier that way."

The men all stepped forward and introduced themselves, shaking hands with Frank.

"I've got enough coffee left for a pot or two, boys," Frank said. "And some food for a meal this night . . . or morning rather. You boys look like you could use some strong coffee and some hot food."

"That would indeed be wonderful, Frank," John Garver said.

"I'll get my horse and we'll start cooking. And we've got to see about your horses too."

"We picketed them, Frank," Jackson Mills said. "We may be dudes, but we knew to do that much."

"And we were lucky in another aspect," Horace Vanderhoot said. "We all got horses that were saddled."

"You really were lucky. Be back in a couple of minutes."

Frank fixed a proper fire, first digging a small pit, then lining the outside with large stones and fixing a place for the coffeepot to rest. Then he sliced up all the bacon he had and fixed a skillet of pan bread.

"It isn't much but it'll jerk a knot in an empty belly," he told the men.

"I'm salivating already," Paul Edwards said.

Over coffee and bacon and pan bread, Frank began bringing the men up to date, starting with, "I might as well let you have the bad news first. Maxwell Crawford is dead. I buried him myself. He was a brave man at the end."

"Oh, my God!" Hugh Dunbar said. "Poor Maxwell."

"What about our wives?" Bernard Harrison asked.

"They're all right. All of them. They're waiting in South Raven for your return."

"Will we return, Frank?" Edmund Greene inquired.

"You bet we will. We'll sleep a few hours and be on the trail come morning. It's going to be rough, 'cause I'll be taking you cross-country. It's the safest way."

"You're the boss, Frank," Delbert Knox said. "Whatever you say do, we'll do it, without question."

"How many of those horrid people did you dispose of?" Fuller Ross asked.

Frank looked at the man who had offered his wife to the outlaws in exchange for his own well-being. "I killed several of them," he said shortly.

Fuller picked up on the scorn in Frank's tone. "Whatever you might have heard about my actions, they are nothing but lies."

"You are the one who is a damn liar, Fuller!" Horace said. "You are an utterly despicable cad! I loathe you!"

Frank used a piece of bread to sop up some of the grease in the skillet. He said nothing, preferring to stay out of the building argument. Let the friends settle it among themselves. If it could be settled.

"Those thugs were threatening to kill me!" Fuller said. "I had to do something to stop the beatings. Any of you would have done the same."

"We didn't," Paul Edwards said. "I would have

willingly died rather than offer my wife to them to stop the abuse. And told them so," he added softly.

"When we return to the city, Fuller," Horace Vanderhoot said, "I shall see to it that your actions are made public. I want all our business associates to know what sort of person you really are. Do not speak to me after this. I want nothing more to do with you."

The other men nodded their heads in agreement, Delbert saying, "The venture you and I planned together is now null and void, Fuller. I would rather go into business with a poisonous serpent."

"You can't mean that!" Fuller protested. "My God, I have a lot of money tied up in that project."

"As I do," Delbert replied. "I will gladly take my losses to be rid of you."

"I'll get even with you," Fuller said. "All of you. You'll see. I'll get even."

"Don't press it, Fuller," Aaron told him. "Or I will personally do Mavis a great favor and make her a widow this night."

"You can't mean that! Listen to what you are saying."

"Shut up," Jackson said. "Just shut your mouth, Fuller. Or I shall give you a thrashing you will never forget."

Frank poured another cup of coffee and rolled a cigarette.

Fuller moved away from the others, and sat down with his back to a tree. He mumbled to himself.

Frank leaned back, easing his wounded leg. Horace noticed the movement and asked, "Are you badly hurt, Frank?"

Frank shook his head, which still ached slightly. "Not bad. I've been hurt worse. It's just a flesh wound."

"Is there nothing you can do for it?"

"Come first light, I'll look for some tree moss and cover it with that. It works to prevent and heal infection. It's an old Cheyenne Indian treatment."

"Tree moss?" Edmund Greene asked. "I never heard of such a thing."

"It works," Frank told him. "I've used it before."

"You've been wounded before?"

Frank smiled. "Several times. A lot worse than this."

"Are you in much pain?"

"Not much. Let's finish up this coffee and then try to get a few hours sleep, boys. We've got a hard pull ahead of us come morning."

"I swear I don't believe I will ever be warm again," John Garver said.

"Be thankful there were bedrolls behind those saddles," Frank told him. "And say a little prayer that the snow holds off until we get back to town."

"Did my wife say anything about me while you were with her?" Fuller Ross abruptly asked Frank.

"She mentioned a few things," Frank admitted.

"What things?"

"This and that," Frank said.

"Let's try to get some sleep," Horace said. "Fuller, what happens to you and Mavis is something the both of you will have to work out when we get back. Good night."

Frank sat long by the fire after the others had gone to sleep. *If* we get back, he thought.

Twenty-six

Frank and the freed hostages started out just after first light. The men rejected Frank's idea that they head for Boise, and insisted they return to South Raven.

"It's rough country, boys," Frank told them.

Frank's statement was met with stony silence.

Frank shrugged. "All right," he said, swinging into the saddle. "Let's do it."

The Easterners put the miles behind them without complaint. Frank knew they must all be hurting from the many beatings they had endured, and his opinion of the men rose considerably as the miles passed. On the evening of the second day out, the land was dusted with a light snow. But the morning sky dawned a bright blue and the men pushed on. Frank killed a deer later that day, and everybody went to sleep that night with a full belly. The saw no signs of the kidnappers.

Over breakfast, with Frank using the last of the flour and lard, Bernard Harrison asked, "What do you think happened to our kidnappers?"

Frank shook his head. "I don't know. But I doubt we've seen the last of them. At least as far as I'm concerned."

"You want to explain that?" Aaron asked.

"I messed up their plans for riches. They won't

forgive me for that. And they won't forget. I'm going to have some ol' boys looking to kill me."

"I'll pay you a thousand dollars for every one of them you kill," Fuller Ross said.

Frank stared at the man for a few seconds. "I'm not a manhunter, Fuller. I don't kill for money."

"Then I'll find someone who will," Fuller replied.

Frank shrugged his response. "Your option."

Fuller had been riding alone, at the end of the column. None of his former friends would have anything to do with him. Frank suspected that when the group returned to the business world, Fuller would be in for a lonely and very rough time of it. And he was going to face it alone, without support of family. He had heard some of the other women talking about Mavis's plans to leave her husband.

"Why don't you hunt the men yourself, Fuller?" Jackson asked. "I can assure you, you will have ample time to do so."

"What the hell do you mean by that?" Fuller snapped.

"Oh, I suspect that once the business community learns of your despicable behavior in this matter, you won't find many men willing to have anything to do with you."

"And you'll be just delighted to spread the word about me, won't you?"

"If asked, I shall tell the truth," Jackson replied.

"And so will I," several others stated in unison.

"Bastards," Fuller cursed them.

Frank stood up and put a stop to the bickering. "Mount up," he told the group. They pushed on.

They encountered no trouble of any kind as they made their way toward South Raven, and that puzzled Frank. He could not understand why Sonny and the others gave up so easily. Perhaps they thought they were being attacked by a large force. Maybe by the time they rounded up their horses, they figured it was too late to catch up with the escaped hostages. Frank just didn't know. But he felt he would . . . when some of those involved in the kidnapping caught up with him. And he was sure that would happen. He kept a sharp eye out for any trouble on the way back to South Raven, but no trouble materialized.

"We'll be in town tomorrow afternoon," Frank surprised the group by saying during a supper of rabbit meat he'd trapped earlier that day. "Y'all can get you a good meal and a hot bath then. And see the doctor if you like."

"That's wonderful news, Frank," John said. "But most of our wounds have healed since we left the old fort."

"I think it's the cold pure air," Horace said. "Am I correct, Frank?"

"It's got something to do with it, for a fact."

"I wonder if the stage is running yet," Edmund said.

"Probably," Frank told him. Then he looked over at Jackson Mills. "You and me better have us a little chat, Jackson. Before we get to town."

"About what, Frank?" Jackson looked up, a puzzled expression on his face.

"About that fellow you hired to kill me."

"I beg your pardon?" Jackson sat up straight.

Frank related what Doc Raven had told him.

Jackson shook his head. "Dr. Raven is badly misinformed, Frank. I paid no one to kill you. Whoever this man is, he lied. Why, I don't know. But he lied."

Frank stared at Jackson for a moment. He believed him. More mystery to an already very strange situation.

"This man, he resembled me?" Jackson asked.

"I guess so," Frank replied. "He sure said he was you."

Jackson nodded his head slowly. He cut his eyes to Fuller Ross. The man refused to meet his gaze. "You son of a bitch," Jackson said, his tone filled with rancor.

Fuller did not reply.

"You betrayed me for a few dollars, didn't you, Fuller? You wanted me dead, didn't you? Answer me, damn you!"

"What's going on here?" Horace demanded.

"I haven't done anything," Fuller said.

"I entered a business arrangement with Fuller just weeks before we came out here," Jackson said. "It's rather complex, but the important point is this: Should either of us die, the living partner would benefit greatly. I thought it was merely a standard contract between friends. I see now what Jackson really had in mind."

"You can't prove anything!" Fuller yelled.

"Now, wait a minute," Frank said, holding up a hand. "I don't understand any of this." He paused for a few seconds, then slowly nodded his head. "Unless the man never intended to kill me. He was set up to pretend to kill me, in the hopes he would tell me who hired him, and I would confront the man."

"And you would kill me," Jackson concluded. "It's something Fuller would do. Very complicated. So complex it didn't stand much of a chance of working. That's the manner in which many of his business deals are written. Complex and unworkable . . . except to his advantage." He looked again at Fuller. "You are beneath contempt."

"You can't prove any of this!" Fuller shouted.

"Oh, shut up, Fuller," Delbert told him. "You're a damn snake in the grass. Now that I have a moment to reflect, I did see you talking with a stranger right after we arrived in town. I didn't think anything of it until now. I saw you, or thought I did, give the man something. You were setting this up then, weren't you?"

"Prove it!" Fuller yelled. "You can't prove it. You can't prove any of it. It's all conjecture. You don't have a shred of evidence that will stand up in court."

Jackson stood up and walked over to the man he'd once called friend. He stood for a moment, then slapped the man across the face.

Fuller staggered back, anger flushing his face, reddening it. "Damn you!"

"I challenge you, Fuller," Jackson said. "Name your weapon."

"Are you insane?" Fuller yelled. "You must be crazy."

"You better pick a weapon, Fuller. I'm warning you. I will have my satisfaction, one way or the other."

"I'm not going to fight you, Jackson."

"You're a coward," Jackson said. "If you won't choose weapons, I will. Pistols. Name your second."

Fuller looked wildly around him, fear evident in his eyes. "I won't fight you, Jackson. You're making a mistake. I didn't ask the man to kill Frank. I just wanted to scare . . . I . . . uh . . ." He realized he was only digging himself a deeper hole, and gulped a couple of times. He closed his mouth and shook his head.

"Get a pistol, Fuller," Jackson told him, his voice cold and flat-sounding.

"No! I won't do it. You can't make me."

Jackson began cursing Fuller. He cursed him until he was out of breath. Fuller stood still in the middle of the clearing, shaking his head.

Jackson walked to the man and hit him in the

mouth with his fist. Fuller went down, his mouth
bloody.

"Get up and fight me, you bastard!" Jackson
yelled.

"No," Fuller said.

Jackson drew back his foot and started to kick
the man. Fuller cringed in anticipation of the kick.
Jackson thought better of it and stepped back,
standing for a moment, looking down at the man
he'd once called friend. "You're a pitiful excuse
for a man, Fuller." He spat on the prostrate Fuller,
the spittle striking the man in the face. Fuller did
nothing. "Mavis will be far better off without you.
And I shall personally see she is well supported,
with your money, for the rest of her life." Jackson
turned his back to Fuller Ross and walked away.

Frank looked at Fuller. The man was a coward
through and through. Probably had been all his
life, and after this, Frank thought, the man would
be an outcast among all those who knew him. That
is, once the full story about what happened out
West was told and retold, and it surely would be.

"Let's all calm down and get some sleep," Frank
told the group. "We'll be pulling out at first light."

The entire town turned out to stand and watch
Frank lead the very bedraggled group of men into
South Raven. The citizens stood in silence and
watched.

Frank reined up in front of the saloon/hotel,
and wearily swung down from the saddle just as
Doc Raven walked up and stood for a moment,
counting heads.

"You've done the impossible, Frank," the doctor
said. "You've brought them all back . . . and in one
piece too."

"More or less, Doc," Frank said, limping over and stepping up onto the boardwalk. "Some of them are missing some teeth."

"You're a little worse for wear yourself," Doc Raven observed.

"I'll be all right. The bullet went right through my leg without hitting anything vital. I treated it with tree moss."

"I used it during the war. It works. I don't know why, but it does."

The men stood and watched as the wives of the freed hostages came out and greeted them. Mavis was not among them. Fuller stood alone by his horse, looking very uncomfortable.

"That one," Frank said, nodding toward Fuller, "is one sorry human being."

"The women told me all about him," Doc Raven replied. "And the news spread very quickly. Fuller Ross will not be treated with much warmth in this town."

"Any of the kidnappers been spotted in this area?"

"No. And the road is open, the stages running."

"The telegraph wires up?"

"Yes. And humming with the stories about the kidnapping. Every lawman in the West knows about it."

"Was my name left out of the story?"

"As far as I know, yes. But it's only a matter of time. You know that."

"I'll be gone by then. How's Dog?"

"Missing you. He mopes around. Horse is settling down. He even let a stranger pet him the other day."

"Amazing."

"I think you've been a bad influence on him."

"Very funny, Doc. Well, I think I'll go play with

Dog for a few minutes and then clean up. I need a bath in the worst way."

"I won't disagree," Doc Raven said with a smile.

Before either man could say another word, Dog came barking and running up the street and practically jumped into Frank's arms. After about a minute of frantic face-licking and pawing and barking, the big cur began to settle down.

"I think he missed you, Frank," Doc Raven said, smiling.

"He smells like flowers, Doc. What'd you do, give him a bath with some sort of women's perfumed soap?"

"Yes. And I can tell you he didn't like it one damn little bit."

"I don't blame him. I'm surprised he didn't attract every female dog in the county."

"He did. The poor boy was worn down to a frazzle. I had to take him home with me and keep him in the house so he could get some rest."

Fuller Ross came running up the street, all wild-eyed and panicky, shouting, "She's got a knife. Says she's going to castrate me. Help!"

Mavis appeared at the end of the street, holding a very large butcher knife. "Come back here, you little weasel!" she shouted.

"You go to hell!" Fuller yelled. "You're crazy, woman. Let me explain."

"There is nothing to explain, Fuller," Mavis told him. "And if you try, I'll cut your lying damn tongue out."

"You tell him, sister!" a woman shouted from the boardwalk.

"Turn him into a gelding, girl!" Sister Clarabelle yelled. "I'll hold him down and you can do the nut-cuttin'!"

"*Whoa!*" Fuller hollered, looking frantically around

him for someone, anyone, to help him. No one volunteered.

"You, Edith," Clarabelle yelled, pointing to a woman across the street. "Block that alley on your side. Bertha, you and Zelda take the street. Don't let the scum get past you."

"*Good God!*" Fuller yelled, panic in his voice. "Somebody help me."

"Not me," Doc Raven said. "I make it a point not to get in the way of a woman holding a large knife."

"Nor me," Frank said.

"Me and Winifred will cover this side," a woman yelled.

"Good girl, Henrietta," Sister Clarabelle shouted. "We'll all work tegether and get the worthless scum and cut him."

"This is getting out of hand," Doc Raven said. "I think these ladies mean it."

"I never doubted it," Frank replied.

Mavis began slowly advancing up the street, waving the butcher knife.

Fuller began backing up.

"Late stage is comin'," someone shouted. "Clear the street. They're comin' fast."

"Damn!" Henrietta said.

Fuller made a dash for the livery and made it. The last anyone saw of him for that day and a couple more days was Fuller on a mule, riding bareback, heading for the timber. He was dressed only in his long-handles.

Twenty-seven

After a long bath and dressing in clean clothes, Frank had his healing wounds checked by Doc Raven.

"They look good, Frank. Nothing I can do now. You'll have a permanent scar on the side of your head, but you've got a good head of hair that will cover it."

"How about the men's wounds?"

"Nothing serious. They all just had the stuffing beat out of them. Some of them lost teeth."

"And one lost his wife," Frank replied.

"For a fact," Doc Raven said with a smile. "That's was Thompson's mule he stole getting away from his wife. Thompson told me a while ago that the mule will take him to the farm . . . eventually. Ross will probably sleep in the barn until Mavis calms down."

"Did anyone take the knife away from her?"

"One of the ladies from the church got it. I gave Mavis a sedative that will keep her knocked out for hours."

"Any news come in with the stage?"

"Nothing of any importance. You expecting any?"

"I don't think those outlaws have given up, Doc. I just don't see them giving up that easy."

"What are you thinking, Frank?"

"That they'll come back here and pull something."

"Why?"

"You're too cut off here. One snip with wire cutters on either side of town and you'd be easy targets for outlaws on the rampage."

"We've got two stages a day now, Frank. The schedule was changed since the road opened."

"Hours apart, Doc. Besides, so what? A driver and a guard are going to help you against forty or fifty heavily armed outlaws?"

"A lot of men in this town are good shots, Frank. You know that. War veterans and Indian fighters and buffalo hunters."

"I know all that, Doc. But if the gang were to slip in close and hide, a few at a time, then strike real fast . . ." Frank shook his head. "Maybe I'm seeing danger where there is none. I hope so. I just can't understand why they gave up the way they did."

"Well, that puzzles me too," the doctor admitted. "But I can't see them attacking a town. Even the way you described it. Too many of them would get shot to pieces."

"Maybe," Frank said. "Well, anyway, I'm going to get some supper and then hit the hay." He smiled. "Literally. I'm going to sleep in that little room in the livery."

"Sweet dreams."

"See you in the morning, Doc."

Frank slept well and deeply that first night back in town, awakening about an hour before dawn, Dog asleep on the floor at the foot of the bunk. Frank put on water to boil for coffee, and then washed up, splashing cold water on his face to help him get the sleep out of his eyes. He stretched until his joints creaked, and then let Dog out to do his morning business.

Now fully awake, standing by the small potbellied stove, Frank could not shake the feeling that the outlaws had not yet finished with the freed hostages, the town, or with him. Especially with him.

Frank dressed in the new clothes he'd purchased at the general store, then sat down on the edge of the bunk. While he smoked and drank coffee, Frank carefully cleaned his six-gun and then his rifle. Maybe he was wrong about the outlaws attacking the town . . . but he didn't think so. However, he didn't want to spread panic in the town with false rumors.

He stepped out of the livery into the cold early morning and walked to the cafe. It had just opened and he was the first customer. He ordered breakfast and a pot of coffee. He was just sugaring his coffee when Doc Raven walked in and sat down at the table with him.

"You're up early," Frank commented.

"I've been thinking about what you said yesterday afternoon, about the outlaws attacking the town. Maybe you're right, Frank."

"And you think we should do what?"

"I'll talk to a few people. But not the community at large. I don't want to start a panic."

"Exactly my thinking, Doc."

The men ate their breakfast, drank coffee, and smoked and talked for a time. Doc Raven excused himself, saying he had to check on a patient out in the country. "I'll be back by mid-morning, Frank. See you then."

"Take care, Doc."

Moments after Doc Raven walked out of the cafe, Old Bob walked in and sat down at the table with Frank. Before Frank could say a word, Bob said, "I been thinkin' about something, Frank. It's been wallowin' around in my head and I can't get shut of it."

"Oh?"

Bob poured him a cup of coffee. "How come them no-counts who kidnapped the Easterners just up and rode off after you attacked the old fort?"

"I don't know. I've wondered the same thing for days."

"I think they're up to something."

Frank waited while Bob took a swallow of coffee.

"Don't make no sense that they would just up and ride off. Unless they figured you was a part of a big posse."

"That could be it."

"I think that mayhaps they might be ridin' back thisaway to hit the town."

"So do I, Bob."

"I talked to Phil at the saloon last night and he thinks the same way."

"And you propose we do what?"

"Get ready for one hell of a fight."

"How are you going to do that without alarming the whole town and setting off a panic?" Frank asked.

Bob shrugged his shoulders. "I don't know."

"Well, when you figure that out, you let me know."

"Riders coming in," the waitress announced, walking over and staring out the front window. "Five of them."

Bob twisted around in his chair and took a long look. "I don't know none of 'em. Never seen 'em before. But they shore look capable of startin' trouble."

"You always announce the arrival of strangers?" Frank asked the waitress.

"No, sir," she replied. "But since the trouble I've been suspicious. And I woke up this morning feeling sort of jumpy."

The five men reined up in front of the saloon

and sat their saddles for a moment. When they determined the saloon was closed, they dismounted and walked to the cafe and stepped inside.

"Mornin'," one said to the waitress. "How's about some coffee and some food?"

"Got plenty of coffee. Breakfast is bacon and eggs and fried potatoes with biscuits on the side."

"Sounds good to us. Pour and serve."

"Got any honey to sweeten them biscuits?" another asked.

"Cost you extra," she replied.

"We can pay. Bring it on."

Frank was stealing some hard looks at the five men while their attention was on the waitress. One of them looked familiar, but he couldn't put a name to the face or dredge up where he knew the man from. But he had definitely seen him before. He had never seen the other four.

"When's the livery open?" one of the strangers asked.

"When I get ready to open it," Bob said. "And that's gonna be in about another hour or whenever I finish a pot of coffee. Whichever comes first."

"We want to stable our horses when you do."

"I didn't figure you wanted to buy the place," Bob replied. "It ain't for sale noways."

"You 'bout a cantankerous old coot, ain't you?" another of the hard cases asked. "What put the ants in your pants this early in the morning?"

"And you got a smart mouth for a newcomer to town," Bob popped right back. "You better rein it in some."

"If I don't?" the mouthy stranger asked.

"Then you and your horse can ride on," Bob told him.

The man pushed back his chair and stood up. "I don't have to take that kind of crap from the likes of you!"

Frank stood up, his hand near the butt of his .45. He said nothing. Just stood there.

"You buyin' into this argument, mister?" the hard case asked.

"Could be." Frank's words were softly offered, but they held a clear note of warning.

"Then maybe my friends will decide to buy in too."

"Then I reckon there'll be a lot of blood on the floor of this cafe," Frank responded.

"That don't have to happen if that old coot would apologize."

"When hell freezes over," Bob said. He pushed back his chair and stood up, brushing back his coat, exposing a holstered pistol. "I ain't no gunfighter, but I reckon I can hook and draw in time to get lead in at least one of you."

The stranger's friends pushed back their chairs and stood up. The situation in the cafe suddenly grew very tense.

"I know you," the man Frank thought he'd seen before said to him. "I disremember your name, but I've seen you somewheres."

"Could be."

"You from Texas?"

"A long time ago."

"You a lawman, right?"

"I've toted a badge from time to time," Frank said.

"I think you threw me in jail one time. After you beat hell out of me. Matter of fact, I'm shore it was you. I always said if I ever seen you again, I'll kill you. Right now is as good a time as any, I reckon."

"I reckon so," Frank replied.

"You got a name?" the stranger asked.

"Everybody has a name," Frank said.

"You 'bout as smart-mouthed as your old fart

friend, mister. I'm just tryin' to find out somethin'
to put on your tombstone."

"Don't worry about my tombstone," Frank replied with a very tight smile. "You'd best be wor-
rying about your own grave marker." Frank had
already picked out the first two of the riders he was
going to put lead in. And out of the corner of his
eye he had seen the cook lift a sawed-off shotgun
and get ready to let it roar. The waitress was obviously Western born and reared. She was ready to
hit the floor behind the counter. She didn't appear
to be overly frightened, just ready to kiss the floor.

"Huh?" the rider questioned. "They's five of us
and only the two of you. And I don't figure that
old coot is even gonna be able to clear leather. And
you're flappin' your gums about *us* gettin' planted?
Mister, you're addled in the head."

"No," Frank countered. "I'm just real sure of
myself, that's all."

"Duke," the fifth member of the group said.
"I've seen that hombre before. I think he's a bad
one."

"Do tell, Bert? Well, he don't scare me none. I
think he's all mouth and nothin' else. I want an
apology from both of them."

"How about me?" the cook asked from the
kitchen. "Do you want me to apologize too?"

A couple of the hard cases cut their eyes. All they
could see through the narrow space between the
counter and the kitchen were the twin barrels of
the old Greener.

"Damn!" one muttered. "All of a sudden, I ain't
likin' this a-tall."

"That cannon do change things some," his partner acknowledged.

"I want to know your name, mister," the mouthy
one demanded of Frank. "I got a right to know
who I'm facin'."

"Frank Morgan."

All the puff and bluster seemed to vanish from the five hard cases. Their shoulders slumped noticeably. Several of them cussed softly, their eyes wide.

"I'm out of this," one said. "I'm a-sittin' down and puttin' my hands on the table. You watch me, Morgan. I'm through."

"All right," Frank said. "Do it."

The man sat down and placed both hands on the tabletop.

"Me too," another said. "This was all just a misunderstandin', that's all. It ain't no killin' thing." He sat down.

"Then there were three," Frank said. "That makes the odds get all evened up, don't you think, boys."

"I ain't a-feared of you, Morgan," the mouthy one said. But his words seemed to lack much conviction. "I still think you're the one that whupped me and tossed me in jail. And I swore to kill you for doin' it."

"How about you other boys?" Frank asked. "You still in this game?"

"I'm foldin'," one of the others said. "Sittin' down. You hear me, Morgan?"

"Then sit."

He sat, relief clearly showing on his face.

"Okay, Sanders," the mouth said. "It's me and you. You still game for the play?"

"I'm game. I'll take the cook."

The cook laughed at that and said, "I doubt it, stranger." He eared back the hammers on the Greener, the sound enormously loud in the suddenly very quiet cafe.

"Make your play," Frank said.

"Now!" the mouth shouted, and grabbed for his pistol.

Twenty-eight

Frank shot the mouth twice just as the man's hand touched the butt of his pistol. He shifted the muzzle of his Colt just as the cook's shotgun roared. The mouth had just hit the floor when Sanders's head blew apart, the full loads of both barrels catching him on the side of the head and very nearly decapitating him . . . What it did do was make a big mess on the wall.

The waitress slowly picked herself up from the floor and was peeking over the edge of the counter. She grimaced at the sight, shook her head, and said, "I better get the mop bucket and some rags."

"I didn't even get to trigger off a shot," Bob complained. "I must really be gettin' slow. Damnit to hell anyways."

"But you stood tough beside me," Frank said. "That counts for a hell of a lot, Bob."

"It do, don't it?" Bob said, his eyes shining bright.

"For a fact, partner."

Bob stood a bit taller at the word "partner."

Frank shifted the muzzle of his Colt toward the three men sitting quietly at the table. "You boys have some explaining to do. Get to it."

"What do you mean?" one asked.

"Who are you and what are you doing in this town?"

"Can't you toss a blanket over Sanders yonder?" another said, glancing toward the hard case with most of his head missing. "That's a disgustin', awful sight to look at."

Half a dozen locals had crowded into the cafe, including the undertaker. "I'll get a sheet," the undertaker said.

The waitress began busying herself mopping up the blood, wiping off the wall, and trying to keep from puking. She finally said, "Excuse me," and ran out the front door.

"You can put up that hogleg," the third hard case said to Frank. "We ain't gonna throw no lead."

"Talk to me," Frank replied. "Answer my questions."

"We was 'posed to meet some ol' boys here in town. Got a wire in a town where we was stayin' west of here."

"What ol' boys?" Frank asked.

"Max Parsons and Red Henson. They said they had some work for us."

"What sort of work?"

"They didn't say and we didn't ask."

"What kind of work do you boys do?"

"Near'bouts anything that pays."

"Such as robbing and killing?"

"Oh, no, sir, Mr. Morgan," another of the hard cases blurted out. "We ain't prone to do nothin' like that."

"Oh, I'm sure that's true," Frank said sarcastically. "Just like Parsons and Henson are model citizens, right?"

The three men fell silent.

The undertaker returned with a sheet and tossed it over the man with part of a head. "You boys got money to pay for the funerals?"

"We got some hard money, yeah. And some

greenbacks. We don't want nothin' fancy for 'em. No wailers and moaners. Just a box and a hole."

"That's what you'll get. Some of you boys help tote these bodies out of here and over to my place, will you?"

The bodies of the dead men were carried out and the waitress returned, a little pale-looking, and resumed her cleaning up.

"I think you fellows are holding back on me," Frank said. "I think you know a lot more than you're telling. Maybe a few days in jail will loosen your tongues."

A local stepped forward. "Mr. Morgan, I was appointed temporary city marshal while you was gone. You want me to lock them up?"

"Yes. I'll come over to the jail and talk to them later." Frank waggled the muzzle of his Colt. "Get up and shuck those gunbelts, boys. Then move out."

"You're makin' a mistake," one of the gunhands said. "We ain't done nothin'. We don't know nothin'."

"Maybe time will jog your memories," Frank said. "Move!"

Frank followed the men out onto the boardwalk, and stood while the marshal marched the trio over to the jail. Then he walked back into the cafe, got a sack of biscuits and a few slices of fried bacon for Dog, and went back to the livery and watched while Dog ate. When he was finished, Dog curled up on the floor beside the bed and went to sleep.

Frank left the door to the small living quarters open, so Dog could come and go out of the room, then walked back up the boardwalk toward the cafe. On the way, he met Bob.

"I spoke with Eaton over at the general store and with Slattery at the apothecary," Bob said. "They think that them damn Olsen boys will surely come back here with some hoodlums and try to pull something. They'll stand ready."

"Good. How about some of the other locals?"

"I told the cook over to the cafe and he's with us all the way. He said he'd talk to his brother and tell him about it."

"All right. Start talking it up to people you know can use a gun and will stand. I don't think we've got a lot of time to waste."

"I don't either, Frank."

"Has anyone seen Fuller Ross?"

Bob laughed at the memory of the last sighting of the rich Easterner. "Not that I know of. He's probably holed up in Thompson's barn. It's his wife I'd worry about. 'Specially if she gets her hands on another knife."

Frank smiled and nodded his head. "I'm going to move around some, Bob. Take care and keep your eyes open."

"Will do."

Frank walked on for half a block. A local trotted across the street and hailed him. "Mr. Morgan! Marshal Burton wants to see you?"

"Who?" Frank asked, puzzled for a moment. Then it dawned on him who the man was talking about. "Oh. Sure. He in his office?"

"Yes, sir."

"I'll get right over there."

"Them troublemakers I put in jail want to talk to you, Mr. Morgan," the newly appointed town marshal said. "Whilst you're doin' that, I'm gonna go get me some breakfast. Close the front door when you're done."

Frank walked to the short row of cells and stood staring at the three men for a moment. After a moment of silence, he said. "Well, what it is, boys?"

"We want to make a deal with you, Morgan."

"What kind of deal?"

"We'll tell you what we know, you turn us loose."

"How do I know you have anything to say I want to hear?"

"We do, and you can believe that."

"What about?"

"Sonny and his gang."

"All right. It's a deal."

"Well, Sonny ain't from the city original."

"So?"

"He run off there about ten years ago. After he kidnapped a miner and his wife in California. He killed 'em both after he got the ransom money."

"Nice fellow, isn't he?"

"Matter of fact, he ain't. I don't trust him a-tall."

"That's why we agree to level with you, Morgan," the second man said. "We want to get gone from here 'fore Sonny and his gang hit the town."

"Yeah," the third man said. "We're afeared he'll find us in jail and think we talked and kill us all."

"How do I know you won't join up with Sonny as soon as I turn you loose?"

"You don't. But we'll give you our word we won't."

"Your word?"

"It ain't worth much, is it?"

"Not a whole hell of a lot."

"It's all we got, Morgan. We got eatin' money, and that's all."

"Where is Sonny and his gang now?"

"Out yonder somewheres." The outlaw waved a hand.

"When's he going to hit the town?"

"Today. This afternoon, I think. We was 'posed to get into place and wait for them to strike. Then we was to hit the bank whilst the gang shot up the town and grabbed up them rich women again."

"And any other women they could . . . for pleasuring, you know," another outlaw added.

"And then kill them when they were done?"

"Yeah. I wasn't too keen on that part. Killin' women ain't somethin' I ever done. I've kilt men for money, but never no woman nor child."

"How big is his gang?"

"That we don't know. That's the God's truth, Morgan. Don't none of us know that. But I 'spect they's forty of 'em at least. Maybe more."

Frank nodded his head. "All right. It's a deal. But you get the hell out of town and you keep riding. If I see you back in this town, I'll kill you. Understood?"

"We understand. And you don't have to worry about seein' us again. We're gone, Morgan. Fast as we can get to our horses, we'll shake the dust of this town."

Frank found the keys and unlocked the cells. "Git!"

The three outlaws got.

Frank found Bob and told him what the outlaws had said.

"You believe what them yahoos told you?" the liveryman asked.

"Yes, I do. As far as the attack on the town goes. As for their not taking part in it, no. I think they're probably riding hard for Sonny's location right now. We'll see them again. And when I see them, I'll kill them. I warned them."

Bob looked for a moment into Frank's very cold pale eyes. He suppressed a shudder. "So how much time you figure we have?"

"Couple of hours, maybe less, maybe more."

"You damn calm about it, Frank."

"No point in getting into a panic. That won't help solve the problem. Pass the word to the townspeople, Bob. Let's get ready for a fight. But do it quietly. Women and kids and the elderly in the safest location you can find."

"That would be the church, I reckon. It's mostly stone. I'll have the folks put food and water in there."

"All right, sounds good. Let's go. We don't have a lot of time to get ready for one hell of a fight. I'll warn the Easterners and then meet you back at the livery. That'll be where we make our stand."

"Good location. We can control most of one end of town."

"Let's get moving."

Frank found the Easterners and warned them what was coming.

"Damn that Sonny!" Vanderhoot said. "He came highly recommended."

"The people who recommended him might well be a part of the kidnapping, Horace. I'd look into that when you get back to the city."

"I'll do that, Frank. Now then, we can all shoot, and I think you know by now we'll stand and fight. Where do you want us?"

"Right here in the wagons, I reckon, Horace. Put the women in the center and form a human circle around them."

"The way the settlers used to fight the Indians?"

Frank smiled. "Pretty much, Horace."

"Consider it done. We'll hold our own."

"I know you will. Good luck."

Phil stopped Frank as he walked back toward the livery. "The telegrapher just told me the wires are down, Frank. Looks like the attack on the town is real."

"I never doubted it. You spreading the word?"

"Yes. I've told people to gather up all the ammunition they can lay their hands on and get ready for a fight."

"There might be fires, Phil. Tell the people to fill water barrels and have buckets handy. And don't panic. That's what the outlaws are counting on."

"Will do, Frank."

Frank walked the town and nodded his head in approval at what he saw. The citizens were preparing for a fight and going about it without panic. Those stores that had opened early were being closed up, and the people were arming themselves. Animals were being taken off the street and stabled. In small groups, the old, the young, and many of the women were moving toward the church, most carrying packets of food.

Frank walked to the livery and filled all the loops in a cartridge belt. He tucked a spare six-gun behind his belt and picked up his rifle.

"You stay in this room," he told Dog. "You hear me?"

Dog wagged his tail.

"I'll take that as yes." Frank stepped out to the front and waited. There was nothing else he could do.

Twenty-nine

Frank rolled and smoked a cigarette, all the while wishing he had a cup of good strong coffee to go with it. After a few minutes he said to hell with it and went back to his quarters in the livery, added more wood to the potbellied, and put some water on to boil. Just as Frank added the coffee, Bob walked in, carrying a sawed-off double barreled shotgun, a bandolier of shells looped across his chest.

"I reckon the townspeople are as ready as we'll ever be," Bob said. "Damned if it isn't warmin' up outside. By now we should have had at least one good snow. This is shapin' up to be a strange winter."

Frank did not ask if any of the outlaws had been spotted. If they had, the air would have been filled with gunfire. "This weather suits me just fine, Bob. I want to get down south some before we get snowed in."

"I was kinda hopin' you'd stick around, Frank. The town folk like you just fine."

"I didn't get the nickname of Drifter because I stay very long in one place, Bob."

"That could change."

"Probably won't, though. I enjoy wandering, most of the time. I want to see everything I can that lies west of the Mississippi River."

"How about east of it?"

Frank shook his head. "Doesn't interest me. Too damn settled. Too many laws that are too restrictive."

"I can shore agree with that. When the war ended, I beat it back to the West as fast as I could. Never had no desire to go back East." He looked at Frank for a few seconds. "Never had no urge to settle down with a woman and raise kids?"

"Not in a long time, Bob. Besides, I'm too old to be thinking about raising kids." Frank smiled. "I don't have the patience for it."

"You didn't have no kids from your marriage?"

"You know about that?"

"Accordin' to the books and articles about you, you was married once."

"I was married briefly, a long time ago. Had a son. He doesn't like me very much, and really, I don't blame him. We didn't know about each other during his young years. He was raised kind of fancy back East."

"Went to them fancy schools, hey?"

"Oh, yes."

"I don't have much use for most Easterners." Bob punctuated that by spitting on the ground. "Most city folks, that is. I met a lot of good country boys from the East durin' the war. But them damn Eastern city folks give me a pain in the butt."

Frank laughed softly. "Theirs is a different way of life, Bob. For a fact."

"And it'll git worser as the years go on, I betcha. They got more damn laws than fleas on a coyote. And they don't know how to deal with criminals neither. Hang 'em or shoot 'em, that's the way I see it. I think if you take a life whilst commitin' a crime, you give a life. I think that's only fair, don't you?"

"Yes, I do. But times are changing, Bob."

"I hope I don't see them changes out here. Not in my lifetime." He fell silent for a moment. "Frank? You notice anything sorta queer?"

"What do you mean?"

"It got real quiet all of a sudden. Real still like."

"Yes, I noticed that."

"Them damn outlaws is comin', ain't they?"

"I think they're already here, Bob. I think they've probably been slipping in close for several minutes."

At the other end of town, a dog began barking. Frank and Bob heard the owner calling the animal, and the barking stopped.

"They're here," Frank said.

Beside him, Frank could sense Bob tensing. "Where? Can you see any of them?"

"Not yet. But they're working their way into town."

"How do you know?"

"I just know, Bob. I've lived my life on the edge of a knife, so to speak. These things either come to a man naturally, or you're dead."

"I reckon so, Frank."

Both of them stepped back into the semidarkness of the barn when they heard a shot coming from the far end of town.

"Take the back, Bob. Get up in the loft."

"Right." He paused and turned around. "Good luck, Frank."

Frank smiled and nodded his head.

Bob climbed up the ladder and disappeared amid the bales of hay.

Frank heard another shot, which was followed by a scream of pain, then the word "No!" shouted out. That was followed by another shot. "Goddamn you!" the man shouted. Then silence.

"That sounded like Martin O'Dell," Bob called

from the loft. "He lives in the last house on the other side of Main Street."

"Married?"

"Widow. His wife died 'bout three years ago."

"They're lootin' the O'Dell house!" a man yelled. "I think they've killed Martin."

"Stay where you are," another local shouted. "Don't go out into the street."

"I got to see about Martin! I got to!"

"Who is that?" Frank called up to Bob.

"Jack Harvey," Bob called.

"If he goes out into the street, he's dead."

The local ran out of his house and into the street. Half-a-dozen shots immediately slammed the morning. Jack Harvey was stopped cold and turned around by the impacting lead. He fell to the street and lay still.

"He never would listen to no one nohow," Bob called from the loft. "I got to get back to the rear of the barn. Them outlaws got to show their ugly faces sooner or later."

"Smoke starting to come from the O'Dell house," Frank said. "The outlaws have fired the house." Frank listened as a woman's screaming shrilled the morning air.

"Bob? Was Harvey married?"

"Yeah. I 'spect that's her screamin'."

"You people in town!" a man's voice shouted. "Listen to this woman holler. You like that? My boys are pleasuring themselves with her."

"Does that make you big brave men?" a local yelled.

"This is what we're gonna do with all the women in town!" the outlaw hollered.

"That's Sonny," Frank said.

"We want the Easterners and Frank Morgan!" Sonny yelled. "You give us them and we'll ride out. How about it?"

"Good plan," Frank muttered. "Turn the locals against us."

Mrs. Harvey began shrieking and begging for someone to help her as she was brutalized by the outlaws.

"Let's give them the outsiders," a man called from the middle of the small business district. "We don't owe them folks nothing."

"Aw, shut up, Chris," another local called.

"Yeah," Phil called from the saloon. "Shut your mouth, you damn coward."

Mrs. Harvey's begging and screaming continued unabated.

"We got some outlaws behind the barn, Frank," Bob called. "They've ringed the town." Bob's shotgun boomed. Outside, behind the barn, a man yelled in pain. "I didn't kill him," Bob called a moment later. "But for shore he's out of the game."

"How many pistols you have, Bob?" Frank called.

"Two. They might overrun the barn, but they'll pay a hell of a price 'fore they get it done, you can bet."

"Nothing happening up here. I'm moving to the rear."

"Come on. I 'spect it's gonna get lively 'fore long. I might need the help."

Frank walked to the rear of the huge livery and chanced a look outside. He could just make out what he thought might be a man's leg, showing through the slats of the bottom of a chicken coop. Frank took aim and squeezed off a shot.

"Oh, hell!" a man yelled. "I'm hit. My knee is busted." He started cussing.

Bob's shotgun boomed above Frank, and part of the old coop blew apart, and so did the gunman with the busted leg.

"I thought I might as well put him out of his misery," Bob called.

"I sure believe you did," Frank answered.

"Is that you, Morgan?" a man called.

"Yeah."

"It's me, Red Henson. I'm gonna kill you, Morgan."

"If I don't kill you first," another gunslick shouted.

"Who the hell are you?" Frank questioned.

"Paul Hardin, you bastard."

"I thought I killed you and your buddy, Moses Gunther back at the fort."

"Naw. You must have been dreamin'. But I'm damn shore gonna put lead in you, Morgan. What do you think about that, Drifter?"

Frank had a suspicion that they were trying to keep him talking so they could better pinpoint his location. He offered no reply, and instead slipped to his left, near to the far wall, and peeked out through a wide crack. He could see just a portion of a man's leg: a boot and part of the leg just below the knee. Frank took aim and let his Colt bang.

The man's leg flew out from under him and he hit the ground hard and rolled. Rolled just enough to present a clear target. Frank squeezed off another shot before the man could get behind cover, and the lead dusted the outlaw, hitting him in the side and blowing out the other side.

"You bastard!" Hardin yelled. "You kilt Harry. Me and him was pards. I'm gonna get you, Morgan."

Frank did not reply. He hit the floor as the lead started flying through the old boards of the livery. Frank crawled away. He slung his rifle up into the loft, then jumped up and grabbed hold of a rafter, swinging himself up to the loft. He picked up his rifle and moved to a window in the rear of the loft. The outlaws were busy laying down a withering field of fire, all directed at the ground floor, where they believed Frank to be.

Frank sighted in a man about fifty yards from the livery, crouched beside an outhouse behind a store. He squeezed the trigger and the man tried to stand up. His legs wouldn't support his weight and he toppled over. He did not move.

Frank's shot was not noticed by the outlaws behind the barn. It was lost in the roaring of their own gunfire.

The townspeople were fighting back. Up and down Main Street, and in the rows of houses that made up the residential area behind the business area, the sounds of gunfire could be heard. The surprise attack by the outlaws had failed. Now it all came down to which side could outlast the other in this confrontation.

That question was momentarily answered when a man shouted, "Let's get out of here. This ain't workin', boys."

"Hold your ground," Sonny yelled. "We can do this. Miller, you and Brownie get inside the general store. Fill up that farmer's wagon in the rear. Get everything we need."

"Grab some wimmin," somebody else yelled. "I got me an itch I cain't scratch."

"Yeah," another outlaw hollered. "I think they're all in the church. Let's go there."

Sonny quickly reacted. "No!" he shouted. "Seize the town first. Use your heads, men. The women can wait. They'll be here. But kill the men first. And don't forget about the bank full of money."

"The man isn't entirely stupid," Frank muttered. He moved to the front of the livery, hoping to get a shot.

An outlaw tried to run across the wide main street. Before Frank could get off a shot, the townspeople opened fire. The outlaw was hit at least half a dozen times by rifle and pistol fire. He spun around in the street like a crazed top before falling to the ground. He tried to rise but could not. He died in the middle of the street.

"Two of you keep Morgan and that old fart pinned down in the barn!" Sonny yelled. "Rest of you concentrate on the stores. Take them one by one by sheer force. Move, damnit. Let's go, boys. Some of you get among the wagons of the Easterners. I want those people alive for ransom. This time we won't screw it up. Move, boys!"

"I want me a taste of them women," an outlaw yelled.

But the outlaws had not reckoned on the renewed courage of the city men. When the outlaws moved to take the wagons, they were met with a hail of buckshot from shotguns in the hands of angry city men who were quickly adapting to the ways of the West when it came to dealing with outlaws.

"To hell with the dudes!" one outlaw shouted after seeing his buddy cut in half by a shotgun blast at very close range.

"To hell with this town!" another yelled. "This ain't workin'. Let's get gone from here 'fore we all get kilt."

"Fall back and regroup!" Sonny shouted over the gunfire. "Fall back east to the edge of town and let's talk this over."

The two men behind the livery slipped away unhurt.

"We won the first battle," Bob called. "But it ain't over. They'll be back, you can bet on that."

"That they will," Frank replied. "And we'd better be ready for anything."

Thirty

The O'Dell house blew up, bits and pieces of the structure sent flying through the air by the heavy charge. A large timber landed directly on the body of Jack Harvey, crushing the dead man.

"Dynamite," Bob said. "Now they're gettin' serious about this fight."

"Hold your position," Frank called to Bob after carefully checking out the terrain behind the livery barn. He could spot no one. "I've got to put a stop to this right now." He climbed down the ladder from the loft.

"You got a plan?"

"No. But I've got to do something."

"That might mean gettin' yourself killed, Frank. Let's talk about this thing."

"You see any of Sonny's gang from your position?"

"No one close. They've pulled back toward the edge of town. They's a couple of them hidin' behind that empty building 'bout fifty yards to our left."

Frank walked to his quarters and knelt down beside Dog, petting the animal for a few seconds. "You stay here," he said softly. "Be safe, ol' boy. You hear?"

Dog wagged his tail and licked Frank's hand.

Back at the rear of the livery, Frank called up to

Bob. "I'm going. You hold down the place and watch your butt."

"Will do, Frank. You take 'er easy."

Frank ran from the livery to Bob's small house. His move drew no fire. He took a deep breath and ran to the side of the outhouse, again drawing no fire from the outlaws.

"I don't think them thugs behind the empty building can see you, Frank," Bob called softly. "But I can't get no clear shot at them. If you can make the ditch, you'll stand a better chance. It's deep, but it's gonna be muddy as hell."

Frank lifted a hand and ran for the ditch that ran the entire length of the business district. There were a couple inches of water in the ditch, and it was cold. Crouching low, Frank carefully worked his way toward the far end of town, occasionally chancing a quick look over the edge of the ditch. The screams from the Harvey house had ceased. The woman had either fainted, or the outlaws had killed her to shut her up. Frank hoped it was the former.

"You townspeople listen to me!" Sonny shouted from the other side of the block. "We'll blow up your damn town and kill you all if you don't give us the Easterners and Frank Morgan. You hear me?"

"This damn safe is a monster," a man yelled from the bank. "We'll never get this thing open."

"Blow it open," Sonny yelled.

Frank could not make out the words of the reply, for just at that instant, someone opened fire from a building on Main Street. Frank didn't doubt the outlaw's words about the safe being a monster, for he'd seen it once when visiting with Doc Raven in the bank/stage office. And he doubted the outlaws had enough dynamite to blow it open. What they would probably wind up doing was destroying the building while the safe remained intact.

"Morgan!" a man yelled behind him.

Frank threw himself to one side just as the outlaw's gun boomed, the slug tearing up dirt at the lip of the ditch.

The outlaw fired again, and again missed.

Frank didn't miss. His bullet tore into the mans chest and turned him around. Frank was out of the ditch and running before the hard-hit man tumbled to the ground.

"Did you see Morgan, Lucky?" someone yelled.

Lucky didn't reply. His luck had run out.

Frank reached the rear of a building and paused there for a moment, catching his breath.

"Lucky?" the man again shouted. "Lucky! Damnit, you bes' answer me, boy! Did you see Morgan?"

Frank slipped to the side of the building and glanced up the narrow space between the buildings. It was clear except for the broken bottles and other trash that littered the ground. He stepped into the space and carefully made his way toward the street.

When Frank was halfway to the street, a man ran into the space, a rifle in his hands. The unshaven man, dressed in very dirty, trail-worn clothing, stared at Frank for a couple of heartbeats and then yelled, "Morgan!" He lifted his rifle.

Frank shot him. The man stumbled backward, a startled look on his features. He lifted the muzzle of his rifle, and Frank put another .45 slug into him. This time the man went down. He stayed down.

Frank turned and ran back toward the rear of the building.

"Howie, was that you?" a man yelled.

Howie, if indeed that was Howie that Frank had

just sent into the cold bony arms of death, did not reply.

A few seconds later the man shouted, "Howie's down and so is Lucky. Morgan's on the prowl. Got to be him."

"Five thousand dollars and first go at the prettiest woman in town to the man who kills Morgan!" Sonny yelled.

Frank opened the back door of a building, and knew immediately by the smell he had stepped into the back room of the saddle shop. He could also smell the strong odor of fresh blood and relaxed bowels and bladder. He didn't have to see the body of whoever it was to know the man was dead.

He walked through the workroom and into the showroom. There, he saw the sprawled body of the saddle-maker. The man had caught a bullet in the center of his forehead.

"One more local paying a heavy price," Frank murmured. He wondered if the man was married with a family.

"Where'd the son of a bitch go?" The shouted question came from outside, jarring abruptly into Frank's musing.

Hard gunfire rattled the morning, coming from the stone church's location.

"Leave the church alone," a man hollered. "That's where all the women is. Don't shoot at the church, you might hit one of them."

"Well, them damn women is shootin' at me!" a man shouted. "What the hell am I supposed to do?"

"Leave them be," Sonny yelled. "We can deal with them later. Get that damn bank vault open."

"Morgan's disappeared," another outlaw yelled. "I ain't got no idea where he went."

A shotgun boomed and a man yelled in pain.

"The bitch done shot me in the ass!" the man hollered. "Oh, hell, my ass is on far!"

The shotgun boomed again.

"Jesus Jumpin' Christ!" another man screamed. "She's shot *me* in the ass! I'm ruined, boys. Somebody kill that damn woman!"

Frank smiled. He had a pretty good idea who that woman might be.

"Way to go, Clarabelle," a woman yelled. "Shoot the scum again."

"I was right," Frank muttered.

"I want her," an outlaw yelled. "That's Sister Clarabelle. She's my type of woman."

"Lonesome Howard," Frank whispered.

"Well, you can damn sure have her," a man yelled. "You and her would make quite a pair. Ain't neither one of you got a lick of sense."

"Shut your blasphemous mouth, Stoner," Lonesome hollered. "She's a good Christian woman."

"She's a fat pig is what she is," Stoner replied. "And you're a damn idiot!"

"I'll kill you when we get done with this town," Lonesome yelled in reply. "I'll kill you in the name of the Lord."

"Shut up, the both of you," Sonny shouted.

Frank chanced a glance out the busted front window of the saddle shop. None of the outlaws were in sight. He had no target . . . yet.

The gunfire in the town had dwindled down to only sporadic firing.

"Whoopee!" an outlaw yelled. "I done found me a high-yeller nigger gal! I likes them young nigger gals. I—"

A shotgun blast shattered the morning, followed by a man's thudding to the boardwalk. Frank smiled. He had a hunch that Grandmother Marvella had given the outlaw a taste of her shotgun.

"Johnny!" a man yelled. "Johnny!"

"Johnny's dead on the boardwalk," a man yelled. "He caught a full load of buckshot in the belly. Damn near tore him in two."

"Who killed him?"

"Some damned old nigger woman. Looked like she was about a hundred years old."

"You shoot her?"

"Naw. I couldn't get a shot off."

Frank wondered briefly why Marvella didn't take Bessie to the church. He didn't have to wonder long. Clarabelle suddenly hollered, "You damned godless heathens! Leave this town, all of you!"

"If we don't?" Frank recognized the voice of Brooks Olsen.

"Marvella and me will wipe out the whole filthy lot of you!"

Clarabelle had hooked up with Marvella. Frank smiled at that. Now *that* was quite a pair, for sure.

"You fat pig!" Brooks hollered. "I'm gonna shoot you personal. Right in your big fat ass just to see you jump and holler."

"Then I'm gonna hop on and poke that good-lookin' high-yeller girl!" Martin yelled.

"The hell you will!" Bessie yelled.

Frank finally got a chance to put lead in an outlaw when one showed himself near the mouth of an alley. Frank lifted his rifle and sighted the man in, squeezing the trigger. The outlaw rose up on tiptoe for a couple of seconds, then pitched forward onto the boardwalk. He drummed his boots for a moment, then passed on into eternity.

"Where'd that shot come from?" Sonny hollered.

"I don't know," a man shouted. "I couldn't tell. Somewheres acrost the street."

"Where's that doctor who lives here?" Sonny yelled. "I got two men with buckshot in their asses."

"I ain't seen him, Sonny," Brooks called. "I reckon he's out of town."

"And we have plenty more buckshot where that came from, you sorry pieces of buffalo turd!" Clarabelle yelled.

"Ain't she somethin'?" Lonesome Howard shouted. "I mean to tell you boys, that there is my kind of woman."

"And you're a damned old hypocritical fool!" Clarabelle yelled.

"I think I love you, Sister!" Lonesome hollered.

"That makes me want to puke!" Clarabelle quickly yelled.

"I'm gonna grab you up and tote you off into the woods, Sister," Lonesome shouted. "We can be the modern-day version of Adam and Eve."

"Now I *am* gonna puke!" Clarabelle said.

"You'll learn to love me, Sister. I'll grow on you."

"Like a big ugly wart!" Clarabelle shouted.

"My God, ain't she somethin'!" Lonesome said. "Talk dirty to me some more, Sister. I'm gettin' all excited."

"Crazy son of a bitch!" Frank muttered.

"You fellas ready to blow that safe?" Sonny yelled.

"Not yet," came the reply.

"What the hell's the holdup?"

"A fuse long enough for us to get clear."

"Hurry up, will you!"

"We just about got it. Couple more minutes and she'll blow."

"Get clear, everybody!" Sonny yelled.

Frank slipped back outside and headed for the ditch behind Main Street. He didn't want to be close to the bank/stage office when the dynamite blew. He had a hunch the explosion was going to take out several buildings and kill or maim anyone close to the blast. And he suspected the huge safe would still be intact.

Frank made the ditch without being spotted, and found a relatively dry part of the depression in which to belly down. Wouldn't be long now.

"You better hunker down, Sugar Bugger," Lonesome called to Clarabelle. "When that dynamite blows, it's gonna be like the end of the world for a few seconds. I wouldn't want nothin' to happen to a single hair on your precious head."

"Sugar Bugger!" Clarabelle hollered.

"Yep. You my precious Sugar Bugger," Lonesome yelled.

Clarabelle then told Lonesome to kiss a certain part of her rather vast anatomy.

"I'm gettin' more and more worked up, my precious flower."

Frank couldn't make out Clarabelle's reply, but he was certain it was less than complimentary.

"You're an idiot, Lonesome!" an outlaw yelled.

"I'm in love!" Lonesome hollered. "Praise the Lord."

In the ditch, Frank grimaced at the words from the Bible-quoting killer.

"Everybody ready for the big blow?" an outlaw yelled.

"Everybody get down!" Sonny called. "Light the fuse!"

"It's sputterin'!"

Frank braced himself.

Thirty-one

The explosion created a concussion that blew out every window along Main Street. Bricks, glass, and chunks of wood were blown high into the sky, and hens stopped laying and nearby cows stopped giving milk. When the debris began raining down the larger chunks knocked holes in roofs and awnings and killed two outlaws by landing on their heads.

The stage office/bank building and both buildings on either side of it were completely destroyed.

The huge safe was moved back about a foot, but was undamaged except for a few scratches.

"Damn!" Frank whispered when the ground stopped shaking and his hearing returned.

He raised up and peered over the edge of the ditch just in time to see an outlaw he knew was part of Sonny's group run into the alley, both hands filled with six-guns. Frank shot him.

He shoved a couple of fresh rounds into his rifle and rolled out of the ditch, scrambling toward the buildings.

Lonesome Howard came stumbling out of an alley, shaking his head. "Sweet Pea, darling, are you hurt, my precious flower."

Clarabelle gave him a blast from her shotgun.

Luckily for Lonesome, it was a shell filled with birdshot, and most of the shot missed him.

"Take that, you heathen!" Clarabelle yelled.

"Does this mean you don't love me anymore, Sugar Bugger?" Lonesome yelled, running back toward the debris-littered alley.

Clarabelle gave him another blast just as Lonesome reached the alley, the buckshot missing him and knocking holes in the building.

"You bitch!" Lonesome hollered. "I could have give you a good life. Now I'm gonna have to kill you for rejecting my affections and breaking my heart,"

"The man has become as crazy as a lizard," Frank muttered.

The debris that was once part of the empty building on one side of the stage office/bank began moving and an outlaw hauled himself out of the rubble and stood up, looking dazed and very disoriented.

"Where's that damn horse that threw me?" he said. "I ain't never seen a horse that I couldn't ride. Put a loop on him and get him over here."

"Get down, you damn fool!" a man yelled at him.

The dazed outlaw took one step and the floor gave way. He fell up to his waist in the jagged hole and was stuck there.

"Can't you people do anything right?" Sonny hollered.

"Oh, go to hell, Sonny!" one of his men yelled.

"Who said that?" Sonny shouted.

No one replied.

The assault against the town of South Raven appeared to be a standoff. The town had lost three buildings along Main Street from the explosion, and one house due to fire. The outlaws had about a dozen men dead. Only one woman had been taken by the outlaws, and as far as Frank could tell, only three or four local men had been lost.

Frank tried the back door to a building, and it was unlocked. He stepped into the storeroom of a dress shop and walked to the front. The show window was gone, shattered by the blast. Frank slipped to the front, broken glass crunching under his boots, and looked out. He could hear the sounds of hooves fading away from the far edge of town. Several of the outlaws were heading out, giving up on the plan to take over the town.

For whatever reason, something that would surely never be known, a lone outlaw chose that instant to try to run across the wide main street. A dozen guns barked, and a dozen bullets fired by local men hit the outlaw and sent him spinning around and around in the middle of the street. He was dead before he hit the dirt.

The old adage that had been repeated dozens of times came to Frank's mind. You don't buffalo a Western town. Westerners just won't let it happen.

Frank listened intently as the sounds of several more galloping horses reached him. More outlaws were giving up the fight and hauling their ashes out of town.

"Let's get the hell out of here!" a man yelled. "This ain't workin' out."

"I'm with you, Shorty," an outlaw yelled. "I'm pullin' out."

"Come on, Sonny," yet another man called. "It's all over. Let's get out while the gettin' is good."

"Yeah," Lonesome Howard shouted. "I'm with you boys. Let's get goin'. Morgan? You hear me, Morgan?"

Frank waited silently in the shop.

"I'm gonna make it my life's ambition to hunt you down and kill you. You hear me, Morgan?"

"You're at the end of a long list, Lonesome," Frank murmured.

"Get to the horses, boys!" Sonny yelled. "There's

always another day and another town. We're done here."

"Get me out of here!" the outlaw stuck up to his waist in the floor yelled. "Goddamnit, don't leave me here."

"You're on your own, Davy," a man yelled. "Sorry. Good luck to you."

"You rotten no-goods!" Davy yelled, trying without success to work his way out of the hole in the floor.

"So much for honor among thieves," Frank said.

"We'll take care of Davy," Clarabelle yelled. "We'll hang him!"

"I'm gonna kill you too, Sugar Bugger!" Lonesome Howard yelled from the far end of town. "You'll regret spurning my love."

"Oh, go to hell, you crazy windbag!" Clarabelle shouted.

There was near silence in the town for several minutes, the only sounds the rapidly fading hooves of the outlaws' horses as they made their getaway from the town that had proved itself too tough for them.

Davy had ceased his struggling and cussing, resigning himself to being taken prisoner.

Frank stepped out of the dress shop and stood on the boardwalk, looking up and down the wide main street. No shots came at him. The town was clear of outlaws . . . live ones anyway. All except for Davy.

Frank heard the clop-clop of horses' hooves, and looked up toward the other end of town. Doc Raven was driving into town. He reined up and stood up in his buggy, staring in amazement at the carnage in his town. He spotted Frank and sat back down, clucking at the horse, driving up to Frank.

"What the hell happened, Frank?"

Frank quickly explained, ending with, "The

townsfolk beat them off, Doc. They stood together proud and solid."

The stone church began emptying of women and kids and the elderly. Bob walked up to Doc Raven and Frank.

"You reckon they'll be back, Frank?" Bob asked.

"I doubt it. They got a pretty good licking this time around. I don't think they'll want seconds. Is Dog all right?"

"Fit as a fiddle. I just gave him a couple of biscuits I had in my pocket, and he gobbled them right down."

Doc Raven looked over at the ruins of the stage office/bank and smiled. "That safe cost me a lot of money. Looks as though it was worth the price paid."

"Get me out of this damn hole!" Davy shouted.

"Let me get my office ready to receive patients," Doc said. He glanced over at Davy, who was frantically waving his arms. "The locals first," he added.

Frank walked the town, checking each business and home for any dead or wounded. Mrs. Harvey's throat had been cut, the last brutal act of Sonny's gang. Frank covered her with a blanket and walked on. The general store has been looted, and the farmer's wagon that had been behind the store driven off, loaded with stolen supplies. Several more homes had been looted by the outlaws, but all in all, the town of South Raven had come out of the assault looking pretty good.

The bodies of the dead outlaws were buried in a mass grave.

"Don't worry about rebuilding," Horace Vanderhoot said. "We shall pay for everything."

"Yes," Delbert Knox agreed. "Whatever the cost.

This tragic event was our fault. It's the least we can do."

"Has anyone seen Fuller Ross?" John Garver asked. "Not that I really give a damn what happened to him."

No one had.

"I hope the outlaws got him. I hope I never see him again," Mavis said bitterly.

Her remark pretty well summed up the feelings of all the Easterners.

Frank saddled up, and for over an hour tried to pick up the trail of the fleeing outlaws. But when they scattered, the gang broke up and rode off in all directions. Frank gave it up and rode back to town. He strongly suspected that he would see many of the survivors again. Especially Sonny. Many would be carrying a powerful grudge against Frank.

"I'll be pulling out in the morning," he told Bob. "There is no more I can do here. I don't think Sonny and his gang will be back."

"Well, I'll shore be damn sorry to see you go, Frank," the old liveryman said. "But I understand. And I'm with you about them outlaws. I think they took them a good bite of this town and didn't like the taste."

Frank smiled. "I believe you're right about that, Bob. I'm going to provision up now. But first I'm going over to Doc Raven's office and turn in this deputy U.S. marshal's badge. I never did like to tote a badge around."

In the doctor's office, Frank held out the badge. Doc Raven smiled and said, "Oh, you can have that. It's no good."

"What do you mean?" Frank asked.

"A deputy U.S. marshal was through here about ten years ago. His horse threw him; startled by a rattlesnake. The fall broke the man's arm. I set it.

The marshal was so grateful he gave me that badge as a souvenir. It's worthless."

"You mean . . ." Frank didn't finish it, just looked at the doctor.

"I thought it might give you more confidence if you didn't know the truth." Doc Raven chuckled. "It worked, didn't it?"

Frank started laughing. He was still laughing as he walked out of the doctor's office.

Thirty-two

Frank said his few good-byes late that afternoon, and pulled out before dawn the next morning, the packhorse Bob had given him trailing on a lead rope. Frank headed south. Days later he reined up in front of the general store in a tiny village in Nevada. Wasn't much to the town: a combination store/saloon and a couple of other buildings. Frank stepped down from the saddle and slapped the dust from his clothing, then walked into the store.

"Howdy," the man behind the counter said. "You look some tuckered, mister."

"I don't feel like running any footraces, for sure," Frank replied. "Got a place where a man can get a bath in this town?"

"No, sir, we sure don't. Barber died last year. I 'spect the town will be nothin' but a memory in a couple more years. Minin' played out, near'bouts everybody left."

"Sorry to hear that. How about a cafe?"

"Don't have one of those either. But I can offer you a plate of beans and a cup of coffee."

"That sounds good to me. Where did the people who left settle?"

"Over west and some south of here. Winnemucca. I'm headin' over there myself if I can ever find anyone stupid enough to buy me out."

Frank laughed and took the plate of beans and bread, got his cup of coffee, and walked out to the front of the store and sat down. Dog had found a shady spot and was asleep. The store owner walked out and sat down beside Frank.

"What's in those other buildings?" Frank asked.

"Nothin'. I'm all that's left."

"You must not get much business."

"Comes and goes. Whole bunch of men rode through here a few days ago. Rough-lookin' bunch, they was. But they had money and didn't mind spendin' it."

"Cowboys?"

"I don't think so. If I had to guess, I'd say they was runnin' from the law. But I didn't ask," he quickly added.

"Yeah, that's best," Frank said. "Dealing with those types, a man best be careful about the questions he asks."

"You mighty right. 'Specially when them crazy Olsen boys is in the bunch."

Frank tensed for a few seconds. "Olsen boys?"

"Horse thieves from up north of here. Both of 'em 'bout half crazy."

"Never heard of them."

"They used come down this way to steal horses." The man shook his head. "Both those boys are crazy in the head."

The store owner left Frank alone for a few moments, and Frank finished his meal, sopping up the juice with a thick hunk of bread and giving that to Dog. Dog ate it, got a drink out of the horse trough, and went back to sleep.

The store owner returned with a plate of scraps for Dog and more coffee for Frank.

"Those hard cases who rode through here," Frank said. "Which way did they head out? I want to avoid running into them, if possible."

"I heard one of them say something about Virginia City."

"Long ride."

"It ain't bad now. Take the stage road from Winnemucca down to Reno. Several places along the way to stop and provision up. And get a shave and a bath if you like."

"I would like that. Anything between here and Winnemucca?"

"Not a blessed thing. Some sheepherders and a few farmers scratchin' at the ground is all."

Frank poured another cup of coffee, rolled a smoke, and tried to pay the man for the food. "No, sir. You don't owe me a thing. I'm just thankful for the company. You sure look familiar to me, mister. You been through here before?"

"Not this way."

"You got a name?"

"Frank Morgan."

The man was still sputtering when Frank swung into the saddle and rode away,

Frank didn't push Stormy on the way west. He was in no hurry. He had been to Virginia City years back when it was a rip-roaring mining town. Now, so he had heard, the town was only a shell of what it had once been. Frank had also learned that the silver taken out of the mines at Virginia City was forty-five percent gold. When the United States Congress enacted the demonetization of silver, the Comstock Lode was already beginning to play out. By 1880, it was all but over for Virginia City.

Frank wondered if Molinelli's Hotel was still there and taking in guests. If it was, he would sure get a room there. It had been a very nice place when he had last stayed there. And Frank wondered if his old friend Nick Barton was still there; that was the reason he was traveling to the mining town.

Frank sighed as he rode west by southwest. He never figured on Sonny's bunch having the same destination in mind as his. But Nick was getting on in years, and Frank wanted to see him one more time. The men had been friends for twenty-five years, their friendship dating back to the War of Northern Aggression.

"To hell with Sonny and his pack of outlaws," Frank said. "I'm going to see Nick."

Days after leaving the lonely store owner, Frank was making camp by the stage road, along the banks of the Humboldt River, when he heard the sounds of approaching horses. He straightened up and turned around. Two men were walking their horses toward his camp. He recognized them as two men who had been in town and had ridden out with the bunch who joined Sonny.

"You boys looking for me?" Frank called.

"We shore ain't lookin' for Santa Claus," a no-account called Burke said.

Both men swung down from their saddles and stepped to one side, facing Frank, about fifty feet away from him.

"We been trailin' you for days," the other no-account said. Frank recalled that someone had called him Sandy.

"You found me," Frank replied. "Now what?"

"Now we kill you," Burke said.

Frank smiled. "You can't be any plainer than that, I reckon. But killing me won't be easy, boys. You better give that some thought."

"Nothin' to think about, Morgan," Sandy said. "You caused us to lose out on thousands of dollars of ransom money. We aim to get some of your hide for that."

Dog had moved silently off to one side, watching and listening intently.

"I'm kind of fond of my hide, boys. I don't like to part with any of it."

"We don't give a damn what you like, Morgan," Burke snapped. "When we get done killin' you, we gonna cut off your head and put it in a gunnysack and collect the bounty for it."

"Do tell?"

"We just tole you, Morgan," Sandy said. "Are you deef?"

"No, my hearing is fine. But I think both of you are stupid."

"Huh?" Burke asked.

"Stupid," Frank said. "As in ignorant. Do you understand that, or would you like me to further explain?"

"You're dead, Morgan," Burke said.

"Then make your play, Stupid."

Burke grabbed for his gun and Frank shot him in the belly. Just as Sandy was leveling the muzzle of his six-shooter, Frank put a hole in his chest. Both men went down in the dirt. Burke lifted his pistol, and Frank drilled him in the head, the .45 slug entering his right eye and blowing out the back of his head.

Sandy dropped his pistol and hollered, "I'm done, Morgan. I'm finished."

Frank walked over and kicked the pistol away from the man. "You're a damn fool, Sandy."

"I know it. But Burke said 'tween the two of us we could take you. I reckon he was wrong, weren't he?"

"Sure as hell looks like it to me."

"I'm hard hit, ain't I?"

"I'd say so."

"I ain't hurtin' none yet."

"That's good. But get ready, it's coming."

"You a cold man, Morgan."

Frank said nothing in rebuttal. A few yards away, Burke farted in death. Sandy grimaced at the sound. "I'm skirred, Morgan," he admitted.

"I'm no preacher, Sandy. Far from it. But if there's something you want to get off your chest, I'll listen."

"What the hell good would that do me now?" The man's voice was surprisingly strong considering the seriousness of his wound.

Frank shrugged and stood up.

"Where are you goin', Morgan?" Sandy asked, panic in his voice. "You ain't gonna ride off and leave me here alone, are you?"

"No. I'm going to get a spade."

"To bury Burke?"

"To bury both of you."

"You rotten son of a bitch! You didn't have to say that."

"You asked." Frank walked to the packsaddle and removed a short-handled shovel. He looked around for a good place to dig the graves. His eyes noticed a shady spot, and he headed toward it.

"Oh, God!" Sandy hollered. "I'm hurtin' somethin' awful, Morgan."

Frank ignored the cries. There was nothing he could do.

Frank dug two shallow graves. He dragged Burke's body to one and rolled him in. He did not go through the man's pockets nor take his boots or gunbelt. He tossed Burke's pistol into the grave with him and quickly shoveled in the dirt.

"Ain't you gonna say no words?" Sandy asked.

"No," Frank replied. "There is nothing to say."

"He was a good man."

"That's certainly debatable."

"Huh?"

"Never mind."

"Maybe I ain't gonna die, Morgan."

"Maybe not."

"You gonna stay with me and see?"

"If you're still alive in the morning, I'll take you into the nearest town and leave you with the doctor."

"That's mighty white of you, Morgan."

Frank said nothing. He set about making a pot of coffee and laying out some scraps of food for Dog.

"You gonna see to your dog 'fore you see to me?" Sandy asked.

"There is nothing I can do for you."

"I hate dogs."

"Your option, I reckon."

Frank listened to Sandy bitch and moan while the water boiled. He made his coffee and poured a cup, then rolled a smoke.

"Morgan?" Sandy said, his voice suddenly very weak.

"What is it?"

"They's blood a-comin' out of my mouth."

"And you want me to do what about that?"

"Pray for me, Morgan."

"The next time I talk to the Lord, I'll be sure and mention you, Sandy. I sure will."

"I think you're lyin' to me, Morgan. I don't think you'll say nothin' 'bout me to the Lord."

Sandy began gasping for breath. He tried to sit up and could not. "Morgan!" he shouted, then was still.

Frank laid his coffee cup on the ground and told Dog to stay put. He walked over to Sandy and knelt down, trying to find a pulse. He could not. He watched for some sign of breath. There was none. Frank buried the man beside his buddy, then looked heavenward.

"Here's two more for You, Lord. Do with them

as You see fit. I said I'd mention Sandy to You. And I did it. Amen."

Frank stripped saddles and bridles from the horses and turned them loose. He kept the men's rifles and several boxes of .45 and .44-40 ammo. He left the rest of their gear in the open. Somebody would be along who needed it. Sandy and Burke damn sure didn't need it any longer.

Frank fixed some supper, and just as the last light was fading, he rolled up in his blankets and went to sleep. He pulled out for Virginia City the next morning.

"Sorry, stranger," the bartender said. "I hate to tell you, but Nick was killed a couple of years ago."

"Gunfight? Nick?"

"Oh, no. Nick wasn't no hand with a gun. Robbers killed him and took his poke. Left him in an alley. It was a right nice funeral, though. Lots of folks liked Nick."

"I'm sure they did," Frank replied. "Did they catch the men who did it?"

"No," the bartender said, eyeing Frank closely, his gaze suddenly wary. "But ever'body knows who done it. Just couldn't prove it."

"And who might that be?"

"What's your name, mister?"

"The name is Frank Morgan and I asked you a question."

"Ah . . . yes, sir! Couple of fellows name of Jess Center and Gene Dale."

"They still around?"

"Yes, sir. They'd be shootin' pool right about now, I reckon. The billiard parlor is right down this street." He pointed. "Thataway."

"Thanks."

"Mister?"

Frank turned around to face the bartender. "Yes?"

"Are you really Frank Morgan? *The* Frank Morgan?"

"That's my name."

The bartender gulped a couple of times. "I thought you was dead, Mr. Morgan. I mean . . . that's the word I got a few months back."

"Somebody lied."

"I guess so."

Frank walked out of the saloon and headed for the marshal's office across the street. Frank shoved the door open and stepped inside. The marshal was seated at his desk, and stared at Frank for a few seconds.

Before the marshal could speak, Frank said, "Were you wearing that badge when Nick Barton was killed?"

"What? Ah . . . I mean, yeah, I was. Terrible thing about Nick. Who the hell are you?"

"Frank Morgan. Why didn't you arrest the men who killed him?"

"Frank Morgan!"

"Nick was a good, decent man. He's grubstaked a hundred men and never asked for a penny in repayment. If Jess Center and Gene Dale killed him, why in the hell didn't you arrest them?"

"Frank Morgan!"

"Is your tongue stuck, Marshal? I asked you a question."

The marshal shook his head. "The men alibied for each other, Mr. Morgan. Was Nick a friend of yours?"

"Yes. He was. Let me see the report on the killing."

"Well, now, say . . . I don't have to show you anything. I . . ."

"Let me see the goddamn report!"

The marshal gulped a couple of times and went to a filing cabinet. He rummaged around for a moment and handed Frank a couple of sheets of paper. Frank read the report and tossed the papers on the desk. "That is a bunch of crap. The men were bloody and had hundreds of dollars on them when they were questioned. They didn't have jobs and couldn't explain where they got the money. Everything points to them being guilty."

"I know that. But I wasn't the investigating officer, Mr. Morgan. The county done that. I had nothing to do with it. The deputy who questioned them is gone. He quit and took off for somewhere else. I don't know where he is."

Frank stared at the marshal for a few seconds.

"That's the truth, Mr. Morgan. I swear it."

"All right. I believe you."

"What are you going to do?"

"First off, I'm going to take a bath and get a haircut and a shave. Then I'm going to change clothes. Then I'm going to get myself a good meal. That's going to take a couple of hours. Then I'm going to look up Jess and Dale."

"That's about the time I was plannin' on ridin' out and servin' papers on a fellow."

"I think that might be a real good idea, Marshal. Why don't you do that."

"I will. I sure will. Two hours, you say?"

"Just about."

The marshal looked at the clock on the wall. "That would be right at two o'clock."

"Close enough."

"I'll be back in town in time for supper. Say . . . six o'clock or so."

"I'm sure I'll see you then. Have a pleasant ride, Marshal."

"You enjoy your stay in town, Mr. Morgan."

"I plan to do just that."

Thirty-three

Frank bought a new black pinstripe suit, a white shirt, and a black string tie, then went to the barbershop for a bath and haircut and shave. He walked over to a cafe and had a very tasty plate lunch and several cups of coffee. He stood on the boardwalk outside the cafe for several minutes, smoking and watching the foot traffic come and go, then crossed the street and entered the billiard parlor. After a couple of minutes of watching the games, he walked up to several loafers.

"I'm looking for Jess Center and Gene Dale. Will somebody point them out, please."

"Ain't we the polite one, though?" a loafer said, a nasty tinge to his voice. "Dressed up to the nines too."

Another loafer took a long look into Frank's eyes and said, "Uh, they ain't here, mister. You'll probably find them over at saloon 'crost the street."

"Thanks," Frank said. "Appreciate it."

"You're so welcome," the mouthy one popped off.

Frank glanced at the young man, then decided not to push it. The smart-mouth wasn't worth the time or effort. He walked out of the pool hall, taking note that the loafers were following him. He walked over to the saloon, the billiard parlor ne'er-do-wells a dozen steps behind him. Stepping inside, he spotted the Olsen boys, Brooks and Martin, standing at the bar. Several other men who had chosen to ride off with Sonny were scattered around the huge saloon.

This is going to be interesting, Frank thought.

"Frank Morgan," a man seated at a table said. "Good God!"

"Where?" another asked.

"He just walked in."

"Somebody go fetch the marshal," another suggested.

"I seen him ride out of town about an hour ago."

"Damn!"

"Morgan!" Brooks Olsen said, turning and spotting Frank.

The saloon fell silent, all eyes moving toward Frank as he walked to the end of the bar. A suddenly very nervous bartender took Frank's order for coffee.

"You made a bad mistake followin' us here, Morgan," Brooks said.

"I didn't follow you," Frank said. "I don't make a habit of following a trail of coyote crap."

"Huh?" Brooks stepped away from the bar. "You callin' me a turd?"

"If that's the way you choose to take it, yes."

"I should have killed you back in South Raven."

"Try it now, Brooks," Frank said, his words cold.

"You callin' me out, Morgan?"

"Yeah," Frank replied softly. "That's what I'm doing, you crazy bastard."

Brooks grabbed for iron and Frank shot him. Brooks's boots flew out from under him and he hit the cigarette- and cigar-littered floor. Martin jerked his six-gun, the muzzle just clearing leather when Frank's bullet tore into his chest. The Olsen cousins died on the floor. Martin's hand was stuck up to the wrist in a spittoon.

One of the loafers from the billiard parlor yelled, "Look out, Jess! He's in town after you and Gene."

Frank dropped to the floor just as the two killers opened fire. Their bullets shattered the mirror and numerous whiskey bottles behind the bar. Frank triggered off a snap shot that hit one of the pair in the hip and knocked him spinning into a table.

"I'll kill the son of a bitch, Jess!" Gene shouted as he jumped up into a chair for a better shot at Frank.

Frank shot him in the belly, then jerked out his spare six-gun from behind his belt just as Jess was crawling to his feet, holding onto the edge of a table with one hand, his other hand filled with a pistol. Frank finished him with one shot to the head, and Jess died with his mouth open and his brains leaking out of the gaping hole in his forehead.

"Somebody kill that bastard!" Gene groaned, on his knees, trying to rise to his boots.

No one stepped up to take the offer.

Frank got to his feet and walked over to Gene, kicking the man's pistol away from him, then quickly reloaded his Peacemaker.

"Somebody better get the doc," the bartender said, his voice shaky. "And tell the undertaker he's got some customers too."

Frank looked at the pool hall loafers, still standing near the door. "Any of you want to deal into this hand?"

They didn't.

Frank pointed toward Jess and Gene. "They killed Nick Barton, and any of you that were here when it happened know they did."

"I knowed it all along," a man said. "But folks was afraid of them two."

"Not much to be afraid of," Frank said.

"Hell with you, Morgan!" Gene gasped. "If that bastard had give us the money instead of makin' a fight of it, he'd still be alive."

"Are you saying it's Nick's fault he was killed, and not yours?" Frank asked.

"Damn right!" Gene said.

"You all heard him confess he and his buddy killed Nick," Frank told the gathering. "If he lives, hang him."

"With pleasure," another local said.

Gene groaned and fumbled at his boot, coming out with a tiny derringer in his hand. He pointed it at Frank and pulled the trigger. The cartridge misfired and Gene threw the gun at Frank.

"This just ain't your day, is it, Gene?" a local asked with a snicker.

"My bowels is burnin' up," Gene replied. "I hurt somethin' turrble. And I don't think they's a damn thing funny about it."

Frank motioned for the bartender to hotten up his coffee.

The men who had ridden off to join Sonny's gang had quietly left the saloon.

"I ain't seen a good hangin' in months," a local said. "Maybe Gene will live long enough to climb the gallows steps."

"You go to hell!" Gene told him.

"Don't forget that you owe me five dollars, Gene," another bar patron called. "I want my money."

"When hell freezes over," Gene said. Frank sipped his coffee and waited.

The doctor and the undertaker entered the saloon together. The undertaker checked the dead, the doctor knelt down beside Gene. "Some of you boys carry him over to my office," the doctor said. "Carry him easy now. He's badly hurt."

"Don't move me!" Gene hollered. "My innards will fall out."

"Well, then, you can die here on the saloon floor," the doctor told him. "But it might take several hours or several days."

"Get him out of here," the bartender ordered. "He'll run off all my business waitin' for him to croak."

"You're a foul, black-hearted sot," Gene told the bartender.

The bartender shrugged his indifference.

Frank sipped his coffee.

The doctor stood up and motioned for some men to carry Gene out. He then turned to Frank. "So you're Frank Morgan, the shootist."

"I'm Frank Morgan, yes."

"You're very nicely dressed for a depraved killer."

"Is that what I am?"

"So I've heard."

Frank turned away and watched as the bartender began sweeping up the broken glass behind the long bar.

"Here comes that new young feller from the newspaper," a man called, just as a bar girl sidled up to Frank and nudged him with a hip.

"I'm available," she whispered.

"Good for you," Frank said.

"And reasonable," the soiled dove added.

"Some other time," Frank told her.

"Whatever," she said, and moved away.

The young reporter entered the saloon and took a look at the carnage. "My God!" he said. "This is terrible."

"You should have been here eight or ten years ago," a man said. "This ain't nothin'."

The young reporter turned to Frank. "Sir, are you really Frank Morgan?"

"That's my name."

"I would very much like to interview you."

"I don't give interviews. Sorry."

"Hell with him!" Gene hollered as several locals tried to pick him up. "What about me? I'm the one who got shot."

The reporter ignored him and stepped up to the bar. He maintained some distance from Frank.

"This feller's hand is stuck in the spittoon," the undertaker said. "We might have to bury him with the spittoon."

"The hell you will!" the bartender said. "Them things don't come cheap. Cut off his damn hand."

"You have to be joking!" the reporter said, challenging the bartender. "That is barbaric. We're talking about a human being here."

"So?" the bartender asked. "Hell, he's dead. He ain't gonna miss a hand. But them spittoons come all the way from St. Louis."

"This is ridiculous!" the newspaperman said. "If you pull hard enough, I'm sure you can free the man's hand."

"You want to git down here and jerk, boy?" the undertaker asked.

"I would rather not."

"Then shut up."

Frank tossed a coin on the bar. "For my coffee."

"It's on the house, Mr. Morgan," the bartender told him. "It's been a real pleasure having you."

"I damn sure tried to do that," the soiled dove muttered.

A local whispered in her ear.

"A dollar!" she hollered. "Are you joking?"

Frank finished his coffee and turned from the bar, heading for the door.

"I hope you rot in hell, Morgan!" Gene moaned.

Frank stepped out onto the boardwalk and headed for the hotel. A good supper and a night's sleep and he'd be gone from this place. Virginia City had lost its appeal.

Thirty-four

Frank headed northwest, toward the little town of Reno. After the shoot-out in the saloon, he had visited the grave of his old friend, provisioned up at a general store, and then returned to the hotel. He had left the hotel only once after that, to feed Dog at the livery. He took his supper in his room and went to bed early, pulling out before dawn.

Frank had no specific destination in mind. He was just drifting. He had finally put all thoughts of a permanent home out of his mind . . . at least for most of the time. It seemed that no matter where he went, someone was there to challenge him, and he suspected that even should he move to the more civilized eastern part of the nation, even in New York City, it would eventually be the same. More than likely the challenges would not come from gunfighters, but instead from local bullies and loudmouths—people that Frank had long thought really had no useful or productive place in society.

"But where or when, then, is my place?" Frank questioned aloud. "Where the hell do I fit in the overall scheme of things?"

He could come up with no answer to his question.

I'm a rich man, relatively speaking, he thought. I'm no railroad baron or wealthy rancher, but I certainly have ample funds to do whatever I wish to do—within reason, that is. Yet all I do is end-lessly drift.

What the hell am I looking for?

Dog's sudden growling brought Frank out of his musings. He reined up at the smell of wood smoke.

"Easy, boy," he told Dog. "Settle down."

Dog immediately ceased his snarling.

Frank sat his saddle for a moment, listening and smelling the wood smoke as it drifted through the stand of timber he was in. He figured he was about half a day's ride from Reno, and had planned on making it that day.

A man appeared out of the brush and timber and stared at Frank for a few seconds, then lifted a hand in greeting. "They's two of us around a noon fire and we ain't got much, stranger," the man called. "But we'll share if you're friendly."

"I'm friendly," Frank said. "I got bacon and po-tatoes if you're hungry."

"That would hit the spot for sure. Come on in and light and sit."

The two men were drifting cowboys out of Wyo-ming, looking for a warmer clime to winter.

"Gets cold in Wyoming," the one called Jim said. "Right down to the bone."

"For a fact," Frank agreed. "I pulled out of Idaho for the same reason." Frank held out his cup and the man filled it. "You boys got any particular spot in mind to light?"

"Nope," the cowboy who had been introduced as Curly said. "For once we saved our summer wages and now we're just seein' the country. You?"

Frank shook his head. "Thought I'd check out parts of California. Hadn't been there in some time now."

"You got a name, mister?"

"Frank."

"You look sort of familiar," Jim said. "I know I've seen you somewhere before."

"Could be," Frank said. "I do get around."

"Are you the law?" Curly asked.

Frank laughed. "No. Although I have worn a badge from time to time."

Curly looked at him for a few seconds, and then set his cup down on a flat rock by the fire. "You're Frank Morgan. Good God! You're Frank Morgan!"

Jim spilled half of his hot coffee on his leg, and jumped up hollering and slapping at his leg. "Frank Morgan!" he finally said, settling down. "You're jokin'!"

"That's my name, boys."

"Are you after someone, Mr. Morgan?" Curly asked.

"No. And the name is Frank. Not Mister. I'm just drifting, boys. Just trying to keep out of trouble, that's all."

"Well, we're right glad to howdy and shake, Frank," Jim said. "We've been hearin' stories 'bout you for years."

"You can believe about one out of every ten," Frank said with a smile. "Those big-city writer fellows tend to exaggerate a mite."

"I read me an article 'bout you just a few weeks ago in some magazine," Curly said. "I disremember who wrote it. Said you'd killed seven or eight hundred men."

Frank chuckled. "Not quite, Curly." He stood up. "Let me get some bacon and potatoes from the pack and we'll get some food cooking. You boys want some pan bread?"

"Hey, now," Jim said. "That sounds great. We can have us a regular feast."

Frank spent the night with the two drifting cowboys, talking and drinking coffee for hours after an early supper. He pulled out the next morning, heading for Reno. In Reno, he decided to satisfy his growing curiosity about how things had worked out back in South Raven and sent a wire to Doc Raven.

"I'll be back in a few hours to check on any reply," he told the telegraph agent.

To his surprise, Doc Raven replied quickly. The body of Fuller Ross had been discovered hanging in an old barn just outside of town. The man had committed suicide. He had left a note saying how sorry he was for what he had done. Wilma was staying in South Raven. She and Doc would be married after a respectable mourning time for her late husband had passed. The Easterners had all gone back to New York City. Marvella and her granddaughter, Bessie, would be staying in town. Bessie was attending school there.

Doc hoped that Frank would someday return to South Raven. He would always be welcome there.

Frank folded the paper and put it in his wallet. "Things worked out," he muttered. "I reckon they always do."

The local law, all armed with shotguns, were waiting for Frank when he returned to the hotel. Their message was very brief and to the point.

"We don't want you in this town, Morgan," the sheriff said. "Buy what supplies you need for the trail and get out."

"I haven't caused any trouble here," Frank said, "and I don't intend to."

"Trouble follows you, Morgan," the sheriff said. "We've got a couple of hotheads in town. They don't amount to much, but I don't want them shot down in the street. And that's exactly what will happen if they brace you. And they will."

"You know that for a certain?"

"They're over at a saloon now, getting liquored up and making their brags. Move on, Morgan."

"My horse is tired, Sheriff."

"I feel sorry for your horse. Make your camp a few miles out of town. Get going, Morgan. Right now."

"All right, Sheriff."

The sheriff and his deputies escorted Frank back to the livery, and waited and watched while he saddled up, rigged up the packsaddle, and rode out of town.

"I kinda feel sorry for him, Sheriff," a deputy said. "All he wanted was a meal and a bed."

"He chose his life," the sheriff replied. "He could get out of it any time he wanted to."

"How?" another deputy asked.

"All he has to do is quit gunfightin'," the sheriff replied. "It's easy. But men like that don't want to quit. Hell with him."

At a tiny crossroads hamlet on the California/Nevada border, Frank had stopped to rest and water his horse and get himself something to drink. When he stepped out, the outlaw Russ Temple was waiting. Russ had a pistol pointed at him, the hammer back.

"That damn dog of yourn like to have caused me to lose my arm back yonder in the livery, you son of a bitch," Russ said. "Now, I'm gonna kill you and then I'm gonna kill that damn dog of yourn."

"You've got the gun," Frank said.

"Damn right, I have. And I'm gonna enjoy this moment for a mite longer. I like to see you sweat, Morgan."

"Don't count on that, Temple. It's a cool day."

"I think I'll gut-shoot you, Morgan. Just to see you cry and beg."

A cat suddenly darted into the wide road, a dog running after it. The cat yowled, and Russ cut his eyes for an instant. That was all the time Frank needed. He drew and fired, the bullet hitting Russ in the lower belly and doubling him over. Frank's boot hung up in a broken board and he lost his balance, falling backward and landing on his butt just as Russ fired, the slug digging up splinters and driving them into Frank's cheek.

Frank fired again, this time from a very awkward position. The bullet hit Russ in the neck and almost decapitated the gunslick. He died in the dirt in front of the general store.

"Bastard!" a man yelled, running out of the barn next to the store. Frank recognized him as a gun-hand he knew only as Post.

Post snapped off a shot at Frank that missed. Rolling to one side, Frank got off a shot that hit Post in the leg and knocked him down.

Another gunny ran out of the barn and fired, the bullet hitting Frank in the fleshy part of his left arm. Frank returned the fire and the third man went down, a bullet in his chest, just as Frank was reaching for his short-barreled Peacemaker.

Frank tried to get up, and found that he had broken the heel off his left boot. He sat up and looked at the men sprawled in the street. Russ was dead and from the way they looked, the other two weren't far behind him. The entire shooting episode had taken about fifteen seconds.

"My God, mister!" the store owner shouted as he came rushing out. "What in God's name brought all that on?"

"I guess they didn't like my looks," Frank replied as he took off his bandanna and tied it around the wound in his arm.

"It'd been a damn sight easier on them if they'd just told you that." He stared at Frank for a moment, then yelled, "Ophelia! Come quick. I told you this man looked familiar. It's Frank Morgan. It really is him."

Ophelia rushed outside, followed by two kids, a boy and a girl, in their mid-teens. They stood in the doorway and stared first at the bodies in the street, then at the man sitting on the edge of the porch, a bloody bandanna tied around the wound on his arm.

"We don't have a doctor here, Mr. Morgan," the store owner said. "Closest one is about a two-hour ride away."

Frank shook his head. "I've got some medical supplies in my pack. The wound isn't that serious. I'll be all right."

"You sure?"

"I'm sure. You wouldn't happen to have any coffee made, would you?"

"We sure do, Mr. Morgan," Ophelia said. "Julie, you run go get Mr. Morgan a cup of coffee. Move, girl."

"Damn you to hell, Morgan!" Post groaned. "I can't stop the bleedin' in my hip. It's a-gushin' out."

"Probably hit a vein," Frank told him.

"The bullet traveled up into my innards," Post said. "My guts is on fire."

"Your face is bleeding, Mr. Morgan," the teenage boy said. "I'll get some liniment from the store."

"I'd appreciate that, boy. Thanks."

"Somebody get me to a doctor," Post yelled as several of the tiny hamlet's residents gathered in the street to stare and point and whisper.

"You got a horse," Frank told him. "Go look for a doctor."

"I'm bad hurt!" Post hollered. "I cain't go by myself."

"That's your problem," Frank said, taking the cup of coffee from Julie. "Thank you, miss."

"I got a wagon," a local said. "I reckon I could haul him over to the doc's office."

"I can pay," Post said.

"You damn sure will," the local replied.

"Load him up and tote him off," the store owner said. "Some of you others help me tote off the dead. Looks bad havin' them in the road like that. Bad for business."

"You can have whatever's in their pockets for burying them," Frank told the growing gathering of locals. "And their horses too."

"That's fair," a woman said. "I can sing a song over them."

"And I'll moan and holler," another woman said.

"This'll be a right nice funeral," a man added. "Somebody go get the preacher and tell him to bring the Good Book."

"I'll go get some shovels," another man said.

"I ain't dead yet," the chest-shot gunhand moaned. "Y'all cain't bury me whilst I'm still alive."

"Man has a point," a local said.

Frank managed to roll a cigarette, and sat on the edge of the porch, drinking his coffee and smoking.

"I reckon we ought to report this to the sheriff," a man said.

"Aw, hell," another said. "They'll be a deputy through here in a couple of days. We can do it then."

"Will somebody get me to a damn doctor!" Post groaned.

"Keep your pants on," he was told. "The team's bein' hitched up now."

"I'll be dead by the time that's done," Post griped.

"That would shore solve the problem," the man agreed.

"I got the liniment, Mr. Morgan," the boy said, handing Frank a bottle. "And some clean rags."

"I'll go around back and doctor myself," Frank said. "And get me a clean shirt."

"You got anything you want to say to me, Morgan?" Post asked. "Since I'm probably bein' hauled off to my deathbed?"

"Yeah," Frank told him. "Good-bye!"

Thirty-five

Frank found a nice spot in the timber, on a ridge overlooking a stream, and settled in for a week or so of rest. Plenty of time for his wound to heal. Each day he carefully cleaned the bullet wound and put a fresh bandage on it. The wound on his face was minor at best, and it healed rapidly.

Frank was right on the edge of the Sierra Nevada Mountains, and it surprised the hell out of him one night when he was awakened by the cold and found himself in the middle of a snowstorm. He quickly built up the fire, and as soon as it got light, he packed up and moved further west and south.

He had plenty of time to think, and finally got it through his head that what was left of Sonny's gang—and that probably numbered thirty or so—was hard after him. Most would quit the hunt after a few months, but some would never rest, feeling that Frank had cheated them out of many thousands of dollars in ransom money and they wanted him dead.

"All right," Frank whispered. "So I find me a place to hole up for a time."

This area was dotted with abandoned cabins, built by men looking for their fortune in gold. Most never even found color and moved out, wiser and busted. But their cabins remained. Frank would find one and settle in.

A few miles off the stage road, and only a couple of miles from a small town, Frank found a small cabin that was in pretty good shape and settled in. The first thing he did was shoot a deer so he would have meat. He hunted around and pulled up a bunch of wild onions to flavor up a big pot of stew. Then he built a fire and made a pot of coffee and relaxed.

Because of the splinter wounds on the side of his face, Frank had not shaved in days. He continued to let his beard grow, trimming it occasionally to keep it even. It changed his looks dramatically. After several days, Frank decided to ride into town for supplies.

As soon as he reined up in front of the general store he knew he had made a mistake that was too late to rectify; at the hitch rails in front of the saloon, across the street from the store, were more than a half-dozen horses that Frank recognized, including Lonesome Howard's.

"Howdy, mister," the clerk said, as Frank entered the store.

Frank returned the greeting. He pointed toward the saloon. "Looks like the town is busy this day. What's the occasion?"

The clerk grimaced. "Trouble-hunting drifters. They've been here for about a week. I hear they're hunting Frank Morgan."

"Is Morgan in this area?" Frank asked innocently.

"Those gunhands think so. Something about a bounty on Morgan's head."

"Well, let me buy a few things and get gone. I don't want to get caught up in the middle of a gunfight."

"I'd like to see Frank Morgan come ridin' into town and tangle with those ne'er-do-wells. I bet he'd kill everyone of them."

"Six or seven to one?" Frank shook his head. "Those are long odds, friend."

"Frank could do it, I bet. He's the fastest man that ever packed iron. I just read a story about him. Why, he's killed hundreds of bad men. And that ain't even countin' Indians."

The stories just keep getting wilder and wilder, Frank thought as he handed the man his grocery list.

"I'll fill this right quick, sir," the clerk said.

"Well, I'll just be damned!" a man said from behind Frank. "It's Frank Morgan. Turn around and face me, Morgan."

"Frank Morgan?" the clerk said, a puzzled look on his face. "Where?"

Frank was standing next to a barrel of ax handles. He dropped his hand to the barrel.

"Right in front of you, stupid!" the man said, taking several steps forward. "Turn around, Morgan, damn you!"

Frank turned, one hand sliding an ax handle out of the barrel. He conked the man on the head with the wood, and the outlaw sank to the floor without so much as a grunt.

"Are you really Frank Morgan?" the clerk questioned.

"Yes," Frank said, jerking the unconscious man's Colt from leather and tucking it behind his gunbelt. "Now fill that order for me."

"Oh, my God!" the clerk said. "Look, Mr. Morgan." He pointed.

Lonesome Howard and the other outlaws had left the saloon, and were walking across the street toward the general store.

"I'll take it outside," Frank said.

"I sure would appreciate that, sir," the clerk replied, rubbing his hands together nervously.

Frank stepped out onto the boardwalk and stood

there. The six outlaws stopped in the middle of the street, surprised at seeing Morgan.

Lonesome Howard was the first to speak. "That beard don't work, Morgan. I'd know you anywhere."

"And you intend to do what, Howard?" Frank asked.

Before Lonesome could reply, a rather portly gentleman wearing a badge on his coat stepped out of a building and shouted, "Here now, you men! What is going on?"

"Carry your butt out of here, Fat Man," a man Frank knew only as Max told the marshal. " 'Fore you git it shot off."

"I beg your pardon?" The marshal's question was filled with indignation.

"Shut up and get your fat ass back inside," Nils told him. "Does that make it any clearer for you?"

The other outlaws laughed as the marshal retreated into his office.

"I told you I'd kill you someday, Morgan," Lonesome said. "Now's the time."

"You got it to do, Howard," Frank called. "I'm damn tired of this. Drag iron."

Lonesome's hand snaked his six-gun out of leather. Frank shot him just as Lonesome was leveling his pistol. Frank's bullet cut through Lonesome's belly and blew out the man's back, on the left side. Lonesome cried out and went down to his knees in the dirt.

Frank jumped to one side as the other outlaws grabbed for iron. Frank put lead into one, and the impact of the .45 caliber slug turned the man around. The others filled the cool air with lead. But Frank had changed positions again, quickly moving to the other side of the alleyway.

"Kill the bastard!" Nils yelled.

Frank drilled him in the brisket, doubling the man over. Nils sat down hard in the street, right smack on a very recent pile of horse droppings. He yelled out a rather apt description of what he was sitting in, then fell over face-down in the dirt.

Max fired, the bullet cutting and burning a shallow groove into the top of Frank's shoulder. Frank grunted in pain and leveled his Colt, putting lead into Max's chest. Max went down slowly, much like a puppet with broken strings, sinking to the dirt. He stretched out in the street as if going to sleep— he would do that forever.

The remaining outlaws broke and ran for their horses, jumping into the saddles and galloping away. Frank let them go. He walked out into the street, feeling the warm flow of blood ooze down onto his arm and chest from the wound in his shoulder. He walked up to Lonesome, still on his knees, both hands holding his punctured belly.

"The Lord will punish you for this, Morgan," Lonesome gasped.

"Are you serious, Howard?"

"I am the sword of the Almighty," Lonesome whispered.

"Well, I hate to tell you this, Howard. But your blade got a little dull."

"You're a damned sinner, Morgan! You'll burn in the hellfires."

"Here comes the doctor, Howard. Maybe he can save your worthless hide."

"If he does, I'll come lookin' to kill you, Morgan." Howard fell over to one side and lay in the dirt gasping.

"You want to sell me your ranch, Howard?"

"Hell, no!"

"I'll give you a good price for it."

"I'd . . ." He coughed up blood. "I'd sooner give it to a damned Injun."

"Now, that's not a very Christian thing to say, Howard. I'd take real good care of it."

Howard told Frank where to stick everything he owned. When he finished, he was out of breath and very nearly out of time.

"Shame on you, Howard. Going to meet the Lord with those suggestions on your lips."

The town doctor walked over and looked at Lonesome Howard. "He's done for. I think your bullet tore up his liver and kidney."

Lonesome told the doctor where to stick his opinion.

"Hell with you too!" the doctor said, and walked over to where Nils lay, all sprawled in the horse crap.

"This one might live." He motioned for some men to move Nils to his office.

The second man Frank had shot was not long for this world. Frank's bullet had dusted him from side to side, and the man had already lost consciousness.

"I hear the angels singin', Morgan," Lonesome murmured. "They're comin' to carry me home on wings of comfort."

"You hold onto that thought, Howard," Frank told him.

"I'll tell you this, Morgan," Lonesome managed to say. "Sonny's gonna kill you. He's already puttin' together another gang."

"All right, Howard. Thanks."

Lonesome Howard closed his eyes and died.

Frank walked over to the general store and paid for his supplies, picking up a can of Cuticura Anti-Pain Plaster and a bottle of Dr. Sherman's Pricklyash Bitters. He walked out of the store and began to stow his supplies on the packsaddle's canvas packs.

"You want me to take a look at that shoulder?" the doctor asked, walking up to Frank.

"It's all right, Doc. Just a burn, that's all."

"The man who was taken to my office just died."

"Tough luck."

"You're a cold bastard, Morgan."

"But a live bastard, Doc."

"For the time being at least."

Frank managed a smile and swung into the saddle. He nodded at the doctor and rode away, back toward his cabin.

"He was only defending himself, Doc," the store clerk said.

"I have no use for gunfighters," the doctor said tersely. "It would have benefitted the country had Frank Morgan been killed this day."

"How, Doc?" a local asked.

"Yeah," another questioned. "The man's a living legend."

"A legend written in blood," the doctor replied. He walked away, back to his office.

The store clerk looked down the road Frank had taken. Morgan was out of sight. "I feel sorry for the man," he said.

"Yeah?" another local questioned. "Well . . . I'll tell you this: We ain't heard the last of Frank Morgan."

Thirty-six

Frank loafed around the cabin for a week, eating, drinking coffee, chopping some wood, and taking care of the wound on his shoulder. Eight days after the shoot-out on Main Street, Frank said to hell with it. He packed up, saddled up, and rode out, taking a northwest route of travel.

Stormy was glad to be back on the trail, and Dog was just as happy to be seeing some new country and encountering and checking out new sights and smells.

Frank picked up a newspaper in a small town and read about an attempted bank holdup in a Southern California town. Sonny and a half-dozen members of his gang were caught and being held for trial. All of them were under heavy guard. According to the newspaper writer, Sonny and those gang members who were caught would spend the rest of their lives in prison.

"Good," Frank muttered. "That's where they belong."

In a small town in Northern California, Frank stepped out of a barbershop after a bath, haircut, and shave, all decked out in freshly laundered and pressed clothes. Frank carried his pistol tucked behind his waistband, for this town discouraged the open carrying of firearms. Frank was enjoying a quiet meal in the cafe when the sheriff and one of his deputies walked in and uninvited, sat down at the table with Frank.

"You Frank Morgan?" the sheriff asked in a low voice.

Frank nodded his head.

"You hunting someone?"

"No," Frank replied.

"Then why are you here?"

Frank smiled. "To get cleaned up and have my clothes laundered. And to rest my horses and get something to eat."

"You going to have a drink at the saloon?"

"I might."

"I wouldn't."

"You want me to get out of town, Sheriff?"

"I would appreciate that, Mr. Morgan."

"Even though I've broken no laws."

"There are hotheads in this town, Mr. Morgan. Young squirts who might take it upon themselves to brace you. I don't want a shoot-out in my town."

"Neither do I."

"Good. I'll have your supplies packed up and you can be on your way soon as you finish your meal."

"Hospitality is sort of thin around here, isn't it, Sheriff?"

"Actually, we're a right friendly town here, Morgan. And a safe one too. And I intend to keep it that way."

"You might find this hard to believe, but I'm basically a peaceful man. And I'll leave your town as soon as I finish this fine meal. But I hope you don't ever brace the wrong gunhand one of these days, Sheriff."

"Thanks for the advice, Morgan. Look here, you could hang up your guns anytime you wanted to."

Frank looked at the sheriff for a long moment. He shoved his plate of food away and stood up.

Just before he walked out the door, he said, "And how long do you think I'd live if I did that, Sheriff? How long?"

The sheriff knew the answer to that. He shook his head and refused to reply.

Look for
William W. Johnstone's
next novel

WARPATH OF THE MOUNTAIN MAN

Coming in July 2002
from Pinnacle Books

Here's a sneak preview. . . .

Smoke Jensen was in front of the hardware store, looping the reins of his horse around the hitching rail, when he heard the gunshot. Sometimes, in drunken play, shots were fired into the floor, or in the air, and most of the citizens of Big Rock had learned to tell the difference between the sound of a shot fired in play and one fired in anger.

This shot, fired at ten-fifteen Tuesday morning in October, was fired in anger.

Suddenly a man burst from the front door of the bank, which was located about two blocks west of the hardware store. It was Rich Flowers, one of the bank tellers.

"They're robbing the bank! They're robbing the bank!" Flowers shouted. "Help, somebody, they're . . ."

That was as far he got before a masked man appeared in the doorway of the bank, clutching a bag in one hand and a pistol in the other. The masked man raised his pistol and fired at Flowers, hitting him in the back. Flowers fell face-down in the dirt.

From all up and down the street there were screams and shouts of fear and alarm. Citizens of the town scrambled to get out of the way, running into nearby doorways, ducking behind watering troughs or around the corner of adjacent buildings. Three more masked men appeared in the bank door, firing their weapons indiscriminately. There

was a scream from inside Mrs. Pynchon's dres
shop, followed by the crash of glass as a woma
tumbled through the window and fell onto th
boardwalk, bleeding from her wound.

"Clear the street, clear the street!" one of th
bank robbers shouted, waving his pistol. "Every
body get off the street!" He punctuated his de
mand with more pistol shots.

Although most of the citizens obeyed the banl
robbers' orders, Smoke Jensen did not. Instead h
strolled, almost casually, to his horse, where h
pulled his rifle from its saddle holster. Then, jack
ing a shell into the chamber, he stepped out int
the middle of the street, raised the rifle to hi
shoulder, and fired at one of the bank robbers. Th
man went down.

"What the hell!" one of the other robber
shouted. "Where did that come from?"

"Down there!" another said, pointing to Smoke

The robber aimed at Smoke and fired, but he
was using a pistol, and he missed. Smoke returned
fire and didn't miss.

Now there were only two robbers left.

"Get the money and let's get out of here!" one
of the two shouted. The other robber tried to re
trieve the moneybag from the hands of one of his
dead partners, but Smoke put a bullet in his leg
and he went down, too.

The last robber, seeing that he was alone and
outgunned by the man with the rifle, threw his pistol down and put his hands up.

"Don't shoot! Don't shoot!" he shouted. "I
quit!"

Keeping the robber covered, Smoke walked to
ward him. By now, most of the townspeople realized that Smoke had everything under control, and
they started coming back into the street, heading
toward the bank and the two robbers who were left

alive, one standing with his hands up, the other, groaning and bleeding, lying in the dirt.

"Who are you, mister?" asked the one who was still standing.

"Why do you need to know?" Smoke replied. "We're not going to be friends."

Some of the citizens of the town, close enough now to hear the exchange, laughed.

"Mister, you just been brought down by Smoke Jensen," someone said. "And if it's any consolation to you, he's beaten many a man better than you."

By now Sheriff Monte Carson was also on the scene, and he took the two robbers into custody.

"What about my leg?" the wounded robber asked. "I got me a bullet in my leg. I need a doctor. I'm your prisoner, and the law says you got to get me a doctor."

"We've only got one doctor in this town, mister," Monte replied. "And right now he's seeing to Mrs. Pynchon and Mr. Flowers. You better hope neither one of them dies, 'cause if either of them does, you'll both be hung for murder. Let's go." Monte made a motion toward the jail.

"I can't walk on this leg, I tell you."

"Couple you men . . . help him," Monte said.

With assistance from two onlookers, the wounded man and his uninjured partner crossed the street and entered the jail.

"We've got two nice rooms just waiting for you," Monte said, opening the doors to adjacent jail cells.

"When's the doctor going to look at my leg?"

"When he gets around to it," Monte answered. "In the meantime, if I were you, I'd just lie on the bunk there and take it easy."

"It hurts," the wounded prisoner insisted.

"Yeah, I reckon it does. What are your names?" Monte asked.

"I'm Jack Tatum," the uninjured man said. He

nodded toward the other robber, who had taken Monte's advice and was now lying down. "His name is Billy Petrie."

"Tatum?" Monte said. "I've seen that name." He opened the drawer of his desk and took out a pile of wanted posters. After looking through several of them, he pulled one out. "Ah, here it is. This is you, isn't it?"

Monte turned the poster so Tatum could see it.

WANTED
JACK TATUM
For Murder and Robbery
$5,000
Reward to be paid
DEAD OR ALIVE

"Only five thousand? They're a bunch of cheapskates." Tatum snorted. "Hell, I'm worth more than that."

"Proud of it, are you?" Monte asked. He pulled out a tablet and began writing. "I reckon I'd better get a telegram off. No doubt some folks are going to be happy to hear that you are out of business."

"Sheriff, what are you going to do about that fella that murdered my two friends?" Tatum asked.

Monte looked up from his desk. "I beg your pardon? Did you say murdered?"

"Yeah, I said murder, 'cause that's what he done. We wasn't shootin' anybody, we was just shootin' in the air to clear the street. Next thing I know, that bank teller was down, then that woman come crashin' through the window, then Fuller and Howard, then Billy was shot. The guy doing the shooting—Jensen, I think someone said—was a crazy man, sending bullets flying everywhere. You ask me, he's the one who should be locked up in here."

"Are you trying to tell me that you didn't have anything to do with shooting Mr. Flowers or Mrs. Pynchon?"

"That's what I'm telling you," Tatum said.

"I'll give you this, Tatum. You've got gall, telling a lie like that when the whole town saw what you did."

"Well, now, some folks may have seen it one way and some the other," Tatum replied. "We are going to get a trial, aren't we? Or, do you plan to just hang us?"

"You'll get a fair trial," Monte replied. He paused for a moment, then chuckled. "Then we'll hang you."

Dr. Spaulding came into Monte's office then, and set his bag on the corner of Monte's desk.

"How's Mrs. Pynchon?" Monte asked.

"She'll be all right. The bullet went all the way through her upper arm, but it didn't hit any bones."

"Rich Flowers?"

Doc Spaulding shook his head. "Dead. He was dead before I even got to him."

"That's a shame. Flowers was a nice man."

"Yes, he was. And the really sad thing is, Edna, his wife, is going to have a baby."

"Damn, that's a shame. What about the two bank robbers? Both dead?"

"Yes."

"Listen, Doc, I want you to do me a favor. Take the bullets out of the bodies. No doubt the court will need them for evidence."

"All right. I understand one of your prisoners is wounded?"

"Yeah, he's on his cot back there. He took a bullet in his leg."

"I'll take a look at it," Spaulding said, picking up his bag and heading toward the cell.

"Sheriff," Tatum called.

Sighing, Monte looked up at him. "What is it now, Tatum?"

"I want to see a lawyer. That's my right, ain't it? To see a lawyer?"

"You have that right," Monte agreed.

"And if I don't have one, you have to appoint him?"

"That's right."

"Then appoint a lawyer for me and get him over here," Tatum demanded.

In the cell next to Tatum, Billy Petrie started screaming.

"Hold still, young man," Doc Spaulding said. "If I don't get this bullet out, you're likely to lose that leg. Here, here's some laudanum."

The laudanum took effect, and the prisoner's screams turned to a few moans and groans. Dr. Spaulding, ever the caregiver, spoke in quiet, reassuring tones as he worked on Petrie.

Monte was just finishing his telegram when Dewey Wallace, a recently hired deputy, came in.

"Whoowee, the town is really buzzing over all the excitement this morning," Wallace said, walking over to the little stove to pour himself a cup of coffee.

"Is Welch seeing to the bodies yet?" Monte asked.

"He had his measuring tape out before they were cold. Want a cup of coffee?"

"No, thanks," Monte said. He tore the sheet of paper off his pad. "As soon as you finish your coffee, take this down to the telegraph office."

"All right," Wallace said. Sipping the coffee, he looked at the sheriff's message, then whistled. "You think they'll pay Smoke Jensen that reward?"

"I don't know why they shouldn't," Monte said.

Wallace walked over to the jail cells and stood just outside the bars, looking at the two prisoners as he drank his coffee. "So, what were you fellas thinkin'?" Wallace asked. "Did you think we're such a small town you could just come in here and rob our bank, then leave without so much as a fare-thee-well?"

Tatum glared at the deputy, but he said nothing.

"Quiet, huh?" Wallace said, chuckling. "Well, I reckon you won't be so quiet when we string you up." Holding his hand beside his neck to represent a rope, he made a jerking motion, then gave his impression of a death rattle. He followed that with a laugh. "Yeah, you won't be so quiet then," he said.

"Wallace, get the hell away from the cells and quit bothering the prisoners," Monte said. "Take that telegram down to Western Union like I told you."

"All right, Sheriff. Whatever you say," Wallace said, draining the rest of his coffee.

As Wallace was leaving, Doc Spaulding came back from Petrie's cell.

"I don't know what I was thinking when I hired that boy," Monte said.

"Ahh, he'll come around," Spaulding said. He dropped a small piece of lead on the corner of Monte's desk. "Here's the bullet I took from his leg."

"What is it? A .44-40?"

"Is that what Jensen was shooting?"

"Yes."

"Then that's what it is. Of course, it's pretty hard to tell the difference between a .44 and .44-40, seeing as they are so close to the same size and weight."

"That's true," Monte agreed. He had opened a small notebook and was looking through it. Then, when he found what he was looking for, he groaned. "He's not going to like this."

"Who's not going to like what?" Doc Spaulding asked as he closed his bag.

"Sam Covington is next in line to be the public defender."

Doc Spaulding chuckled. "You're right," he said. "He's not going to like it."

"I'll tell you who else won't like it. Norton, the prosecuting attorney. If anyone can make a case out of this, it will be Sam Covington."

"Covington's good, all right."

"Good has nothing to do with it. As far as I know, every lawyer in the county is good. But Covington is more than good, he is ruthless. He'll do anything it takes to win a case, any case. It doesn't matter to Covington whether something is right or wrong or whether someone is guilty or innocent. All that matters to him is who wins. And who loses."